GAMMA QUEST

BOOK 3

FRIEND OR FOE?

MARVEL®

GAMMA QUEST

BOOK 3
FRIEND OR FOE?

Greg Cox

Illustrations by George Pérez

MARVEL®

BP BOOKS, INC.
NEW YORK

BERKLEY BOULEVARD BOOKS, NEW YORK

Special thanks to Ginjer Buchanan, John Morgan, Ursula Ward, Mike Thomas, Steve Behling, and Dwight Jon Zimmerman.

X-MEN & THE AVENGERS: GAMMA QUEST:
Book 3: FRIEND OR FOE?

A Berkley Boulevard Book
A BP Books, Inc. Book

PRINTING HISTORY
Berkley Boulevard paperback edition / June 2000

All rights reserved.
Copyright © 2000 Marvel Characters, Inc.
Cover art by Julie Bell.
Cover design by Claude Goodwin.
Book design by Michael Mendelsohn.
This book may not be reproduced in whole or in part, by mimeograph or any other means, without permission.
For information address: BP Books, Inc.,
24 West 25th Street, New York, New York 10010.

The Penguin Putnam Inc. World Wide Web site address is
http://www.penguinputnam.com

Check out the Ace Science Fiction/Fantasy newsletter,
and much more, at Club PPI!

ISBN: 0-425-17038-1

BERKLEY BOULEVARD
Berkley Boulevard Books are published by The Berkley Publishing Group,
a division of Penguin Putnam Inc.,
375 Hudson Street, New York, New York 10014.
BERKLEY BOULEVARD and its logo
are trademarks belonging to Penguin Putnam Inc.

PRINTED IN THE UNITED STATES OF AMERICA

10 9 8 7 6 5 4 3 2 1

"What is the odds . . . so long as the wing of friendship never moults a feather?"

—Charles Dickens (1841)

"With every end comes a new beginning. . . ."

—Henry McCoy (1996)

ACKNOWLEDGMENTS

As always, credit is due to Stan Lee and Jack Kirby for creating the X-Men, the Avengers, and the incredible Hulk, as well as to all the talented writers and artists who have fleshed out the Marvel Universe for the last three decades.

In addition, a few reference works proved singularly valuable during the writing of this trilogy, including: *A Guide to Marvel Earth* (TSR, 1998), *Xavier Institute Alumni Yearbook* (Marvel, 1996), *Wizard's X-Men Special* (Wizard Press, 1998), *The Iron Manual* (Marvel, 1993), *Cerebro's Guide to the X-Men* (Wizard Press, 1998), plus way too many back issues and graphic novels to list here. I also recommend *The Grand Tour: A Traveler's Guide to the Solar System* by Ron Miller & William K. Hartmann (Workman, 1993), which served as a useful primer on lunar geography.

Finally, thanks to Sumi Lee for help with the German, to the gang at rec.art.comics.xbooks for obscure Marvel trivia, and to Karen and Alex for letting me live at the computer.

Prologue

Their names were the Scarlet Witch, Rogue, and Wolverine. The first was a member of the acclaimed super hero team the Avengers, the other two were members of the controversial group of mutants known as the X-Men. All three were mutants—humans with extraordinary powers. They had been prisoners—guinea pigs, actually—of the super-villain known as the Leader. They had escaped from his hideous laboratory. But, instead of breaking free on Earth, they had discovered that their prison was on the moon.

The stunned prisoners were only seconds from extinction, gasping soundlessly upon the barren surface of the moon, their lungs desperate for oxygen that was nowhere to be found amidst the desolate lunar landscape. The two mutant women, Rogue and the Scarlet Witch, had already succumbed to unconsciousness while only Wolverine's superhuman endurance had kept the feral X-Man alert for a few heartbeats more. He knelt in the fine gray powder beside his fallen comrades, clutching his throat with both hands.

This won't do, the lethal Leader concluded. Like the incredible Hulk, he had been mutated by gamma radiation; like the Hulk, his skin was green; unlike the Hulk, the gamma radiation had made him a super-genius. Now he was observing the escapees' plight on one of the many closed-circuit monitors lining the curved wall of his control room, located at the center of his secluded headquarters elsewhere on the moon. He still had use for the three mutants, whom could not be permitted to expire so prematurely. With the press of a pale green finger upon the lighted control panel, the Leader retrieved his captives via a trans-mat beam that teleported the dying heroes from the harsh environment outside to the relative safety of a containment cell within the Leader's lunar base.

On the screen in question, the X-Men and the mutant Avenger vanished in a flash of viridescent light that was duplicated, a nanosecond later, a few yards away from where the Leader sat. He rotated his futuristic metal throne 180 degrees until, his back to the wall of monitors, he now faced the cell containing the newly-transported mutants.

Haydn's Symphony No. 1 in D major played softly in the background. The one-way mirror that had until recently divided the control room from the containment cell lay in shards upon the floor, a casualty of his unwilling test subjects' foolish and futile attempt to escape captivity. Thus, nothing but pressurized air stood between the Leader and the three figures who materialized within the gleaming metal sarcophagi they had vacated less than half an hour before. There was one open steel coffin, propped up at a forty-five degree angle from the floor, for each of the wayward mutants. Adamantium clamps snapped back in place around their wrists, ankles, and throats. Automated waldoes went to work replacing the sensors, electrodes, and I.V. lines that the escapees had torn free from earlier. Robotic fingers expertly inserted hypodermic needles into their victims' veins, thrusting the sterilized needles through the thin orange fabric of the captives' matching jumpsuits; finely-attuned heat sensors embedded in the mechanical arms allowed the phlebotomy apparatus to detect the exact location of veins and arteries beneath the subjects' clothing.

Rogue flinched as a sharp adamantium needle penetrated even her invulnerable skin. Neither she nor the Scarlet Witch had regained consciousness yet, but the Leader was both surprised and intrigued to find Wolverine glaring at him from the cramped confines of the savage mutant's sarcophagus. "You!" he snarled, locking his gaze on the Leader's unmistakable countenance: a thin green face surmounted by a swollen, bulbous dome.

Wolverine's blood-rimmed eyes were wild and full of hate. Polished metal claws spasmodically extended from his knuckles, flashing impotently out of reach of his restraints. "Witchie was right! You're the sleazeball responsible for all this!"

"Well, to be quite honest," the Leader replied coolly, his epicene voice holding no trace of alarm at Wolverine's obvious fury, "my newfound partner played some small part in this particular operation."

"Partner? What partner?" Wolverine barked. He writhed within his unbreakable metal bonds, struggling unsuccessfully to break free. "What in blazes are you talking about, you swell-headed scumbag?"

The Leader took no offense at the X-Man's tactless disparagement of his enlarged cranium; *I could hardly expect an atavistic throwback like Wolverine to appreciate my superior cerebral capacity.* Nor did he feel any obligation to alleviate the X-Man's impertinent curiosity, especially since the powerful narcotic flowing into Wolverine's veins through the reattached I.V. line was already causing the enraged mutant's eyelids to droop despite his nearly indomitable will. "I'll getya," he slurred, even as his body slumped within the sarcophagus, held up only by his unyielding restraints. "You . . . c'n . . . bet . . . on't."

Wolverine's primitive display of defiance held no interest for the Leader's elevated intellect. Confident that his errant lab animals had been restored to their rightful place, he spun his chair back around toward the wall of monitors. Now that the would-be jailbreak had been stopped, he wished to assure himself that the rest of his elaborate machinations were proceeding exactly as he had anticipated.

Over three dozen video screens, stacked row upon row, greeted his inspection. His vastly capacious brain easily absorbed data from every monitor simultaneously, allowing him to track events in several arenas at once:

1. Elsewhere in the lunar base, an airlock or two away from the control room, his mindless humanoid servants were already hard at work repairing the rest of the damage left behind by the ill-fated escape attempt, including the gaping hull breach carved out by Rogue when, dragging her fellow prisoners in her wake, the super-strong mutant heroine had smashed her way free of the compound—only to encounter the debilitating vacuum outside. *That must have come as a dreadful surprise,* he assumed, without much in the way of sympathy. *Too bad I never bothered to tell them precisely* where *they were being held.*

Automatic safeguards had protected the control room, along with the bulk of the base, from explosive decompression, while even now his pliable humanoids, immune to the ravaging effects of the lunar environment, were patching over the breach. Chances were, by the time the Leader's partner returned from his own urgent mission, he would not be able to tell that anything had ever been amiss.

Probably just as well, he thought. His current associate had a paranoid and pessimistic disposition, especially where Earth's super-powered defenders were concerned; he would not be pleased should he discover that their captives had managed to escape their bonds, however briefly. *I just know I'd never hear the end of it. . . .*

2. Concealed cameras allowed him to look in on Freehold, his former refuge beneath the Columbia Icefields, where a mixed assortment of X-Men and Avengers had come in search of their purloined compatriots. Captain America, Cyclops, and the Vision comprised the rescue team dispatched to the underground city, site of the Leader's most recent "death," where they had hoped to find clues pointing toward his current residence.

A frown tugged on his thin green lips as he recalled just how close he had come to dying for real during that final battle at Freehold, his gamma-mutated body riddled with bullets during a three-way confrontation between the Leader, the Hulk, and the murderous hordes of Hydra. *That was a narrow escape,* he reflected soberly. *Someday I will make Hydra pay—and dearly—for their crimes against me.*

But not today. Other pawns occupied his attention at present, most notably the various super-powered confederates of his recaptured specimens of mutantkind. He had known from the beginning that abducting Wolverine and the others would draw in the rest of the Avengers and the X-Men, and had planned accordingly.

The mission to Freehold, predictable as it was, was a wild goose chase, perfectly suited to keeping a percentage of his foes occupied while he continued his experiments upon the defenseless bodies of his captives. The Leader had covered his tracks well; no evidence remained beneath the icefields that could betray the existence of his new lunar lair, constructed with the considerable assistance and resources of his current associate. Captain America and company would find nothing in Freehold.

3. Another team of X-Men and Avengers had fared somewhat better, if not for much longer. On Muir Island, off the coast of Scotland, a group of heroes led by Storm, Iron Man, and, as always where the Leader's plans were concerned, the hated Hulk, had vanquished three-quarters of the Gamma Sentinels that the Leader had sent to Muir Island to obtain valuable scientific data from the isle's famed Genetic Research Centre. Three consecutive screens, designated GS-#'s 1-3, through which he had been able to gaze through the cybernetic eyes of each Gamma Sentinel, had gone blank, indicating that a trio of robotic enforcers had been rendered inactive by the Hulk and his uneasy allies.

A pyrrhic victory, that, the Leader thought with a smirk, given the insidious failsafe devices implanted in each of the Gamma Sentinels—and programmed to activate in the event of the robots' capture and/or defeat. *I wonder if Banner will even recognize his handiwork, before it destroys them all.* He stroked his black handlebar mustache in malicious anticipation. *I certainly hope so. . . .*

Granted, his partner, who had infiltrated the heroes' quest in the guise of "Wolverine," was theoretically threatened by the same imminent cataclysm, but the Leader trusted that his formidable associate was fully capable of shielding himself from what was to come; while hardly a genius of the Leader's caliber, his partner possessed cunning and physical faculties enough to guarantee his survival, at least until the Leader had no further need of him.

4. A fourth screen, GS-4, showed another scene, proof that the fourth and most powerful of the Gamma Sentinels remained in operation. Fashioned in the image of the Hulk himself, the surviving Sentinel now stalked the venerable halls of Avengers Mansion, where only a single inconsequential hero, the clownish anthropoid known as the Beast, offered feeble resistance to robot's rampage. The destruction of their stately headquarters, along with the probable demise of the Beast, would further delay and demoralize the Leader's foes.

In short, all was as it should be, throughout the entire Earth, as well as here upon that spinning globe's only natural satellite. The Leader leaned back against his throne, more than pleased with each new development in his unfolding scheme. His experiments upon his mutant specimens, taken in concert with the stolen data his Sentinels had transmitted from Muir Island prior to their undoing, had brought him within hours of his ultimate objective.

Haydn's symphony winded to its close as the Leader sat in contemplation, his long fingers steepled beneath his chin. He had no illusions that he could evade either the Avengers or the X-Men indefinitely; despite all the obstacles and adversaries strewn in their path, a few redoubtable heroes were bound to survive long enough to carry the fight to the moon.

No matter, he thought confidently. By the time the surviving adventurers braved this selenological sanctuary, it would already be too late.

He had more than one surprise prepared for them.

Chapter One

"They're not just Sentinels!" Iron Man announced, his horrified voice electronically amplified. "They're walking, talking Gamma Bombs—programmed to detonate upon defeat!"

The Golden Avenger clicked off the sensor beam emanating from the chestplate of his gold-and-crimson armor. His dire pronouncement echoed off the battle-scarred walls of the Genetic Research Centre. Although Iron Man's helmet concealed his own expression, shock and surprise registered on the faces of the other individuals occupying the remains of Dr. Moira MacTaggert's once pristine laboratory. A quartet of X-Men— the weather-controlling wind-rider known as Storm, the demonic-looking, nimble Nightcrawler, the feral fighter, Wolverine, and the aptly-named Iceman—listened in horror, while even the incredible Hulk looked disturbed by the news. *As well he should be,* Iron Man reflected, given that his human alter ego, Dr. Robert Bruce Banner, invented the very first gamma bomb many years ago.

Iron Man felt a twinge of sympathy for the man inside the monster; as Tony Stark, billionaire industrialist and inventor, the armored hero knew too well the pain of seeing the fruits of one's scientific ingenuity twisted to malevolent and destructive ends. Banner hadn't personally placed these new bombs into the so-called Gamma Sentinels, but Iron Man had to assume that, deep beneath the brutish exterior of the Hulk, some part of Bruce Banner felt responsible for the danger bearing down on them all.

"Are ye quite sure, Iron Man?" Dr. MacTaggert asked anxiously. The Scottish scientist, who was a long-time friend of the X-Men's, wore a battered white lab-coat over her civilian garb. She peered through her glasses at the nearest Sentinel, sculpted to resemble the green-haired super-psychiatrist, Doc Samson. Lying stiff and unmoving upon the debris-strewn floor, the inert robot appeared to be harmless at last.

"There's no mistaking the emissions coming from the Sentinel's power core," Iron Man stated. He glanced across the lab toward a second Sentinel, shaped like the mutated bird-woman known as the Harpy, lying on its side near a shattered picture window looking out onto the North Sea. Protective metal shutters had not stopped the artificial Harpy from blasting her way into the third-floor laboratory. Now the faint morning sunshine snuck through the jagged gap in the shutters, providing little in the way of warmth or hope. "The chain reaction has already started; I estimate we have less than five minutes before detonation."

He stared through the ruptured shutters at the open sky beyond; even with the Avengers' quinjet parked at the docks below the Centre, there was no way they could evacuate the laboratory in time. The explosion of three separate gamma bombs, the third residing inside yet another defeated Sentinel, currently gathering dust in a basement four stories below, would incinerate the entire research complex, the prison that held some of the most dangerous mutant villains, along with most of the surrounding geography, including a few nearby villages. *The death toll, even on this small island, could be horrific,* he realized.

His gaze locked on the X-Men's beautiful leader, the regal African woman codenamed Storm. "Ororo," he addressed her urgently. "You're the only one of us who stands a chance of outracing the blast—if you fly away now, as fast as your winds can carry you."

His own jets, of course, could bear him away from the island at supersonic speed, but he couldn't leave, not while there was still a chance to deactivate the bombs— and save the innocent inhabitants of Muir Island. *I have to try,* he thought, *even if time is running out.*

Storm shook her head. "An X-Man does not abandon her allies," she said firmly, an exotic accent flavoring her words. Her fellow mutants gathered around her, showing equal courage and determination on their faces, regardless of whether those faces were covered by ice, dark indigo fur, or, in Wolverine's case, a forbidding black mask. "The technological is your field of expertise, Iron Man. Tell us what, if anything, we can do to assist you."

"Ain't nothing I can do about those G-bombs," Wolverine grumbled. At least a foot shorter than Iron Man, the stocky mutant didn't look a bit intimidated by the armored Avengers. He sniffed the air warily. "I'd better keep a look-out for that runaway Hulk robot, just in case it gets the idea into its computerized skull to come back and catch us by surprise." He loped toward the exit, adamantium claws extended. "You can find me on the roof," he told the others, "if we ain't all blown to smithereens, that is."

The Avenger did not waste valuable seconds arguing with Storm or her comrades. Instead he turned toward the looming green behemoth standing nearby. "Hulk!" he challenged the surly titan. "Gamma bombs are Banner's baby. Can you—or he—help me disarm these?"

Considering the frequently adversarial relationship between the Hulk and his better half, invoking Banner's name was a risky plot, but Iron Man didn't see where he had any other choice. With luck, the Hulk could look past his perpetual rivalry with his more intellectual counterpart long enough to lend them a bit of Bruce Banner's genius.

The Hulk scowled. "You don't need that weakling, Banner," he rumbled. Concentration dug deep furrows in his sloping brow, and he tapped his temple with an oversized finger. "I got all of his memories right up here."

Iron Man prayed the Hulk was telling the truth. "Let's get to it then," he asserted. "I'll take Samson. You handle the Harpy." That left a replica of the Abomination in the basement, no doubt ticking away like the other time bombs. "Dr. MacTaggert, I don't suppose you know anything about defusing gamma bombs?"

"I'm afraid not," she answered, stepping back instinctively from the Samson-Sentinel. "My specialty's genetics, nae nuclear physics or weapons design."

"What about us?" Iceman asked. The X-Man's body was composed entirely of translucent blue ice. Puffs of wintry mist accompanied every syllable he uttered. Iron Man could feel the intense cold radiating off the young mutant even through his insulated armor. "What can we do to help?"

An idea struck the desperate Avenger. "Get down to that third Sentinel and freeze it as cold as you can. It's almost surely too late to halt the chain reaction, but you might be able to slow it down long enough to give us a chance.''

"Got it," Iceman said, nodding. Coating the floor ahead of him with a slick layer of frozen moisture, he slid toward a yawning pit behind the counterfeit Samson. A robotic version of the Hulk had created the pit earlier, when it leaped from the basement to the roof of the Centre, tearing a hole through every floor and ceiling in-between. Iceman's self-generated track transformed at the brink of the pit into an ice chute that carried the refrigerated X-Man out of sight. Iron Man wished him luck before turning to his own task.

The self-destructing Sentinel perfectly mimicked the appearance of Leonard Samson, Ph.D, taking the form of a large muscular figure with shoulder-length green hair. A bright red vest covered the Sentinel's brawny chest, beneath which surged the miniature gamma reactor that had served as the robot's heart.

Time for a little cardiac surgery, Iron Man thought grimly. Magnifying lenses dropped into place before his eyes. A countdown appeared at the corner of his vision, projected directly onto his retinas by HUD (Heads Up Display) units mounted in his helmet's eyepieces. *4 min 29 sec,* it began to tick down, keeping him perpetually aware of the need for swift action. A pencil-thin laser beam, ideally suited for such delicate work, emerged from the index finger of his right gauntlet.

Before he could get to work, however, a freezing gust of wind enveloped the Sentinel, frosting its synthetic skin and garments. Iron Man's helmet swiveled to one side, and he saw Storm standing by, her open hands elevated before her. The backwash from the frigid blast lifted her hair, whipping the snow-white tresses about her head.

"My arctic winds are not nearly as cold as what Iceman can summon," she volunteered, "but perhaps this can buy you a few more precious seconds."

"Thanks," Iron Man said sincerely. He wasn't sure Storm's icy gusts could actually slow the reaction on a sub-atomic level, not unless she cooled the gamma reactor down to absolute zero, but he wasn't about to look a gift breeze in the mouth; he needed every edge he could get. "Keep it up," he urged her.

His finger-laser sliced right down the middle of the Sentinel's chest. . . .

"Ach du lieber," Nightcrawler muttered, biting down on his lower lip in frustration. *If only there was something I could do . . . !*

Watching Iron Man perform surgery on "Doc Samson's" mechanical innards, while Storm did her best to delay the predicted explosion, Kurt Wagner felt singularly useless. There wasn't much his trademark acrobatics and swordsmanship could avail them in this crucial instance, even if his right ankle hadn't already been crushed by that inhuman facsimile of the Abomination. He considered joining Wolverine on the roof, but Logan hardly needed any help watching out for danger, not with those incredibly acute senses of his. Instead Nightcrawler limped closer to the Samson-Sentinel for a better look at Iron Man's efforts to defuse the bomb, the aluminum crutch beneath the German mutant's shoulder making him uncharacteristically clumsy. *Ouch,* he thought, wincing as the movement caused a sharp pain to throb up and down his injured leg. His long blue tail twitched in sympathy.

Like Moira, he was no expert in nuclear weapons, but he could see that Iron Man had already exposed the Sentinel's internal mechanisms and was now hastily examining a globe-shaped metal chamber located approximately where Doc Samson's heart should be. *A shame that Iron Man's employer, the famous Tony Stark, is nowhere nearby,* Nightcrawler thought, *the man is supposed to be a mechanical genius.* A devout Catholic, the demonic-looking X-Man prayed that some of Stark's brilliance had rubbed off on his armor-plated bodyguard.

"I think I recognize the design," Iron Man called out. "It's similar to the bomb that destroyed that town in Arizona a few years back." Fingers sheathed in flexible steel gloves carefully probed the interior of the Sentinel. "In theory, the damping rods must have retracted into the lower chest cavity—yes, there they are!"

"Yeah, yeah," the Hulk shouted back impatiently. "I figured that out already." Metal and plastic tore apart loudly as the Hulk dissected the imitation Harpy with his bare hands. "Race ya to the finish, Shellhead!"

It occurred to Nightcrawler that the Hulk had been created by a gamma bomb not unlike the ones that now menaced Muir Island, just as gamma radiation had spawned the real Harpy, the original Abomination, and even the malignant mastermind known as the Leader, whom, according to Storm, was believed to be responsible for the Sentinels' unprovoked attack on the Centre. *If even one of these bombs goes off,* he wondered apprehensively, *bathing the entire island with gene-altering gamma radiation, what sort of mutated menaces might emerge from those villages that survived the cataclysm?*

Another Hulk, perhaps? "*Mein gott,*" he whispered, appalled by the frightening possibilities.

"Less than a minute to critical mass," Iron Man reported. He thrust both hands into an assemblage of circuits and cables beneath the spherical reactor. "Here goes nothing."

"Easy for you to say, *mein freund,*" Nightcrawler remarked, "you're the one wearing the protective metal suit." Not that he really thought the Avenger's armor could shield Iron Man at ground zero of a nuclear explosion; he was just trying to lighten the mood as much as possible. If this was indeed to be the end of his illustrious career, Kurt Wagner wanted to go out with a quip on his lips and a smile in his heart. *And a bum ankle,* he reminded himself. *Let's not forget that.*

Something clicked into place within the Sentinel, and Nightcrawler held his breath, waiting for the firestorm to reduce him to atoms. The moment passed, though, and he heard a sigh of relief escape the anxious Avenger's gilded faceplate before Iron Man spun around to check on the green-skinned component of this impromptu bomb squad. "Hulk! What's happening over there?"

The jade giant casually lifted the false Harpy by one enormous pinion, yanked both her wings off, then dropkicked the mutilated Sentinel into the closest corner. "Don't cry so hard you rust, tin man," the Hulk said with a sneer. "This feathered fake ain't ticking anymore."

Nightcrawler recalled that the Harpy-Sentinel had been made to look like a mutated form of the Hulk's late wife. He wondered if that had anything to do with the disdain and violence with which the Hulk had disposed of the disarmed Sentinel, or if the Hulk was just constitutionally cranky? He found himself leaning strongly toward the latter explanation.

Iron Man had better things to do than respond to the Hulk's belligerent gibes. Jets flared from the soles of his iron boots as the Avenger launched himself down the adjacent pit after Iceman. Less than thirty seconds later, he rocketed up from below, carrying a Hulk-sized figure encased in a block of solid ice; through the frosty translucence of the ice, Nightcrawler dimly glimpsed the scaly hide and reptilian features of the Abomination, or at least a reasonable facsimile thereof. His fractured ankle ached as he recalled how the absurdly powerful grip of this particular Sentinel had squeezed his ankle until it shattered. Moira had prescribed him enough painkillers to numb the pain somewhat, but the drugs were not enough to spare him from the memory of that excruciating ordeal. In his mind, he could still feel the splintered bones grinding against each other before he teleported to safety.

A beam from Iron Man's chestplate scanned the Sentinel through six centimeters of ice. "What's the story?" Iceman asked the Avenger, ascending from the basement atop a rising pillar of ice. His crystalline form glistened in the sunlight. "Did the freeze treatment do any good?"

"You slowed the collision rate between the electrons and positrons," Iron Man informed him, "but not enough to shut down the chain reaction." The glowing sensor beam vanished in a blink, but the Avenger's ominous words hung in the air. "It could go any moment," he said; clearly, there was not enough time to crack open the ice, let alone defuse the bomb. *Is that it?* Nightcrawler thought. *Are we doomed?*

Iron Man refused to give up. His helmet turned toward the immense chartreuse goliath over by the window. "Get over here, Hulk," he ordered. "Throw this blasted thing straight up as hard as you can. You probably can't get it high enough fast enough, but it's our only chance!"

He didn't sound very optimistic, but, for once, the Hulk didn't put up a fuss. He bounded across the laboratory in a single leap, then wrapped his massive arms around the frozen Sentinel, lifting it off the floor. Nightcrawler shook his head in disbelief; the Hulk's colossal strength was legendary, but could even those herculean muscles propel the bomb into orbit before it exploded?

Maybe with a little bit of help . . .

"Wait!" Nightcrawler called out. Tossing his crutch aside, he somersaulted over to the Hulk's side and placed a three-fingered hand against the giant's ribs, using the Hulk's unyielding mass to support his weight. "Excuse me, *Herr* Hulk," he gasped, ignoring the sudden burst of agony radiating from his ankle. "Permit me to give you something of a foot up."

BAMF!

Without further explanation, Nightcrawler teleported himself, the Hulk, and the ice-covered Abomination-Sentinel two miles straight up. A puff of sulfurous black smoke greeted their instantaneous arrival in the sky high above Muir Island, as well as a wracking wave of discomfort that left Nightcrawler doubled over in pain and shock. Transporting such a heavy load over so great a distance would have been a strain even under the best of circumstances; in his drugged and debilitated state, the effort had nearly killed him.

Kurt prayed that the Hulk would take full advantage

of the 'port, right before he blacked out and began falling back to earth.

What the heck? the Hulk thought, confused by his unexpected translocation. One minute he'd been down in that Scottish chick's lab with Shellhead and the others, getting ready to fling an Abomination-on-ice for all it was worth; now here he was, up among the clouds. For an instant, he thought he'd been snatched by one of the Leader's patented trans-mat beams. Then he got a whiff of brimstone and realized that the X-Men's resident blue devil had *bamf*ed them both into the sky, giving the Hulk a sizable head start in getting rid of the bomb.

The very thought of owing that mutant gimp a favor, along with the implication that he even needed the help in the first place, fueled the Hulk's anger, adding strength to his already stupendous sinews. He used that extra *oomph* to hurl the ticking Gamma Sentinel away a split-second before gravity seized hold of him. The force of his throw sent him speeding downward, accelerating past the plummeting form of Nightcrawler.

Motivated by a certain crude decency that he would have vigorously denied if queried on the subject, the Hulk reached out for the unconscious mutant as they passed each other on their way to the island several thousand feet below. His outstretched fingers barely missed Nightcrawler's sagging limbs, but, at the last second, he managed to snag hold of the X-Man's ropy tail right above the triangular point at its nether end. Holding onto the tail with a clenched fist, the Hulk dragged Nightcrawler behind him as he plunged through the gray northern sky. "Great," he muttered sourly to himself, a cold wind whipping against him, carrying his words away. "*Now* what do I do with him?"

A blinding flash of emerald light, followed almost simultaneously by a thunderous blast of sound and force, interrupted the Hulk's sarcastic monologue. High above the clouds, at least an additional mile or two from where the Hulk had launched it skyward, the gamma bomb detonated, taking with it a near-perfect replica of Emil Blonsky, the Abomination. *Good riddance,* the Hulk thought, regretting that it wasn't the real Blonsky even as the shock wave hit him, battering his indestructible frame and searing his flesh, which healed just as quickly as it burned away. *Gotta hand it to Banner,* he admitted grudgingly, while his clenched teeth rattled in his skull, *those babies deliver one heck of a kick.*

The impact was enough to loosen his grip on Nightcrawler's tail, which slipped through his gargantuan fingers before he realized what was happening. *Oops!* He groped hastily for the escaped appendage, but seized only empty air. The force of the explosion drove their falling bodies apart, until Nightcrawler was well out of reach.

Above him a spreading mushroom cloud, distinctly viridescent in hue, blotted out the sun, casting emerald shadows over the bean-shaped island below, which appeared to grow larger by the second as the Hulk and Nightcrawler rushed toward the ground. He spotted MacTaggert's think tank near the northern tip of the island, its imposing steel and glass structures standing out amidst the rural villages and rolling hills carpeted in purple heather. The Hulk hoped he wouldn't miss Muir Island entirely and splash into the sea instead; he didn't feel like getting wet.

The fall itself didn't worry him. He'd walked away from every sort of crash landing before and didn't expect that this one would be any different. Too bad Nightcrawler probably couldn't say the same. *Hey, I tried to catch him,* the Hulk thought defensively. *Nobody forced him to* bamf *without a parachute. He knew the odds.*

The elflike X-Man sped earthward like a fuzzy blue meteor, until a purple ray of light swept over him, slowing his descent. The Hulk watched in surprise as the violet beam brought Nightcrawler's freefall to a standstill. His wide green eyes followed the tractor beam back to its source: the glowing projector at the center of Iron Man's chestplate. *Yeah, right,* he thought. *I should've guessed Shellhead wouldn't let the gimp go splat.*

While Iron Man carefully began to lower Nightcrawler to the ground, the Hulk fell past both X-Man and Avenger. He didn't expect similar treatment, figuring he was on his own as usual, so he was caught by surprise when a sudden whirlwind arrived from out of nowhere, lifting him back into the sky well before he impacted with the waiting bedrock of Muir Island. The Hulk gasped out loud, puzzled by the timely twister, until he glimpsed Storm soaring above him, the black fabric wings beneath her arms catching the updrafts carrying her aloft. Her arms were outstretched before her, commanding the weather like a conductor leading an orchestra.

The whirlwind ferried him back to the roof of the Centre, where he found the X-Men and their Avenger buddy waiting for him, Dr. MacTaggert already leaning over the baked and battered form of Nightcrawler as he lay sprawled upon the rooftop. Storm touched down gently seconds after her tamed tornado evaporated back into the cool Scottish air. Miles overhead, the seething mush-room cloud had yet to dissipate entirely. "Praise the Goddess!" Storm exclaimed, eyeing the emerald turbulence with a mixture of awe and disgust. "We have been spared after all."

"You praise her," the Hulk snarled back. "I didn't need any help. And still don't."

Despite his angry words, the sight of the gamma bomb's unleashed atomic fury sent a chill down his spine, forcing him to remember another explosion, years ago in the New Mexico desert, that had changed Banner's life forever—and given birth to the hated and hate-filled being now looking out over the North Sea. *Hi, Mom,* he thought to the bomb's aftermath, reflected in the icy blue waters of Cape Wrath. *Sorry I didn't get you a card.*

Thankfully, the Gamma Sentinels had not totally destroyed the Centre's medlab. Many of the overhead lights were smashed, the walls bore serious dents and jagged scratches, the tile floor was badly scuffed, and at least one bedframe was now a crumpled mass of metal shoved into an unoccupied corner of the infirmary, but there was still enough intact equipment for Moira to immediately treat Nightcrawler for his injuries. An antiseptic medicinal smell, common to medical facilities everywhere, suggested, in a vaguely subliminal fashion, that, despite everything, the medlab was open for business.

Storm stood by, helpfully holding a tray of instruments, as Moira completed her examination of Kurt, now resting in bed beneath a display of sophisticated diagnostic monitors. It pained Ororo to see her friend in such a ravaged state. His once-colorful uniform had been burned away, reduced to charred black rags that were almost invisible against the patient's dark indigo fur. In places, the fine blue fuzz covering his body had been scorched away as well, revealing reddened patches of caucasian skin. Beneath sagging eyelids, his normally incandescent yellow eyes were clouded and streaked with red. Blisters covered his pointed ears. *At least Iron Man caught him as he fell,* she thought, *but look what that hateful bomb has done to him!*

Finished taking his pulse, Moira let go of Kurt's wrist and inspected the monitors above the injured X-Man's head. "He'll live," she pronounced eventually, granting Storm a welcome sense of relief. "He's in shock, his ankle's still broken, and he's picked up some nasty radiation burns, but he should recover in time."

Thank you, Bright Lady, Storm thought. "Are you certain he'll be well, doctor?" Nightcrawler had not truly regained consciousness since his selfless decision to teleport both the Hulk and the bomb away from the island. If only she could be sure that he knew how much his sacrifice had bought them. "I trust your judgment, Moira, but he looks worse than I ever remember seeing him before."

Moira gave her a reassuring smile, then glanced at Wolverine. "Kurt may nae have Logan's mutant healin' factor, but I've learned never t'underestimate the recuperative powers of any X-Man." She took the instrument tray from Storm and laid it down atop an adjacent bed. "You folks take the proverbial lickin', then keep tickin' along more reliably than Big Ben. Have nae fear," she assured the other heroes. "He'll be fine soon enough."

"That's great news, doc," Bobby Drake said. Now that the immediate crisis was over, Iceman had defrosted himself, so that he now looked like nothing more than a brown-haired youth in a pale blue uniform. He stood at the end of Nightcrawler's sickbed, beside Wolverine. Iron Man, not wanting to intrude on the X-Men's bedside vigil, kept his distance, as did the Hulk, who sulked impatiently against an already dented supply cabinet. "Doesn't look like he's coming with us, though," Bobby added.

"No," Storm agreed, shaking her head sadly. She wished they could linger to comfort Kurt through his recovery, but there was no time for delay. Rogue and the Scarlet Witch remained missing, presumably in the hands of a diabolical villain, the Leader, whom Storm herself had never fought before, but whom both the Avengers and the Hulk insisted was a formidable foe. *We must return to our quest,* she realized, hoping that Cyclops, Beast, and Iron Man's fellow Avengers had discovered some means of tracking the Leader to his hidden sanctuary. "The sooner we rendezvous with our comrades at Avengers Mansion, the better."

"I'm coming with you, of course," Bobby insisted. Visiting Moira in Scotland, he had missed the early stages of their hunt for Rogue, but could hardly be expected to stay behind now, especially since, as Storm now recalled, there had once been the early stirrings of a romance between Iceman and the X-Men's missing southern belle; nothing much had come of their flirtation in the end, since Rogue's heart remained inextricably bound with the mutant thief Gambit, yet Storm had no doubts that Bobby wanted to see Rogue restored to safety as much, if not more, than any one of them.

"Great," the Hulk groused, his voice several octaves deeper than Storm would have thought humanly possible. "Just what we need, the human popsicle. The Leader must be getting the chills already."

"Watch your mouth, bub," Wolverine said, spinning around to confront the green-skinned titan. Silver claws jutted from the backs of his gloves and he dropped into an aggressive stance. "I don't see you doin' too much at the moment, except takin' up too much space."

"Oh yeah?" the Hulk shot back, clenching his anvil-sized fists. His heavy tread shook the medlab, rattling the loose instruments on the discarded tray, as he stepped toward Wolverine, eager to renew their longtime rivalry. "Says the sawed-off runt who let that Hulk-Sentinel get away!"

Wolverine bristled noticeably. A low growl escaped his lips, promising havoc on the horizon. "Hey, wait a second, guys," Bobby protested, as alarmed as Storm at the prospect of a super-powered brawl breaking out in the medlab. He stepped between the Hulk and Wolverine, attempting to play peacemaker, but the Hulk effortlessly brushed him aside. Although little more than a tap, the Hulk's gamma-charged backhand was enough to send Bobby tumbling backwards. Only the quick reflexes of Iron Man, who grabbed onto Bobby's shoulders with both gauntlets, kept the de-iced Iceman from landing flat on his back.

"That is enough!" Storm declared with righteous indignation, punctuating her words with a resounding thunderclap that captured the attention of everyone in the infirmary—and probably the rest of the island. "Must we quarrel amongst ourselves even in the presence of our wounded companion? I thought we were united against the Leader, or have you both forgotten that?"

Moira beamed in approval, clearly impressed by

Storm's no-nonsense attitude. "You go, lass!" she whispered audibly.

Blessedly, Ororo's heartfelt admonition had the desired effect; even the brutish Hulk looked slightly abashed. His gigantic fists retreated to his sides and he withdrew to the hallway outside the medlab, his disheveled emerald scalp barely clearing the top of the exit. Wolverine retracted his claws, but his glowering eyes tracked the departing Hulk until the bellicose giant lumbered out of sight. "Sorry about that, darlin'," he muttered to Storm. "Guess there's a time and a place for everything."

"Indeed," she affirmed. Wolverine's reckless behavior disturbed her. The Goddess knew the Hulk was obnoxious, and Logan was not exactly the type to willingly turn the other cheek, but she would have thought he knew better than to rise to the Hulk's bait in the middle of the medlab. For all his deeply-rooted ferocity, the Logan she knew was a wiser and more pragmatic warrior than that, one generally capable of keeping his most violent impulses under a tight rein when necessary. But picking a fight with the Hulk during a vital mission . . . ? That wasn't like him.

Or so she liked to think.

Chapter Two

CNN was the first to report an unconfirmed nuclear explosion in the upper atmosphere high above the Scottish isles. Due to the high altitude at which the blast occurred, no casualties were anticipated, although various nations in Europe and elsewhere had already accused their respective enemies of being responsible for the radioactive explosion, which they condemned in the strongest possible terms. No country or terrorist organization had yet come forward to take credit (or blame) for the unprovoked nuclear incident, but many commentators and self-described experts, in the absence of any hard evidence one way or another, pointed ominously at the remote Balkan nation of Latveria, long suspected of concealing a nuclear arsenal. "Has Dr. Doom finally come out of the thermonuclear closet?" Bernard Shaw asked during a special news bulletin. "We'll be back with that question, after this brief commercial break."

Doctor Doom indeed! I should say not. Tapping gently on his lighted control panel, the Leader muted the audio component from that particular broadcast, one of many he monitored on the profusion of screens laid out before him. Over two hundred thousand miles from the hubbub, securely sequestered in his private control room on the moon, the intellectually over-endowed supervillain sighed in disappointment. Judging from the distressingly deathtoll-free details of the bulletin, he reluctantly deduced that the Hulk and his occasional allies had survived the explosive death spasms of the captured Gamma Sentinels. *I should have known it was too good to be true,* he thought ruefully.

Although saddened, he was not too surprised. Nobody knew better than he, after all, how aggrivatingly hard the Hulk was to kill. His own calculations had projected a 48.83 percent probability that the Hulk and his costumed compatriots would escape death on Muir Island.

"Fine," he murmured softly. He had allowed for that. . . .

Air! I need air!

Logan awoke with a start, surprised to find himself still alive. His freshest memory was of gasping for breath on the moon's lifeless surface, alongside Rogue and the Scarlet Witch. *I'd thought we were goners for sure,* he recalled, *but, wait, hadn't there been something after that?* Racking his fogged memory, he called up vague, fragmentary impressions of cold, analytical eyes observing him like he was a bug under glass, and of a bulging skull whose pulsing hemispheres resembled cabbages on steroids. *That's right,* he remembered all at once. *I saw the main sleazeball himself. The Leader!*

Blinking, he tried to rub his eyes, only to discover that his wrists were pinned to his sides by unyielding metal shackles. "Blast it," he growled. "Not this again."

Sure enough; as his blurry vision came into focus, he discovered that he was right back where he started: crammed into a stainless steel casket, like he was already embalmed and fit to be planted six feet under, except that this stinkin' coffin was leaning upright above the floor. *So much for our great escape,* he thought sourly. *Time for Plan B—whatever the heck that is.*

The wall-length mirror that had once greeted his eyes from this same uncomfortable vantage point was no longer there, shattered by Rogue with a single punch during their botched break for freedom. Now he had a clear view into the control room facing his cell, where row upon row of tv screens looked back at him. No sign of the Leader, though; the crumb's elevated throne sat empty. *I guess even a would-be ruler of the world has to take a break every now and then,* Logan mused. *Fine with me. I ain't in a hurry to see his ugly face again.*

But what about Rogue and the Witch? He frowned, frustrated by the clamp over his throat. Without the convenient mirror, he had no easy way to check on his partners in captivity. He tried to locate them out of the corner of his eyes, but all he glimpsed were the sides of his cramped sarcophagus. He could smell the distinctive scent of each woman, though, so he knew they couldn't be far away. *Probably trussed up just like me.* "Rogue? Wanda?" he called out, hoping to hear Rogue's familiar southern drawl in response, or even the Witch's Eastern European accent. "Are you alright? Can you answer me? Rogue?"

A whiff of ozone teased his super-sensitive nostrils, presaging by seconds a flash of bright light that faded quickly, leaving an unmistakable figure behind. Logan recognized the new arrival immediately. If nothing else, the economy-sized frontal lobes were a dead giveaway, not to mention the fungus-green complexion.

"You can save your breath, my atavistic guest," the Leader said coolly, apparently unruffled by the abruptness of teleportation. His mutated brain was just as bloated as Logan had always heard; he had no idea how the Leader's skinny neck managed to support its weight. "Lacking your truly remarkable recuperative powers, your female associates are unlikely to regain consciousness as swiftly as you have."

The future conqueror of humanity was simply dressed, wearing a better-tailored, freshly-pressed version of the same orange jumpsuits Logan and the other prisoners had been dressed in. Black metallic wristbands, adorned with touchpad controls, granted him easy access to his advanced technology. *Not much of a fashion-plate,* Logan decided; *guess he doesn't want anything to draw attention away from his overflowing gray matter, which, in his case, I bet is more green than gray.* Wolverine's claws slid out of his hands as he looked forward to finding out for himself the first chance he got.

"What's this all about, brain-boy?" he snarled, straining against his restraints. "You got a reason for draggin' us all the way up to the moon, or are you just starved for company?"

Glaring at the Leader with undisguised animosity, Logan waited for the inevitable long-winded recitation. These egghead types, he knew from excruciating experience, could never pass up a chance to blab about their ingenious master plans. How else were they supposed to show off their allegedly superior smarts, along with their oversized vocabularies?

The Leader proved no exception. To Logan's expert nose, the mutated mastermind literally reeked of ego, arrogance, and cologne. "As a matter of fact," he began, "you and your distaff counterparts have proven an invaluable source of genetic data, aside from a few intriguing and as-yet undefinable anomalies where the Scarlet

Witch's powers are concerned. Thanks to my in-depth analysis of your mutant abilities, metabolisms, and DNA, I am almost ready to proceed to the next stage of my grand experiment, awaiting only the return of my silent partner in this enterprise.''

Partner? Logan wondered. What partner? As far as he knew, the Leader had always worked alone. Then again, it had been a long time since Logan had seen any of Department H's intel reports on the Leader's activities. One of the few disadvantages to leaving Canada's intelligence forces had been losing his access to various classified material. He wished he could remember more about the Leader's reported strengths and weaknesses.

''I don't know who'd be stupid enough to trust you,'' Logan told his captor, ''but I'll lay odds that the X-Men will be here looking for us before your idiot partner gets back. The Avengers, too, I figure.'' It seemed safe to assume that the Scarlet Witch's teammates wanted her back.

The Leader chuckled at Wolverine's prediction. ''You may be amused to know, Specimen #3, that my admirably devious associate has already taken your place in the ranks of the X-Men. Indeed, I can assure you that your mutant colleagues do not even know you're among the missing.''

''We'll see about that, bub,'' Logan snarled. He doubted that any imposter, no matter how good, could fool Storm and the others for long. ''And the name's Wolverine, bub, not Specimen anything.'' A red-hot surge of anger flared inside him, sparked by vivid memories of the experiments performed on him years ago in an isolated laboratory in the Canadian wilderness. Being treated like a test animal again touched a raw and painful nerve; it took all his self-control to keep his temper and bloodlust from boiling over. "What about Rogue and the Witch?" he asked, his voice hoarse with pent-up rage. "You come up with ringers for them, too?"

"That was deemed unnecessary," the Leader admitted. "One spy in our enemies' midst seemed more than sufficient." He stepped out of Logan's limited line of sight, perhaps checking on the other prisoners. "Besides, to be utterly frank about it, the womens' abilities would have been significantly more difficult for an undercover agent to mimic."

Yeah, that makes sense, Logan was forced to concede. Even he wasn't exactly sure how the Scarlet Witch's powers worked. He tried to guess who the Leader's sneaky spy might be. Mystique? The Chameleon? Mastermind? It didn't have to be a bona fide shape-changer or illusionist, he realized; these days anyone with a working image inducer could look like whomever they wished, greatly expanding the list of possible suspects. He'd have to drag some more clues out of the Leader before he had a chance of sussing out the second half of this sinister partnership.

A moan, coming from somewhere on his right, distracted Logan from his detective work. "Rogue?" he asked. "Is that you?"

"Wolvie?" She sounded groggy, confused. "Wha' happened? How'd we get back here?" Fury supplanted bewilderment, however, as she laid eyes on the Leader, or so Logan surmised. "Who the—? Ah know who you are!" she blurted angrily, apparently remembering Wanda's description of the Leader. "Wait until ah get mah hands on ya!"

"Pleased to meet you as well," the target of her rage

replied archly. "Welcome back to the realm of the wakeful, Specimen #1. Good of you to join us at last."

"Join ya?" Rogue sounded mad enough to spit. "Why ah'll take ya apart piece by piece, you scrawny, turnip-headed sidewinder!" Logan heard her squirming against her adamantium bonds, keen to teach the Leader a painful lesson in down-home hospitality. He admired her attitude, even if he doubted that it would shake the self-satisfied confidence of the Leader, who pretty much had to have heard worse from the Hulk. "Ah'll kick your fat head all the way back ta Earth!"

As Logan had expected, the Leader ignored Rogue's spirited threats. "You presented me with a singular challenge, Specimen #1," he calmly informed her. "As you may or may not be aware, my considerable mental powers include the useful ability to control the minds of any individual I choose to touch, provided they have not also been transformed by gamma radiation. Unfortunately, as you well know, touching you is an extremely problematic proposition."

"Like I'd even want your oily fingers anywhere near me!" Rogue retorted, madder than ever. Her inability to touch or be touched by someone without absorbing their memories and characteristics was a real sore spot with her, one the heartless Leader apparently had no fear of poking. "You keep your sweaty green hands away from me, you hairless varmint."

Her incensed outburst failed to derail the Leader's train of thought. "My own brilliant super-science has provided a solution to this apparent impasse," he explained. "Based on close examination of your genetic pattern, conducted over the last twenty-four hours or so, I have developed a synthetic compound that I believe will successfully inhibit the proper operation of your unique absorption process." He tapped a control panel upon his wrist. "A compound, which, I should probably add, is even now being introduced into your bloodstream via intravenous infusion."

"You mean, you got a drug that blocks mah powers?" Rogue spoke in a hush, sounding like she didn't know whether to be excited or aghast. "One that really works?"

"Only a short-term solution, to be sure," the Leader divulged. "I doubt if my compound can suppress your parasitic talent for more than a minute or two, but, really, that's all that I need."

Uh-oh, Logan thought. *I don't like the sound of that.*

Neither did Rogue. "Wait a sec," she said apprehensively. "What do you mean?" An edge of panic crept into her voice and Logan swore in frustration, unable to see what was happening less than a yard away. Superstrength rattled her adamantium restraints, but not enough to break her loose. "Get back!" Rogue shouted helplessly. "Stay away from me!"

Her unleashed lungpower, although unlikely to deter the Leader, served to rouse the Scarlet Witch from her drugged slumber. Logan heard the captured Avenger stirring a couple feet to his left, trapped in her own customized sarcophagus, complete with a metal blindfold to prevent her from effectively employing her mutant sorcery. "Rogue?" she called out, and Logan couldn't help noticing the sincere concern in her voice, quite a change from the cold shoulder she had given Rogue when they had first found themselves trapped together in the Leader's chamber of horrors. "What's wrong? Are you in pain?"

The Leader laughed coldly, and Logan heard him step away from Rogue's upraised casket. "Go ahead and answer her, m'dear," he said mockingly, enjoying a joke at his captives' expense. "Tell your fellow test subjects how much better you are feeling now."

"Yes," Rogue answered mechanically. "Ah'm feelin' much better." Logan was shocked by what he heard. The hot-tempered X-Man's voice had been drained of all spunk and defiance; he barely recognized it. *Oh, darlin',* he thought bitterly, *what's that scumbag done to you?*

Unfortunately, he had a pretty good idea; the Leader's insidious talent for mind control was well-documented. "There we are," he announced with smug satisfaction. "No need to keep you locked up anymore." Logan heard the click of the Leader's wrist controls, followed by the sound of metallic shackles springing open. "You may step down from there, Specimen #1."

"Yes," she agreed readily. Her bare feet slapped gently against the smooth metal floor as she landed in front of her former coffin. Moments later, the Leader strolled back into view, followed by a compliant and listless Rogue, displaying none of the justifiable indignation in evidence only a minute before. Her arms, which should have been enthusiastically wringing the Leader's neck, hung limply at her sides. Wide brown eyes, usually full of sass and wicked humor, stared blankly ahead, glazed and unfocussed. Logan had seen Sentinels with more personality.

"Snap out of it, Rogue!" he growled at her, hoping to spark a fire in those snuffed-out eyes. "You can do it, darlin'. Break loose, just like Charlie taught us!"

In fact, Charles Xavier had trained his X-Men in various exercises designed to help them resist telepathic incursions, but just how strong was the Leader's enormous brain anyway, and how did he stack up against the likes of Mesmero, Karma, or the White Queen? *Too bad Chuck or Jeannie ain't here,* he thought, gnashing his teeth. *We need one of our own psi-types to level the playing field.* He was the best there was at what he did, but that hardly included psionic warfare. "C'mon, Rogue!" he urged her. "Don't let him do this to you! Shake it off!"

For one tantalizing second, he thought he saw a glimmer of the real Rogue in that vacant face. Long black lashes quivered and her forehead wrinkled in confusion. Her lips parted and, for a heartbeat, he thought she was trying to voice her own thoughts and opinions.

Then the moment passed. Animation fled from her features, which relaxed into unthinking lassitude. Without any prompting from the Leader to do so, the enslaved X-Man made no response to Logan's angry pleas. She didn't seem to hear a word he said, unlike the Scarlet Witch, who called out to him desperately. "What is it? Tell me what's happening!"

Logan remembered that the blindfolded Witch could not see a thing. *Probably better off that way,* he thought grimly, but he answered her anyway. "It's the Leader," he spat in disgust. "He's turned Rogue into a friggin' zombie."

"Proving the efficacy of my chemical suppressant," the Leader congratulated himself. "Not that any such precautions are required when it comes to you remaining specimens." He raised his hands before him, methodically cracking each sickly green knuckle, like a pianist getting ready to sit down at his instrument.

Logan saw where this was going, and his heart sank. Leaving Rogue standing stiffly in front of Logan, the Leader disappeared briefly to the left. Wanda gasped once, perhaps surprised by the sudden touch of a stranger's fingers against her face, then she fell unnervingly silent. "For convenience's sake," the Leader instructed her. "You will answer to the designation: Specimen #2."

"Yes." Steel bonds unfastened once more, a metal visor slid away, and the auburn-haired Avenger stepped down from the open sarcophagus. At the Leader's direction, she joined Rogue, padding barefoot across the floor until she came to a stop beside her fellow thrall. "Be careful, #2," the Leader warned her as he paced back to where Logan could see him. "You don't want to get too close to Specimen #1, formerly known to you as Rogue, at least not until we get a pair of gloves on her."

"Yes," Wanda Maximoff answered obediently. Her exotic green eyes were just as empty as Rogue's. Looking at them both, silent and docile, made Logan's blood burn. He didn't know the Scarlet Witch anywhere near as well as he knew Rogue, but that didn't stop him from feeling enraged on her behalf. Nobody deserved to have her free will stripped away like this, and especially not an Avenger who had risked her life to save the whole planet a hundred times over. *This bites, big time.*

Now it was his turn. Logan gritted his teeth, bracing himself for the psychic violation he knew was coming. Was there any chance his high-powered healing factor could overcome the Leader's mental mesmerism? It was a slim hope, but it was the best he had. *Give me your best shot,* he thought defiantly as the Leader approached, his enormous skull obscuring Logan's view of the two entranced super-heroines.

"For what it's worth," the Leader informed him snidely, "you've already made a genuine contribution to my own brand of superior science. The insights I've gained from studying your mutant metabolism, particularly your extraordinary ability to heal, have given me some intriguing ideas as to how to counteract the Hulk's even more astonishing recuperative powers." He smirked beneath his bushy black mustache. "I hope knowing that you've played an instrumental part in the future destruction of the ever-incredible Hulk provides you some measure of comfort—in the brief interval that your mind remains your own."

Unable to reach his tormentor with his unsheathed claws, Logan spit in the Leader's face. He glared at the cerebral megalomaniac through a blood-red haze. "One of these days, buster, you're going to end up at the wrong end of my built-in pigstickers." Visions of bloody carnage flashed through his brain. "I can't wait."

"A rabid animal to the last, eh?" The Leader smirked and lifted his hands toward Logan's exposed face. The fettered X-Man flinched at the touch of clammy, uncalloused fingers. A cold, numbing fog descended over his mind, driving out the red-hot blaze of his homicidal bloodlust like a high-pressure front dispelling a heat wave. *No!* he thought fiercely. *Keep out of my flamin' brain!* He tried to construct a psychic barricade, just like the Professor advised, but the fog was already dulling his mental faculties, making it hard to think straight. Or even think at all.

"No!" he groaned, dragging the words up from somewhere deep inside him. "No, no, no . . ."

Yes?

''Try not to lose all of that innate savagery, Specimen #3,'' his Leader said approvingly. ''I can always use whatever's left.''

Chapter Three

8 *90 Fifth Avenue.* Over the years, the venerable mansion on Manhattan's Upper East Side had opened its doors to many unusual visitors, ranging from alien ambassadors to pagan deities, but Hank McCoy could have done without Avenger Mansion's latest unwelcome guest: an immense humanoid juggernaut that bore an uncanny resemblance to the Avengers' most infamous founding member, the rampaging Hulk.

"Identified: mutant designate: Beast," the menacing simulacrum stated implacably. Two tons of lethal machinery, encased in synthetic green flesh and hair, stepped into the high-tech conference room, rattling the floor with its heavy tread. "Threat assessment: minimal. Immediate priority: termination."

Oh my stars and garters! the Beast thought, momentarily transfixed by the imposing figure barging through the entrance, its massive shoulders shattering the reinforced titanium doorframe. Behind wire-frame reading glasses, the Beast's blue eyes widened in alarm. He gulped loudly, his mouth suddenly dry as the Living Mummy's desiccated bandages.

Despite the invader's picture-perfect impersonation of the Hulk, the Beast recognized the Gamma Sentinel immediately; not only did the murderous robot's speech patterns reveal its true nature, Nick Fury had earlier revealed to the assembled Avengers and X-Men that this new line of Sentinels had been constructed to mirror the physical appearance of various celebrated gamma-mutated monstrosities, the better to provide S.H.I.E.L.D. with plausible deniability should another anti-mutant pogrom be deemed necessary—as they too often were.

"I beg to differ," the shaggy blue anthropoid protested. He looked around quickly for a place to stow his glasses, then decided they'd be safest on his nose. Seeking higher ground, he bounded onto the circular meeting table, nimbly avoiding the pitcher of hot coffee that Jarvis had thoughtfully prepared for the Beast before retiring for the evening. Computer print-outs on the Leader's past activities and bases of operation littered the polished chrome tabletop, which was emblazoned with a stylized capital "A" designed by one of Tony Stark's best graphic artists. "Sorry to say, I fear our respective priorities are fundamentally irreconcilable."

In other words, the bouncing Beast definitely hoped to stay alive. Which wasn't going to be easy, considering that he was currently holding down the fort all by his lonesome, while the rest of the X-Men and the Avengers pursued undeniably urgent endeavors throughout the world. With the exception of Jarvis, the Avenger's faithful butler, the Beast was on his own. *I wonder if it's too late to join the Fantastic Four?* he speculated mordantly, even as the hostile Sentinel (a redundancy if ever there was one) reached out for him with the Hulk's huge hands. "Hulk will smash!" the robot recited, programmed to perpetuate its perfidious imposture for the benefit of any possible witnesses, human or otherwise.

"You will have to do considerably better than that, o' masquerading mechanism," the Beast replied. His powerful legs propelled him upward, out of reach of the

Sentinel's grasping arms. At the same time, one prodigiously dexterous foot flung the entire pitcher of steaming coffee into the robot's face. "Have a heaping helping of mountain-grown java on me!"

The Beast's leap carried him backwards over the table's edge. Somersaulting in mid-air, he landed squarely on the floor behind the round table. He had no illusions that the spilled coffee would drive off the Sentinel for good; trying to repel even an imitation Hulk with nothing more than a hot beverage was tantamount to swatting a stampeding elephant with a lady's fan. At most, he hoped the opaque liquid would foul the robot's optical sensors long enough to buy him a few more seconds.

No such luck. "Switching to sonar targeting," the Sentinel announced. Its cavernously deep voice captured the basso profundo quality of the real Hulk's speech, if not exactly the flavor of his dialogue. "Eliminating physical obstacles prior to termination of mutant designate: Beast."

The sturdy table, around which Earth's mightiest heroes so often conferred, had been securely mounted to the floor, and built to last by the same unparalleled engineering expertise responsible for Iron Man's armor. The Hulk-Sentinel wrenched it free of its steadfast moorings with a single tug, then shoved the dislodged table to the side. Sparks flew, and tortured metal shrieked, as the table slammed into the nearby communications console. A tray of half-eaten finger sandwiches clattered to the floor. Now nothing stood between the Beast and his attacker but a few yards of empty air and a couple of egg-shaped chairs. "Hulk will smash!"

Although spacious enough for its intended purpose, the conference room was too confined to let the Beast take full advantage of his preternatural agility. Fortunately, he had other options at his disposal. "Intruder alert!" he shouted with atypical succinctness. "Activate emergency detainment measures. Command authorization: McCoy-alpha-one!"

Voice-activated security systems came into play, no longer mistaking the disguised Sentinel for the real Hulk, whom had been welcomed into this very meeting room several hours before. Automated panels slid open in the walls, floor, and ceiling, releasing an impressive array of Stark-built and -designed mechanisms, intended to subdue and/or immobilize any uninvited visitors to Avengers HQ. Low-yield plasma guns, descending from the ceiling, blasted the chartreuse behemoth with coruscating bursts of ionized gas that had distressingly little effect on the robot's artificial skin. Capture coils, snaking out from concealed apertures in the floor, wrapped around the Gamma Sentinel like electrified pythons, squeezing the counterfeit Hulk's impossibly muscled arms against its sides while simultaneously delivering a high-voltage shock.

Thank providence that I never gave up my associate Avengers status, the Beast thought. He had retained his privileges, including access to top-secret Avengers security codes, even though his first loyalty remained to the X-Men. As an erstwhile alumnus of both distinguished super-teams, he had been the logical choice to man the communications center while his assorted teammates scattered hither and yon. Then again, no one had anticipated that one of the missing Sentinels would stage a frontal assault on Avengers Mansion.

Blue electricity crackled around the ensnared Hulk-Sentinel, causing the hairs of its emerald scalp to stand on end. The galvanic jolt administered by the coils was capable of overloading the nervous system of any ordinary being—which the Gamma Sentinel, lamentably, was not. Fighting back against the constricting coils, it flexed its mighty arms and strained to break free from the thick cables, each one a full six inches in diameter. The Beast heard concealed servomotors whirring madly within the fraudulent Hulk's huge biceps, and realized that, if he was ever to make a break for it, the time was now, before the mechanical monster was loose once more. "Nothing can stop the Hulk!" it bellowed ominously, increasing the Beast's understandable sense of alarm.

His natural agility matched only by Nightcrawler, and, maybe Spider-Man, too, the Beast leaped and rolled through the blistering barrage of plasma bursts, simultaneously giving the Hulk-Sentinel a wide berth on his way to the exit. The impromptu obstacle course reminded him of many a training exercise back in the X-Men's legendary Danger Room, but this time the stakes were substantially higher. No sooner had he dived through the ruptured doorway into the carpeted second-story hallway outside the conference room, than he heard the unmistakable sound of sundered metal giving way before an irresistible force. The hiss of the electrified cables died out at once, and the liberated Gamma Sentinel barrelled noisily through the wall in pursuit of the Beast, who tumbled down the corridor only a few cartwheels ahead of the lumbering robot. Framed portraits of the Black Panther, Captain Marvel, and other distinguished former residents crashed to the floor, knocked loose by the Gamma Sentinel's charge.

Jarvis appeared at the bottom of a stairway leading

down to the ground floor. The middle-aged Englishman, clad in a dressing gown and slippers, had no doubt been roused from sleep by the bogus Hulk's clamorous rampage. Shocked and confused, he stared aghast at the conflict and destruction upstairs. "Master Hulk! Master Beast! What in heavens are you doing?"

Despite his own peril, the Beast spared a moment to warn the loyal retainer. "Head for the hills, Jarvis, old boy! Contrary to appearances, this rambunctious barbarian is not the Hulk—it's a Sentinel!"

"My word!" the balding butler gasped. Accustomed to the unusual occurrences that so often befell the mansion, he did not require any further explanation. "Understood, sir," he said, moving briskly toward the front door. An ordinary man with no special powers, aside from his uncommon discretion and the ability to brew a first-rate pot of tea, Edwin Jarvis knew better than to stick around the mansion during an assault, where he might well end up a hostage or a casualty. "Good luck to you, sir! I will notify the authorities *post haste.*"

Running atop the wooden bannister at the top of the stairs, the Beast heard the front door open downstairs. *One less thing to worry about,* he thought gratefully, relieved that the veteran manservant had escaped unscathed. He was sorely tempted to join Jarvis in fleeing the house, but that would mean unleashing the relentless Sentinel on the unsuspecting city streets, not to mention sacrificing his home field advantage.

Even now, the Mansion's automated defenses continued to deploy new weapons against the ersatz Hulk. Bean bag guns pelted the Sentinel with weighted bags of silicon gel, concussive vibranium missiles exploded soundlessly against the robot's verdant epidermis, and anesthetizing gas hissed out of pipes hidden above the landing. *Do Sentinels breathe?* the Beast wondered, holding his own breath until he was safely free of the narcotic fumes. *Regretfully, I suspect not.*

Alas, he recognized the ultimate futility of this automated exercise in pest control. Apparatus intended to administer non-lethal amounts of force against the likes of the Grim Reaper or Baron Zemo would inevitably prove insufficient against any mechanoid even approximating the quite literally immeasurable might of the Hulk. The most he could hope for was that the Mansion's state-of-the-art security system would slow the Sentinel down.

"Hulk will smash mutant designate: Beast," the Gamma Sentinel said, mixing its syntax a bit. The Beast recalled that this trespassing automaton was, in fact, an experimental prototype stolen from S.H.I.E.L.D., so it only stood to reason that all of the bugs hadn't been worked out yet. Not that the hijacked robot wasn't perfectly capable of inflicting stupendous quantities of damage on whatever came within reach of its implacable fists, as proven by the brutal ease with which the Hulk-Sentinel uprooted the entire bannister, throwing the Beast off-balance.

"Allez oop!" the X-Man exclaimed. A crystal chandelier hung over the foyer below and the Beast kicked off from the broken bannister, his simian arms stretching out to grab hold of the chandelier, which he used to swing out over the foyer, away from the deadly Gamma Sentinel. Reaching the end of its arc, he let go of the pendent chandelier before it could swing back toward his enemy, whereupon he performed an aerial backflip that landed him feet first upon the ground floor of the Mansion.

Similarly eschewing the stairs, the Gamma Sentinel jumped directly from the landing to the floor below, hitting the bottom with a reverberating thud that shook the whole Mansion and cracked the marble tiles beneath his feet. "Nobody gets away from the Hulk!" he roared, still spewing incriminatory sound bytes as he chased after the Beast, who bolted for the auxiliary elevator at the back of the building.

Best to lure him below, the Beast strategized on the run. The Mansion's sub-basements, where many of the Avengers' most secure facilities were housed, had been triple-reinforced with an adamantium/vibranium-strand ceramic, which just might be enough to contain the Gamma Sentinel until help arrived. If nothing else, taking the fight underground reduced the chances of any innocent bystanders getting caught up in the conflict. *Sometimes I'm so selflessly noble I scare myself,* he thought; dividing one's time between the X-Men *and* the Avengers could do that to a person.

With the world's biggest and most dangerous "Hulk" action figure charging after him, trampling heedlessly over pricy antique furniture that was rapidly reduced to splinters, the Beast arrived at the rear elevator and jabbed the DOWN button with a furry finger. According to the lighted display above the closed metal doors, the actual elevator compartment was currently residing two floors above. *No time to wait,* he thought, prying open the sealed double doors to expose a set of cables hanging in the empty elevator shaft. "Open sesame!"

The elevator car had already begun its descent from the third floor. Nevertheless, the hirsute X-Man seized onto the greasy cables with both his hands and his feet, then slid to the bottom of the shaft, another three stories below the ground floor. "Basement, Level Three," he reported cheerily to an imaginary audience, pressing an emergency release button to open the bottom doors from inside the shaft. "Ladies Lingerie and Disabled Super-Weapons."

He sprang from the shaft into the darkened storage space beyond, pushing the corresponding DOWN button with his big toe as he leaped clear of the open doorway. Mere seconds later, a resounding tremor proclaimed that the Hulk-Sentinel had likewise reached the bottom of the shaft. *Sentinel see, Sentinel do,* the Beast thought, amusing himself at the expense of the killer robot's imitativeness. A margin of a few moments made a tremendous difference, however, as the floor of the descending elevator smashed into the Sentinel before the Hulk's manmade doppleganger had a chance to exit the shaft. The Beast watched with satisfaction as the crushed elevator compartment wrapped itself around the surprised Sentinel.

Unhappily, the collision was harder on the elevator than the Hulk-Sentinel. The Beast had to admire the preeminent quality of S.H.I.E.L.D.'s workmanship; the Sentinel had plainly been built to stand up to most anything. *All the worse for yours truly,* the X-Man thought. Feeling as though he were somehow trapped in an interactive remake of *The Terminator,* or perhaps *Westworld,* the Beast turned his back on the crumpled elevator even as the undamaged Sentinel tore the metal compartment to shreds in order to free itself from the wreckage. *What would Linda Hamilton do in a situation like this?* the Beast wondered. *Probably call for her stunt double . . .*

Seldom visited, the bottommost sub-basement was reserved for the storage of potentially dangerous artifacts and equipment that the Avengers had taken out of the nefarious hands of various defeated adversaries. In theory, all such confiscated apparatus, ranging from a trashed Omni-Wave Projector to fragments of a broken Cosmic Cube, had been rendered harmless prior to storage, but they were kept safely locked away just in case, along with some of the Avengers' own mothballed equipment. Basement Level Three also boasted a private shuttle to a submarine pen on the East River. *Not an option, alas,* the Beast thought with regret; the longer he could confine the chase to the Mansion, the better chance there was that reinforcements, in the form of multiple X-Men and Avengers, would show up eventually. *Avengers, come home!* he exhorted his absent colleagues while he scrambled past stacked crates of disassembled adaptoids and decommissioned dreadnaughts.

Would that I were more familiar with the current inventory . . . ! he wished longingly, ducking around a ten-gallon tank labeled "Liquified Terrigen Mist" and vaulting over an enormous hourglass covered by a plastic tarp. Deep, umbrageous shadows added an aura of mystery to the dimly-lit basement. There might well be something amongst these salvaged souvenirs that he could turn to his advantage, although, realistically, he doubted that there was time enough to get anything up and running, even if he knew what to look for. *Weapons, weapons, everywhere,* he mused, paraphrasing Coleridge, *yet nary a defense for me.*

Instead he bounced up the emergency stairs three steps at a time, racing past the secondary sub-basement (home of the Mansion's thermal power generator and multitasking Stark-Fujikawa super-computer) until he came to Basement Level One. Hearing the Hulk-Sentinel hot on his tail, the Beast bypassed the underground rec room and gymnasium, hopping directly into his final destination: the Combat Simulation Room.

Although not quite as sophisticated as the X-Men's Danger Room, which had the added benefit of advanced Shi'ar technology, the Avenger's combat training system was nonetheless well-equipped to give most any Avenger, past or present, a grueling work-out, while Wakandan-built kinetic dampers in the walls generated impact-absorbing fields that prevented wholesale damage to the Mansion's structural integrity, no matter how wild and woolly the simulated fighting became. *Let's hope T'Challa's gizmos can keep a lid on Sentinel-spawned havoc as well,* the Beast prayed.

Miraculously, his reading glasses had hung on through all his impressive acrobatics. Rapidly installing himself in an armored control booth at the far end of the spacious chamber, the endangered X-Man swiftly scanned a computerized listing of the various training programs available. To his disappointment, he couldn't immediately find an exercise specifically tailored to the Hulk, whose rare stints with the Avengers had been mostly notable for their brevity. "Oh my, this could pose a problem," he whispered at the very moment that the obstreperous automaton barged into the training room. The unstoppable Sentinel advanced across the wide, open floor of the combat simulation area toward the puny control booth, which offered the Beast little protection against the Hulk-like menace bearing down upon him.

"You cannot escape the Hulk, mutant designate:

Beast,'' the Gamma Sentinel warned. The robot's Hulk-ish histrionics were definitely starting to prey on the Beast's nerves. ''Nobody is stronger than the Hulk!''

Maybe. Maybe not. The Beast's questing eyes fixed on just the program he needed. Maybe it wasn't intended for the Hulk *per se,* but the Beast figured that any combat simulation designed to test the mettle of the mighty Thor, Norse god of thunder and the Avengers' premiere powerhouse, might give an imitation Hulk a run for its money. ''Let's ragnarok-and-roll!'' he declared, starting the program with a press of his finger.

Without warning, a force field weighing as much as the Empire State Building crashed down upon the Hulk-Sentinel, crushing it to the floor. At the same time, orange gelatinous goo gushed from vents in the walls, engulfing the trapped titan in a sea of viscous slime that kept the immersed Sentinel from achieving the leverage the robot needed to resist the tremendous force field pressing down upon it. The Gamma Sentinel's awesome strength was useless against the ooze, which it could neither batter nor seize. The robot lay sprawled upon the submerged floor, flattened against the slick wet tiles.

This is more like it, the Beast thought approvingly, humming the score to Wagner's *Gotterdammerung* as he watched the Sentinel struggle futilely in the mucilaginous morass. He mentally tipped his figurative cap to whichever Avenger had conceived of this ingeniously appropriate ambuscade. The genuine God of Thunder, he surmised, might be able to disrupt the force field by summoning a bolt of lightning with his mystic hammer, then miraculously part the sea of goo with a heaven-sent gale; how fortuitously convenient it was that the phony Hulk lacked any such divine prerogatives. ''*Mirabile dictu!''* he rejoiced. ''Will wonders never cease?''

The Beast had about five seconds to bask in well-deserved triumph before the Hulk-Sentinel revealed that it, too, had a few unexpected tricks up its non-existent sleeve. Strenuously raising its face from the floor, the robot's troglodyte-like jaws opened wide and a frosty white slush spewed from its mouth, freezing the orange goo solid in a matter of seconds. *Holy smokes,* the Beast realized at once, *that's liquid nitrogen!* Although unquestionably taken by surprise, he really shouldn't have been; your ordinary, standard-model Sentinel invariably came with all manner of hidden armaments, so why shouldn't this spurious Hulk? Indeed, he had often seen old-fashioned Sentinels immobilize their mutant prey with their patented frigi-blasts.

The flood of ooze hardened quickly. With the once-glutinous mess rendered stiff and brittle, the Gamma Sentinel easily cracked open the translucent shell encasing its muscular frame. Glistening fragments of solidified gel fell away from the prone Sentinel, breaking apart into even smaller pieces. *A most unpropitious development,* the Beast acknowledged.

That left only the constant downward pressure of the force field to pin the robot to the floor. Before the Beast's horrified gaze, the Sentinel gradually rose to its feet, defying the crushing weight with all the indomitable stubbornness of the real Hulk. If the Beast hadn't known better, he would have sworn he was witnessing the genuine article.

That is, until powerful jets flared beneath the Hulk-Sentinel's large green feet, launching him upward at the ceiling like a Saturn rocket. Two invincible fists, raised high above the robot's head, slammed into the top of the training room, smashing the intricate machinery responsible for projecting the vanquished force field. The Beast gulped as his control panel reported the entire Thor sequence off-line. Would he care to initiate the next program on the menu?

Given that, due to the vagaries of alphabetization, the following program was an acrobatic routine designed to test the fabulously feline reflexes of Tigra the Were-Woman, the Beast didn't think that would do him much good. He suddenly found himself envying the inimitable Ant-Man, if only for his ability to shrink out of sight at times like this. *Mother of mercy,* he thought, *is this the end of Mamma McCoy's bouncing baby Beast?*

He had nowhere else to run. He could only watch in ineluctable apprehension as the pseudo-Hulk yanked its fists free from the punctured ceiling, then dropped back to the floor, less than ten yards from the Beast's control booth. Leftover tendrils of smoke leaked from the extinguished jets in the robot's soles. "Targeting mutant designate: Beast," it rumbled. "Hulk will smash!"

The Beast braced himself for the worst, but he never expected the earth-shaking tremor that suddenly rocked the basement, a seismic perturbation that evidently overwhelmed even the vibranium shock absorbers in the walls. The startled X-Man blinked in surprise and, when he opened his eyes again, he thought he was seeing double. *Two* Hulks, identical in size and surface characteristics, faced each other upon the floor of the training room.

Huh? the Beast thought, his extensive vocabulary momentarily deserting him. Since when did Sentinels split like amoebas? And what caused that momentous quake a few heartbeats ago?

Then he noticed that the injuries to the ceiling now included a gaping hole large enough to fly an Avenger through, as made manifestly apparent when Iron Man came diving into the basement chamber, followed almost immediately by Storm. Moments later, both Iceman and Wolverine descended to the floor of the combat arena on a swiftly-growing chute of ice that touched bottom only seconds before the two mutant heroes did. "There's that flamin' Sentinel again!" Logan snarled loudly, silver claws snapping out like switchblades. "Let me at him!"

The Beast literally leaped for joy, grabbing onto the ceiling with his toes so that he watched his friends' timely arrival from a distinctly inverted perspective that lessened his jubilation not one iota. At last, the cavalry had arrived! And what a superlative cavalry it was; the outnumbered Sentinel didn't stand a chance.

But the Hulk—the real Hulk—was less than enthused about their salutary numerical advantage. "Everybody stay back!" he ordered angrily, making it sound more like a threat than a request. Chunks of fallen plaster and masonry were crushed to powder beneath the jade giant's weighty tread. "This tin-plated copycat's mine."

Stalking forward aggressively, Wolverine looked like he was ready to disregard the Hulk's forcefully expressed directive and slice himself a sizable piece of Sentinel. But Storm, landing behind the scrappy Canadian hellraiser, laid a restraining hand upon his shoulder, and cooler heads appeared to prevail. *A most judicious move on Ororo's part,* the Beast concluded; he wouldn't want anyone getting in between the Hulk and his robotic double.

For the moment, it was not too difficult to distinguish the authentic man-monster from his emerald effigy.

"Identified: gamma mutate designate: Hulk," the Gamma Sentinel intoned, betraying its artificial origins. "Recommended course of action: immediate retreat."

Flames jetted from the Sentinel's feet, but the Hulk was way ahead of his twin. "Forget it, gears-for-guts!" he roared, leaping at the escaping invader. "That may be how you got away from Wolverine back in Scotland, but you ain't going to give me the slip." His dynamic leap intercepted the Sentinel's flight plan fifteen feet above the floor. Grabbing onto his S.H.I.E.L.D.-manufactured counterpart with both hands, he dragged the fleeing robot back to earth. The basement shook once more as the two Hulks fought head-to-head and hand-to-hand. Bestial grunts blended with the whirring of internal motors strained to their limits. Looking like he was battling his own reflection in a mirror, the Hulk gave no ground against the Sentinel. Veins the size of elevator cables stood out from his skin, throbbing above great slabs of muscle and sinew. "This puny planet's not big enough for two Hulks," he spat, "so one of us is goin' down, and it ain't goin' to be me!"

Storm and Iron Man hovered in the air above the grappling titans, standing guard in case the jet-equipped Sentinel made another break for it. Meanwhile, Iceman further reduced the phony Hulk's chances of escape by plugging the hole in the ceiling with a seal of ice at least three feet thick. Wolverine alone was left to fume and glower on the sidelines, somehow managing to override his primal yen to join in the fighting. "C'mon, Hulk!" he shouted savagely, like a soccer hooligan watching a losing game. "Tear that friggin' wind-up toy apart!"

At first, the twin Hulks appeared evenly matched. As they whirled and wrestled across the floor, the Beast quickly lost track of which green gargantua was the original and which was the cybernetic clone. *Is it live or is it Memorex?* he wondered, watching one of the Hulks try unsuccessfully to catch his opponent's neanderthal skull in a headlock. Was that the honest-to-goodness Hulk pounding the other one's ears between his fists, or was it instead the soulless imitation that just delivered a battering ram of a punch to his foe's broad ribcage? *If this tussle were on pay-per-view,* the Beast thought, feeling rather like a spectator at Madison Square Garden the night of a heavyweight bout, *the ratings would be ascending into orbit now.*

He eased cautiously out of the control booth. Seeing his chance, he darted across the open floor to join Wolverine. "Lafayette, we are here!" he said exuberantly, slapping his fellow X-Man upon the back. "As you can surely imagine, your fortuitous return is robustly appreciated!"

"Yeah, sure," Wolverine said tersely. A scowl showing below the edge of his mask, he didn't look away from the cataclysmic brawl going on a few yards away. "Glad we could make it."

The Beast raised a quizzical and exceptionally bushy eyebrow. Logan could be moody and anti-social at times, but his present attitude struck the Beast as surprisingly standoffish under the circumstances. "What of Muir Island?" the worried anthropoid inquired urgently. "I see that Bobby is hale and hearty, but what of Moira and Kurt?"

"Alive and kickin', more or less." Logan didn't elaborate, and the Beast opened his mouth to ask for more details, but Logan cut him off with a severe look that brooked no dissent. "Later," he decreed laconically.

Scratching his head, the Beast decided not to press the matter. He could always get the full scoop from Ororo or Bobby if and when the Hulk-Sentinel was disposed of. His own unsated curiosity could wait that long. But what was Wolverine's problem? Merely a foiled desire to butt heads with the Sentinel?

"You are not the Hulk," the mendacious machine insisted as it bludgeoned the real Hulk with its inordinately large fists. The Richter-scale blows did not even raise bruises on the Hulk's invulnerable hide; the indefatigable monster held his own and then some. "You are an imposter," the false Hulk lied, prompted by some preprogrammed imperative to mislead the public.

"If I'm not the Hulk, nobody is!" the Hulk thundered, proving his point by slugging the Sentinel so hard that the flying robot smashed through a reinforced ceramic wall into the gymnasium adjacent to the combat testing area. The two-ton metal monstrosity hit the Avengers' Olympic-sized swimming pool with a splash of truly nonpareil proportions, the impact displacing a miniature tsunami of chlorinated water that poured into the combat arena through the newly-carved gap in the wall. Only the Beast's enhanced agility, and Wolverine's tiger-like reflexes, kept both heroes from getting thoroughly drenched by the oncoming wall of water.

The Hulk, on the other hand, waded straight into the face of the tidal wave, eager to get his vengeful hands on the mechanism attempting to sully his already infamous reputation. "You know why you're not ever going to beat me?" he challenged the Sentinel, cannonballing into the pool after his egregious double. "It's cause you can't ever get as mad as I am right now." Water streamed down his ample head and shoulders as he lifted the pummelled robot high above the shallow end of the pool. The left side of the Sentinel's face had collapsed inward, giving its fraudulent countenance a grotesque and distorted grimace. Blue sparks spurted from a cracked green eyeball. "And, as somebody should've told you, the madder I get, the stronger I get!"

With that, the irate Hulk ripped the Sentinel in half, tearing it apart at its mid-section. High-tech entrails spilled from its sundered humanoid chassis: wires, nozzles, gears, and motors. Internal lubricants, mixed with jet fuel and unignited napalm, bled from severed tanks and conduits, polluting the formerly pristine water in which the Hulk stood up to his knees. The bisected Sentinel's limbs flailed about spasmodically while its computerized mind tried to cope with its grievous condition. "Warning—*zzz*—unit integrity compromised—" it sputtered, bursts of static interfering with its coherence, "—*zzz*—self-repair requirements exceeding defined limits—*zzz*—systemic shutdown—*zzz*—Hulk will smash!—*zzz*—activating failsafe procedure—"

"Aw, shut your trap!" the Hulk snarled in contempt. He hurled both halves of the broken Sentinel into the fouled water swirling around his soaked purple trousers. A less durable being might have been electrocuted on the spot, but the Hulk wasn't even stung by the flashing and sparking that briefly transpired once the robot's exposed circuitry came into contact with the water.

"I guess I proved who the real Hulk is." He leaped from the pool in a single bound, landing hard on the floor of the gym. His monstrous feet left deep impressions in the padded mat beneath a set of trapezes. "Accept no substitutes."

For the first time since the pseudo-Hulk invaded the

Mansion, the Beast allowed himself to fully relax. *All's well that ends well,* he thought, only to be taken by surprise when Iron Man zoomed past him at high speed. The Golden Avenger's boot jets carried him into the gym with such velocity that the befuddled Beast had to wonder what all the rush was about. From where he was standing, the Sentinel was irrevocably kaput, so why such unseemly alacrity?

Iron Man touched down at the far end of the pool, next to semi-sunken remains of the demolished Sentinel. "All right, Hulk," he said grimly, his amplified voice carrying easily across the length of the gym, "you've done your part. Now let me disarm that gamma bomb."

The Beast's jaw dropped, revealing a mouthful of pearly white fangs.

Bomb?

By the time Captain America returned to Avengers Mansion, along with Cyclops and the Vision, the threat of the last Gamma Sentinel had been neutralized in more ways than one. Comparing notes with the entire assemblage of X-Men and Avengers, the star-spangled champion of liberty was glad to hear that the various heroes had survived their respective adventures intact, even if the Scarlet Witch and Rogue remained missing and presumed captured. *But not for much longer,* he vowed, *not if I have anything to say about it.*

"There's just one thing I still don't understand," Cap said to Iron Man. "How did you and your party get all the way back from Scotland before the rest of us could return from Alberta?"

Since the main meeting room had not yet recovered from the Hulk-Sentinel's rampage, everyone had convened in an elegantly appointed parlor on the first floor, one often used by the Avengers for public receptions and to entertain visiting dignitaries. Commemorative plaques and trophies, presented to the Avengers by various grateful communities and organizations, adorned the mantel of a large brick fireplace over which a framed portrait of Tony Stark's deceased parents, the original residents of the mansion, hung proudly. Avengers and X-Men occupied the antique sofas and chairs situated around the parlor.

Iron Man, whose heavy armor would be too much for mere wooden furniture, remained standing. He kept his helmet on to preserve his secret identity from their mutant guests. "It's not hard to make good time," he explained, turning his golden faceplate toward Storm, "when you've got a full-fledged weather goddess ensuring a strong tailwind." Despite the iron mask covering his teammate's face, Cap could readily imagine Tony's charming smile accompanying his words of praise for the X-Men's regal co-leader. Iron Man's alter ego always had been a smooth talker where beautiful women were concerned.

"In addition," the Vision pointed out, his sepulchral voice devoid of warmth or feeling, "we were delayed by the necessity to inform the Canadian authorities of our activities."

That's right, Cap recalled. Although it had been only common courtesy to keep the R.C.M.P. apprised of what he, Cyclops, and the Vision had encountered in that underground city beneath the Columbia Icefields, there was no denying that the lengthy debriefing had cost them a certain amount of time.

"That's one of the few advantages of being an outlaw

organization,'' Cyclops observed. His ruby quartz visor turned toward the mantelpiece, where the Avengers's numerous awards were displayed; Cap imagined that the feared and much-maligned X-Men didn't get much in the way of public testimonials and citations. ''Less paperwork.''

It's a shame Xavier's people don't always get the recognition they deserve, Cap thought, *but they may bring some of that on themselves by being so secretive.* His legendary shield rested against the side of his upholstered armchair. ''Maybe I'm old-fashioned, but I still think there's something to be said for working within the system.''

''You might not feel the same way,'' Cyclops said, his voice taking on a bitter edge, ''if the system hunted patriots with the same enthusiasm it has for chasing mutants.''

''I'm sorry you feel that way,'' Cap answered sincerely, ''but I respect your right to disagree with me on this issue. Certainly, there's a proud American tradition of civil disobedience in a good cause, such as protecting the civil rights of mutants everywhere.''

Cyclops's tone mellowed as he offered Cap something of an olive branch. ''If every American felt the way you do, Captain, then maybe we wouldn't need to operate outside the law, or keep our distance from the authorities.''

Maybe one day you won't have to, Cap thought. He had personally vouched for Cyclops on their mission to Alberta, but he had seen firsthand the wary treatment the X-Men's other leader had received from the officials they'd dealt with on their way in and out of Canada.

Anti-mutant prejudice was no figment of the X-Men's imaginations.

"Enough politics," Iceman blurted impatiently. Having regained his human form, the defrosted X-Man sat on a red damask couch between Storm and Cyclops. "What's all this about the moon?"

The Beast, perching atop a camel back sofa behind the Vision, cleared his throat loudly. "Ahem, that sounds like my cue," he began as all eyes and a visor gave him their full attention. "As you'll recall, S.H.I.E.L.D. provided us with aeronautical information on the Unidentified Flying Object believed to be involved in the heinous abduction of our fair teammates. I'll spare you all the abstruse mathematics and tedious triangulating, but meticulous analysis of the UFO's reported trajectories, conducted by yours truly while the rest of you were gallivanting about the globe, clearly points to Earth's moon as the mysterious vessel's point of origin."

"The moon?" Wolverine snorted skeptically. Too restless to take a seat, the abrasive X-Man paced in front of the dormant fireplace. Although he had retracted his adamantium claws, Logan struck Cap as no less volatile. "I think you cooked your numbers too long, Beastie Boy. C'mon, the moon? Give me a flamin' break."

"I wouldn't dismiss the idea out of hand," Iron Man stated. "It wouldn't be the first time one of our enemies took up residence on the moon. As a matter of fact, the Fantastic Four and I were up there only a few months ago, running interference against Ronan the Accuser."

"We've been to the moon as well," Cyclops said somberly. From his tone, Cap gathered it hadn't been the happiest of experiences. He saw Storm give Cyclops a sympathetic look, and wondered what the taciturn X-Man might have endured on Earth's largest natural satellite. "And we can go there again if we have to," Cyclops affirmed.

The Beast nodded vigorously. "One small step for a man, a giant step for mutantkind. Let us not forget," he lectured in a quasi-academic fashion, "that the baneful Leader has previously demonstrated a marked predilection for establishing his devious domiciles in remote locations. Beneath a glacier, for instance, or aboard an orbiting space platform. What could be more remote and inaccessible than the abandoned stomping grounds of our revered Apollo astronauts?"

A persuasive spiel, Cap thought, but Wolverine still appeared dubious. "So now you're telling me the Leader is really the Man in the Moon. Get real, McCoy."

The Beast blinked his eyes, seemingly taken aback by Wolverine's persistent objections. "But my calculations—? The angles of approach and ascent are incontrovertible."

Iceman, for one, required no further convincing. "I say we go!" he exclaimed, jumping up from the couch. Cap admired the young man's pep and spirit. "If there's any chance that Rogue and Wanda are up there, we've got to check it out."

"I concur," the Vision stated, although the synthezoid's icy reserve could not have been more different from Iceman's youthful enthusiasm. His voluminous yellow cloak was draped over the arms of the small sofa. "I have reviewed the Beast's calculations and concluded that his hypothesis has an 83.6 percent probability of accuracy. In the absence of any other plausible alternative, I can see no other logical course of action."

"Then we are agreed?" Storm asked, searching the faces of the other heroes in the room. "As much as I regret separating myself from our mother Earth, I will gladly brave the barren vacuum of space to liberate our departed friends."

I couldn't have put it better myself, Captain America thought. He didn't know Rogue well, although she had punched him through a park bench, then put him in a coma, during their memorable first encounter, but he had personally taken the Scarlet Witch under his wing when she and her brother first joined the Avengers. Casual jaunts to the moon still felt like Buck Rogers to a wartime relic like himself, yet he'd pilot a starship to the Skrull Empire and back if it meant rescuing Wanda and Rogue from the Leader's clutches.

But would Wolverine go along with the plan? Despite the gruff Canadian's longtime affiliation with the X-Men, Cap regarded Logan as more of a loner than a team player. He'd always been that way, even when they first met back in World War II. It occurred to Cap that Logan was surely the only individual in the room who was older than he was; it felt a bit odd not to have seniority. "Well, Logan?" he asked the other man. "Are you with us?"

"Sounds like a snipe hunt to me," Wolverine said. "But if the rest of you are deadset on blasting off, who am I to raise a ruckus? Count me in."

Good man, Cap thought. Now only the Hulk remained to be heard from. Too large and heavy-set for even the most sturdy of hardwood furniture, the brawny titan loomed at the back of the parlor, blocking Cap's view of a cherry-finish china cabinet. With some difficulty, Jarvis had persuaded the surly giant to trade his damp purple pants for a pair of Hercules's old brown trousers. Even wearing hand-me-downs from the mighty Son of Zeus, the Hulk's trunk-like legs had already torn out the knees of his new pants. "What about you, Hulk?" Cap asked. "Are you in this until the end?"

He half-hoped the Hulk would turn him down. A walking disaster area, the Hulk was also a loose cannon of the highest caliber; he made Wolverine look like Miss Congeniality. The prospect of going into space with such an ungovernable troublemaker was enough to give anyone second thoughts, even Captain America.

Scowling, the Hulk mulled the question over for several moments before answering. "Get this straight," he said finally, sneering at the roomful of Avengers and X-Men. "I don't need any of you costumed clowns to deal with my old pal, the Leader. Once we get to the moon, you'd best stay out of my way." His angry green eyes and hostile expression dared anyone to object. "Still, I can't think of any faster way to get to the moon 'cept by hitchin' a ride with you losers. Just don't push your luck."

Cap rose from the leather armchair to confront the Hulk. *This requires careful handling,* he realized. He didn't want to set off a destructive tantrum that could leave the mansion in ruins; they had already wasted too much time fighting the Hulk back at Niagara Falls. On the other hand, he wasn't about to let the Hulk think he could intimidate the rest of them whenever he felt like it; that would set a dangerous precedent and undermine his leadership. Glancing over at Cyclops and Storm, he could tell they felt the same way. *The Hulk's an Avenger, though, at least sometimes,* Cap thought. *That makes him my responsibility.*

To avoid provoking another senseless battle, he left his shield leaning against the chair. "All right, Hulk," he said firmly. "You've got more experience with the Leader than anybody here, I'll grant you that. You want to launch a preemptive strike against the Leader while the rest of us concentrate on rescuing our friends, fine with me. But don't think you can bully anyone here, or put the mission in jeopardy. You try something like that, and I'll personally make sure you toe the line. Got that, mister?"

A moment of tense silence followed, as everyone present awaited the Hulk's response. Standing firm, Cap kept his gaze fixed steadily on the jade giant's subhuman features, maintaining eye contact. Some people called Captain America a living legend, a label he often felt uncomfortable with, even if it occasionally came in useful in cutting through red tape and taking charge of a crisis. At this moment, though, Cap was willing to trade on his laurels for all they were worth. *If ever my status as a so-called national icon counted for anything,* he thought, *let's hope it carries some clout with the loyal American inside that green-skinned monster.*

"Yeah, whatever," the Hulk grunted, looking away. His huge fists unclenched and his bulging muscles relaxed a little. Shoving the couch aside, he lumbered toward the door. "Let's get this show on the road."

I don't believe it, Cap thought, maintaining a stern expression to hide his relief. *He actually backed down.* Cap figured that was as much of a concession as he was ever going to get from the Hulk. *Sergeant Duffy would be proud,* he thought, recalling the leather-necked old drill sergeant who had tried so diligently to make a soldier out of an unpromising young private named Steve

Rogers, back during the fight against the Axis. He doubted if Duffy had ever had to deal with a recruit as recalcitrant and impossible to discipline as the Hulk.

Cap surveyed the parlor, taking stock of their combined forces: three Avengers, five X-Men, and the Hulk. Nothing to sneeze at, even if transportation posed a bit of a problem. *Now for the hard part,* he thought wryly.

"One more thing, Hulk," he said. The gargantuan brute shot him a dirty look, his annoyed expression asking *now what?,* but Cap pressed on regardless. "The quinjet's going to be pretty cramped as is, with nine of us en route for the moon. It will be a lot easier on all concerned if you'll change back into Banner until we get there."

Wolverine whistled in appreciation. "One thing I'll say for you, Cap," he said, grinning like a wolf on the prowl. "You're not afraid to live dangerously!"

Chapter Four

Even with the Hulk's massive frame replaced by the slender form of Bruce Banner, the quinjet was still packed to capacity. Seated at the helm of the sleek, high-tech aircraft, Iron Man made a mental note to expand the passenger area the next time he upgraded the vehicle. *Maybe if I reconfigure the engine assembly,* he theorized, drawing up imaginary blueprints in his head, *then increase the wingspan to compensate for the added weight. . . .*

His gauntlets had been inserted into customized niches in the helm controls, establishing a direct cybernetic interface with the quinjet's instrumentation. Iron Man had designed the helm to be compatible with both his and the Vision's operating systems, not to mention Hank Pym's cybernetic helmet. The controls could also be operated manually, of course, but Iron Man regarded that as embarrassingly clunky and retro.

Through the polarized plastic windshield, he watched the moon grow steadily larger as the ship neared their destination. They had already left Earth's atmosphere far behind; according to the onboard navigational computer, they were less than an hour away from entering into orbit around the moon, preparatory to touching down on the lunar surface.

First, though, they had to pinpoint the location of the Leader's headquarters. No small task; although the moon was only a quarter of the size of the Earth, they were still talking over fourteen million square miles of craters, mountains, plains, and basins. "How are we doing?" he asked the Vision. "Any luck tracking down the Leader's new address?"

The synthezoid sat beside Iron Man in the co-pilot's seat. A fiber-optic cable linked the solar gem in his forehead to the ship's computer banks. "Affirmative," he reported. "A systematic survey of the most recent lunar reconnaissance photos, provided by S.H.I.E.L.D and Starcore, has detected what appears to be an artificial structure located in the Tycho crater on the earthward side of the moon. This structure, previously unreported, is too small to be seen from the Earth except by the most powerful telescopes. It is a domed structure, approximately one thousand feet in diameter, resting inside the circumference of a smaller crater in the shadow of Tycho's outer walls."

Yes! Iron Man thought, encouraged by the Vision's news. "That's got to be it. How many people could have set up housekeeping on the moon recently?" He quickly reviewed his lunar geography; Tycho, a crater the size of Yellowstone National Park, was located in the moon's southern hemisphere, hundreds of miles from the Sea of Tranquility, where Apollo 11 made history decades ago.

Tycho was also significantly distant from the moon's famed Blue Area, site of alien ruins over ten million years old. Given that the Blue Area currently housed the Watcher, the Supreme Intelligence, and a full complement of Starcore scientists, Iron Man wasn't surprised that the Leader had set up shop in a less crowded neighborhood. *The man likes his privacy, it seems. Too bad he's about to get a whole passel of unwanted visitors knocking on his door.*

A voice piped up from the passenger seats behind Iron Man. "Are we there yet?" the Beast asked waggishly. "I'm not saying that conditions are snug back here, but I find myself pining yearnfully for the wide open spaces of a New York subway at rush hour."

"You can say that again," Iceman agreed. "Just 'cause I can freeze up doesn't mean I want to feel like I've been crammed into an ice cube tray." Iron Man heard the young man squirm within his zero-gravity restraints. "This trip is bringing all new meaning to the term 'icepack!' "

Probably just as well we were never able to contact Quicksilver, Iron Man thought. There wouldn't have been any room aboard for Wanda's brother even if they had succeeded in catching up with the world's fastest mutant, which was no easy task.

A groan from the back reached the armored Avenger's audio receptors. "Are you all right, Bruce?" he asked. The Hulk's human counterpart sounded ill, but Iron Man wasn't too alarmed; weightlessness sometimes had that effect on people. "There should be medication for space sickness in a compartment by your seat."

"That won't be necessary," Banner answered. "You forget, I've probably been to space as often as any of you. I was just reacting to Iceman's joke. I guess I have a low tolerance for bad puns."

"Even after knowing Rick Jones all this time?" Cap remarked, referring to the high-spirited young man who had often ended up playing sidekick to either the Avengers or the Hulk. Rick's personality and sense of humor weren't all that different from Iceman's.

"You have a point," Banner admitted readily. "Maybe it's just that I'm not really used to working with a team, let alone two at once. I'm out of practice when it comes to witty banter."

Iron Man couldn't help noting the dramatic difference in attitude between the soft-spoken physicist and his bestial alter ego. Even after dealing with the bizarre phenomenon for years, along with plenty of other secret identities, Iron Man still found it hard to accept that the Hulk and Bruce Banner were really the same person. Never mind the grotesque physical transformation; the psychological metamorphosis was astounding in its own right.

"If it makes you feel any more comfortable, Dr. Banner," Storm began, "I admit to a touch of claustrophobia myself, under the circumstances."

Maybe we should have taken two ships, Iron Man mused. The X-Men's Blackbird was not equipped for extraterrestrial flights, but a spare quinjet remained parked in a hangar on the top floor of the Mansion. At the time, though, it had seemed unwise to divide their forces when they had so little idea of what to expect at the end of their journey. "Not much longer," he assured his crowded passengers. "There's Luna, dead ahead."

Reflecting the light of the distant sun, the moon filled the quinjet's front window, several times larger than it ever appeared from the Earth. The huge shining disk was pockmarked with the scars of ancient meteorite collisions, while vast basaltic lava plains, left over from primordial eruptions nearly four billion years ago, created dark patches that Galileo and other early astronomers had once mistaken for oceans. Primitive cultures and modern-day pagans worshipped the moon as a goddess, but scientist Tony Stark knew better; Earth's smaller companion was nothing but a dusty rock, locked in orbit around the third planet from the sun.

A radical new scientific theory proposed that the moon had been created deliberately by the enigmatic Celestials back at the dawn of time, but Iron Man wasn't quite ready to buy into that particular hypothesis; as far as he was concerned, the jury was still out on that one. He couldn't dismiss the notion entirely, however. As an Avenger, he knew too well that powerful cosmic entities were at work in the universe.

Thankfully, they were not after Galactus or the Grandmaster today. Judging from past experience, the Leader was dangerous enough. Iron Man located the Tycho crater with the quinjet's radar tracking system and entered the correct coordinates into the navigational computer.

"Better be on guard," Cyclops suggested. He and Storm were strapped into the passenger seats directly behind Iron Man and the Vision. "Who knows what kind of defenses the Leader has? The closer we get, the more careful we should be."

Words to live by, Iron Man reflected. Like Captain America, Cyclops seemed strong on strategy. "Absolutely," he agreed. "I don't intend to be caught napping."

As if on cue, the Vision suddenly lifted his gaze from the control panel. "Attention," he announced emotionlessly. "Sensors detect another spacecraft approaching at Mach 3.84. Coming into visual range now."

The android Avenger was not mistaken. Adrenalin rushed through Iron Man's body as the vessel in question came into view, silhouetted against the white reflective surface of the moon itself. To his surprise, this Unidentified Flying Object was, no kidding, an actual flying saucer! Looking like two shallow soup bowls glued together at their brims, the streamlined silver spaceship glided silently toward them, despite no visible means of propulsion. Its outer rim, glowing with incandescent blue energy, spun clockwise around the saucer's vertical axis. Although it was hard to judge distances against the unusually nearby moon, Iron Man estimated that the saucer was about one-and-a-half times larger than the quinjet. Not exactly an Imperial Star Destroyer, perhaps, but an impressive sight nonetheless.

Gasps rose from the passenger area, proving that his fellow heroes could see the gleaming saucer as well. "Klaatu birada nikto!" the Beast exclaimed. "Where in the sainted name of Carl Sagan did *that* come from?"

"The Tycho crater," the Vision stated matter-of-factly, confirming Iron Man's suspicions. Although none of the S.H.I.E.L.D.'s blurry spy photos had caught the craft's image this clearly, the Golden Avenger had no doubt that they were looking at the same mystery UFO linked to the abductions of both Wanda and Rogue. *Looks like the Beast's calculations were right on-target.*

The saucer looked like an escapee from a 1950's sci-fi movie, but Iron Man recognized the design immediately. "That's a Skrull ship!" he said, eyes wide behind the slits in his helmet.

This was an unexpected new wrinkle. The Skrulls, an aggressive and highly advanced race of alien shape-changers from the Andromeda Galaxy, had nursed hostile designs on Earth for many years, dating back to the earliest days of the Avengers and the Fantastic Four. Less than a year ago, in fact, a Skrull infiltrator had taken Captain America's place for a time, until the real Cap escaped captivity to expose the hoax. The ongoing Skrull menace was a fact of life in the late twentieth century, but Iron Man had hardly expected to encounter them here and now.

"Of course!" the Beast yelped, smacking his forehead with a fuzzy palm. "It all makes sense now. The malignant marionettes that attacked Wanda, and the mobile garments that accosted Rogue, were Skrulls in disguise. They altered their forms to elude detection, then beamed back to their spaceship with their unconscious captives. Besides allowing them to blend in with their surroundings prior to each ambush, their surreal masquerades served to thoroughly obfuscate any subsequent investigation of the kidnappings." The Beast clucked his tongue in approval. "Ingenious, in a treacherous and machiavellian sort of way, that is."

A plausible scenario, Iron Man decided, *which accounted for a number of unresolved loose ends.* His mind rapidly switched gears, racing to accommodate this vital new data with his previous understanding of their mission. "I'm guessing that those phony X-Men who attacked the S.H.I.E.L.D. Helicarrier were Skrulls, too. Maybe even the same ones."

"But what have Skrulls to do with the Leader?" Storm asked, expressing aloud what the rest of them were thinking.

Good question, Iron Man thought. Had the Skrulls entered into an alliance with the Leader? Or had they been mistaken about the Leader's involvement all along? Perhaps the infamous gamma-spawned mastermind really was dead after all, just as the world had been led to believe.

Many provocative possibilities came to mind, but now

was not the time to sort them out, not with the Skrull spaceship bearing down on them. Spinning like a glow-in-the-dark buzzsaw, it approached the quinjet at a 90 degree angle to the quinjet's own plane of orientation. "Evasive maneuvers!" Cap ordered, and Iron Man veered the quinjet away from the path of the incoming saucer. Seventy thousand feet above the moon's surface, he reasoned, was no place to play chicken.

For a second, the Skrull saucer dropped out of sight, but Iron Man knew shaking the saucer wasn't going to be that easy. "The enemy vessel is adjusting its trajectory to intercept us," the Vision reported dutifully. "And accelerating."

This could get bad, Iron Man realized. As part of their United Nation charter, the Avengers carried no offensive weapons on their aircrafts. The quinjet was protected by repulsor screens, but how long could those hold up against whatever futuristic firepower the Skrull ship was packing? Not for a second did he think the flying saucer was pursuing them with peaceful intentions.

"Vision, take over the helm," he instructed. His gauntlets disengaged from the control panel as the synthezoid transferred all key navigational functions to his own station. Unclamping his seatbelts, Iron Man rose from the pilot's chair. The lack of gravity made his armor feel much lighter than usual, and he magnetized his boots to keep from floating off the floor of the cockpit. *Have to make it to the airlock,* he thought urgently. Of all the heroes aboard the quinjet, he was the only one fully equipped to fight in deep space.

The Skrull ship zipped across the front window, firing a bright green beam that barely missed the fleeing quinjet. The Vision executed a flawless Immelmann turn that carried them out of the line of fire, at least for a few more moments. *What was that ray?* Iron Man wondered. *A high-intensity laser? A particle beam?* Skrull technology was millions of years ahead of human engineering, so the possibilities were frighteningly endless.

Moving as swiftly as he could, the Golden Avenger made his way through the passenger area toward the emergency airlock at the rear of the jet. Peering out through one of the starboard portholes, he saw the Skrull saucer coming after them, once more flying perpendicular to the quinjet's horizon. *Must figure they present a thinner target that way,* he guessed; possibly the Skrulls didn't realize the other ship was unarmed. *Maybe that will buy us a little more time.*

The quinjet yawed sharply to the right to evade its spinning pursuer. His magnetized boots kept Iron Man from falling outright, but the sudden change in direction caused him to stumble to one side, almost slamming his iron-plated shoulder into Captain America's head. Luckily, Cap's lightning-fast reflexes had not been dulled by zero-gravity; he brought his shield up just in time to block the blow. "Oops! Sorry 'bout that," Iron Man apologized.

"No problem," Cap assured him. "Get out there and teach those Skrulls whose moon that is." He flashed Iron Man a courageous smile. "Last I heard, Colonel Armstrong claimed that rock for Earth."

Cap's confidence was inspiring. "You bet," Iron Man said, hurrying toward the airlock while the Vision piloted the quinjet through a dizzying series of loops and curves. Iron Man spotted Bruce Banner near the back, looking distinctly green. Mere nausea, brought on by the wild ride, or was the stress and excitement releasing his inner Hulk? Iron Man hoped for the former; the last thing they needed now was for the Hulk to throw a fit.

He had just reached the entrance of the airlock when their luck ran out. A blinding flash of green struck the quinjet on its port side. Iron Man held his breath, waiting anxiously to see if the ship's magnetic force field, and dense vibranium shielding, would be enough to prevent a catastrophic hull breach. He crossed armored fingers while an eerie viridescent radiance flooded the passenger compartment.

The results were far different than he had anticipated, even in his worst imaginings. Instead of the sudden, violent onset of explosive decompression, nothing happened at all—except that the strange green glow seemed to converge on Wolverine, outlining his seated form in a shimmering halo from head to foot. "What the—?" he grunted in surprise, before the light disappeared completely, taking Wolverine with it.

"Logan!" Storm cried out, but it was too late. Wolverine had vanished, leaving an empty seat behind. Still clamped in place, his safety belt and shoulder strap floated above the seat cushions, as thóugh protecting an invisible passenger.

One down, eight more to go, Iron Man thought grimly. Was that the Skrulls' battle plan, to beam them away one by one, just like they had Wanda and Rogue? He had no fear that Wolverine had simply been disintegrated; there were more efficient ways to kill them all if that was what was desired. In his gut, he knew that the tough Canadian X-Man had been beamed aboard the Skrull saucer. Obviously, the quinjet's repulsor screens were no match for the enemy's teleportation ray.

His fellow X-Men stared in horror at Wolverine's vacated seat, but Banner had a different reaction. "That was the Leader's trans-mat ray, all right. I'd recognize it anywhere." Banner's voice sounded deeper, more guttural than before. His face had an unmistakably greenish cast, and his borrowed sweater, which had been a few sizes too large before, was now stretched tightly against an expanding chest. He slammed a clenched fist into his other meaty paw. "I knew that good-for-nothing head case wasn't dead. I knew it!"

Here comes the Hulk, Iron Man thought glumly, but he couldn't afford to worry about that now. He had to get outside, before another X-Man or Avenger went the way of Wolverine. He hastily spun the wheel that opened the airlock and stepped into the pressurized chamber inside. While he waited for the inner door to relock, he performed a quick check on his armor's built-in life support systems. Airtight seals slid into place within his mouth slit and eyepieces. He took a few deep breaths to activate the automatic rebreather in his helmet. Interior heating units prepared his armor for the deadly cold of space. In theory, he could survive the vacuum indefinitely, unlike any of his comrades. Even the Hulk needed to breathe.

What about Iceman? he wondered briefly as the thought occurred to him. *Did the youthful mutant require oxygen in his ice form?* Iron Man pondered the question for a second, then realized that, without any ambient moisture to draw upon, Iceman's offensive capabilities would be severely limited in space, even if he was able to endure the harsh conditions.

"It's up to me," he murmured. Making sure the door to the passenger compartment was completely sealed, he evacuated the atmosphere from the airlock chamber, returning it to the quinjet's reserve air supply. But before he could press the release button on the outer door, another flash of light lit the interior of the quinjet, visible to Iron Man through a transparent window in the inner door. "Blast!" he swore. The Skrulls had scored another hit.

This time the flash was red, not green, and the effect entirely different. A powerful shockwave rattled the quinjet, only partially ameliorated by the aircraft's defensive shields. Sparks flared from a short-circuited control panel next to the outer door, tiny white-hot embers spraying out in all directions rather than falling to the floor. Charred computer chips and bits of circuitry floated freely within the confines of the sealed chamber. *That was no trans-mat ray,* Iron Man realized. *They've broken out the heavy artillery.*

The Skrulls were playing for keeps now, but why? Iron Man was puzzled by the abrupt change in tactics. Why would the Skrulls, working in tandem with the Leader, want to capture Wolverine, but obliterate the rest of them? *Maybe if I knew why they snatched Wanda and Rogue in the first place,* he mused, *I might have some clue as to what the big picture was—and why they grabbed Wolverine.*

One thing for sure, he wasn't going to find out by standing around in an airlock while a bunch of trigger-happy Skrulls took pot shots at his ship. With the automated controls fried by the Skrull energy blast, Iron Man was forced to open the outer door manually. Transistorized servomotors amplified the strength of his armored fingers as he released the emergency clamp, then tugged the thick steel door open. Anxious to engage the enemy, he ignited his boot jets even as the heavy steel door slid away. "Geronimo!" he shouted, flying clear of the quinjet under his own power.

The silence of the void was deafening. All he could hear was his own breathing and the sound of his artificial heart pumping rhythmically inside his chest. He took a few seconds to orient himself, the great swollen moon hanging above him, the familiar blue globe of the Earth receding into the distance beneath his feet. *What a view!* he thought, momentarily awestruck despite the urgency of the situation. Diaphanous clouds veiled the familiar continents and oceans of Terra, while the looming satellite more than dwarfed the fullest moon ever seen from Earth. The famous *Mare Tranquillitatis* alone, where Apollo 11 touched down decades ago, seemed larger and more imposing than any of Earth's seven seas. *All a matter of perspective, I guess.*

He quickly located the Skrull saucer, spinning through space after the quinjet. Rather than retreating back toward Earth, the Vision piloted the Avengers' airship around the moon, clearly keeping in mind their ultimate objective. They had come too far to turn back now, not while their teammates remained prisoners upon the moon and within the enemy saucer.

Using his boot jets as retro rockets, the Golden Avenger accelerated toward the Skrull ship. Before he came within firing range, however, the saucer unleashed another blistering salvo of crimson energy. The deadly ray rocked the quinjet, simultaneously burning away some of the outer heat shields. Having designed the quinjet himself, with a little help from T'Challa's Wakanda Design Group, Iron Man knew the besieged vessel couldn't take much more abuse of that order. *If nothing else, I need to draw the Skrulls' fire away from the others.*

Activating his armor's communications array, he broadcast a warning on every frequency the Skrulls had ever used in the past: "Attention, Skrull vessel. This is Iron Man, representing the Avengers and the planet Earth. You are instructed to call off your attack at once."

Iron Man had yet to meet a Skrull who couldn't understand English, but his hail elicited no response. *Where is Lt. Uhura now that I need her?* he thought, setting his comm unit to repeat his warning at five second intervals. *Let's see if I can get their attention.*

Repulsor beams blasted from his gauntlets, blazing through the vacuum to strike the energized ring propelling the Skrull saucer. Scintillating flashes of azure energy flared to life where his beams intersected the saucer's own protective force field, but Iron Man couldn't tell if his repulsors had inflicted any serious damage on the alien spaceship. To his frustration, it didn't look like it, even after he raised the power of the force beams to their upper limits. A coruscating carpet of sparks raced over the polished exterior of the saucer, and he fired up his chest projector as well, adding a high-temperature thermal beam to the barrage striking against the formerly unidentified flying object. "Leave my friends alone, you pointy-eared reptiles!" he muttered under his breath. "Why don't you take on somebody who can fight back!"

The realization that Wolverine was probably aboard the alien vessel hampered Iron Man, making him reluctant to let loose with the biggest guns in his arsenal, most notably his incredibly destructive pulse bolts. He couldn't risk destroying the saucer while Wolverine was still a prisoner of the Skrulls. But would he be able to save the quinjet, and everyone aboard it, without going all out against the saucer? He might not have any choice.

The combined repulsors and heat ray must have had some effect, since the Skrull saucer abruptly broke off its pursuit of the imperiled quinjet and veered toward Iron Man instead. Spinning through the void, the saucer came after him, throwing off luciferous bolts of crimson fire. *That's right,* the armored Avenger thought. *Come and get me.*

Infinitely more maneuverable than the much larger spacecraft, Iron Man zigzagged through space, skillfully dodging the Skrulls' energy bursts. To further confound his alien hunters, he released a stream of metallic foil confetti from a tubular cache in his armor. With any luck, the ferrous shavings would interfere with the Skrulls' targeting sensors, even though he did experience a twinge of irrational guilt at littering the pristine emptiness of space like this. Who knew, perhaps the moon's meager gravity would someday pull the bits of foil down to its cratered surface, to the confusion of future lunar geologists.

A small price to pay for survival, he decided, rocketing through space a few leagues ahead of the former UFO. Within seconds, however, the saucer was gaining on him. A spear of crimson energy came dangerously close to Iron Man, missing him by less than a yard. At first he thought the Skrulls had accelerated drastically, then his own speedometer display, projected directly onto his retina, reported that, no, it was he who was slowing down.

How is that possible? he wondered. He still had plenty of liquid oxygen to power the micro-turbines in his boots, plus little or no atmospheric friction to retard his flight. Heck, he wasn't even fighting gravity, so what was holding him back? An instant self-diagnostic revealed that an external force was acting upon his armor, impeding his escape. *Some sort of long-range tractor beam,* he realized; he'd been snagged in a wide, electromagnetic net!

Directing even more power to his jets, he tried to break free from the beam's invisible clutches, but it was too strong. The beam soon slowed him to a stop, then began dragging him back toward the waiting saucer, closer to firing range. In less than a minute, there would be no way they could miss him with their hellish death ray. He doubted his own armor plating would fare much better than the battered quinjet's had.

Thank goodness he knew something about tractor beams himself! A battery of sophisticated sensors analyzed the beam holding him, measuring its intensity, wave length, and amplitude. Taking careful note of his sensor's readings, Iron Man spun around until the vari-beam projector in his chestplate was aimed back at the oncoming saucer. He met the Skrullian tractor beam with one of his own, of precisely the inverse amplitude. The colliding wave fronts cancelled each other out, releasing him from the beam's grip.

Iron Man took advantage of his regained freedom to put on a burst of speed that carried him safely out of range of their energy weapons. "Sorry, gang. You'll have to do better than that to take this Earthman out of the picture." His sense of victory gave way to alarm, however, when the thwarted saucer declined to give chase, arcing away in the direction of the quinjet. Apparently concluding that the solitary Avenger was not worth the effort, the Skrull ship resumed its pursuit of the unarmed vessel carrying Iron Man's teammates and allies.

"Blast!" he cursed. Executing a sharp U-turn, Iron Man chased after the same flying saucer he had just successfully left behind. He zoomed through space like a humanoid missile, rockets blazing from his boots. It felt strange not to feel a wind blowing against him as he flew, nor to hear anything outside his armor as he soared through the vacuum. Catching up with the alien spacecraft, he strafed the saucer with his repulsor rays, bombarding the Skrull ship with a beam of accelerated neutrons that exploded impotently against the saucer's force field. Beneath his gilded faceplate, Tony Stark's handsome face grimaced in dismay as he watched the Skrulls close in on the quinjet. Unless he did something right away, the quinjet would explode into a fireball before it even had a chance to make a crash landing on the moon.

Forgive me, Wolverine, he pleaded silently. *I've run out of alternatives.* Cutting off his repulsors, he fired his pulse bolts at the enemy saucer. Phosphorescent bolts of highly-charged plasma crossed the airless abyss between Iron Man and his target, gaining speed and power as they zeroed in on the predatory vessel taking aim on the quinjet; unlike his repulsors, the pulse bolts only increased their potency over distance. Each one was capable of annihilating a tank or two. *I'm probably worrying too much about Wolverine's safety,* he thought hopefully. *Chances are, the bolts will just disable the saucer.*

But his repulsors must have done more damage to the Skrulls' shields than he'd realized. One after another, the discharged plasma bolts struck the spinning saucer, sending it twirling out of control toward the moon. The ship's metal skin melted away, its outer casing dissolving into molten slag. "Oh no!" Iron Man gasped, half wishing he could recall his killer bolts, but knowing he had no choice. The saucer exploded noiselessly as it fell upward at the southern hemisphere of the moon, suspended above them all like a pendulous white breast. Unable to escape the rocky satellite's gravitational pull, the flaming remains of the saucer crashed into the moon like a meteor, carving out yet another crater on its deeply creviced landscape. Iron Man increased the magnification of his optical lenses one-hundredfold, but could detect no signs of life at the crash site; all he saw were a few charred and twisted pieces of alien alloy, two-thirds buried in the deep lunar dust astronomers called the *regolith*. No heartbeats, human or otherwise, registered on his long-distance sonic receptors, and Iron Man felt his throat go dry.

No one had survived the saucer's destruction, not even Wolverine.

Chapter Five

"**A**re you quite certain, Iron Man, that Wolverine perished in the crash?"

Storm could not yet accept the bitter news brought to them by the Avengers' gleaming armored warrior. Logan dead? Although mortal danger was an inextricable element of every X-Man's life, Logan had always seemed a born survivor, likely to outlive them all. How could such an indomitable spirit have been snuffed out so abruptly?

"To be honest," Iron Man informed her, "I doubt that anyone survived the initial explosion in space. He was almost certainly dead before what was left of the saucer crashed into the moon. I'm sorry."

Iron Man had resumed his place at the helm of the quinjet, which still bore the scars of the Skrulls' murderous attack. Blackened electronic components marred the interior of the aircraft while the chemical odor of fire-retardant foam polluted the pressurized atmosphere of the passenger area. Wolverine's vacant seat, between Iceman and the Beast, lingered like an open wound, tearing at Storm's heart whenever she looked behind her. Circumstances could have been so much worse, she realized, had not Iron Man defended the quinjet from the alien warship. All their lives had been saved by the Avenger's prompt action—but at what cost?

A profound sense of loss gripped her. Of all those

whom had received Iron Man's dreadful tidings, she had perhaps been the closest to their departed friend. Although widely different in temperament, they had shared a common appreciation of the natural world and endured many arduous trials together, commencing their careers as X-Men on the same historic occasion. Who could have ever guessed that their parallel journeys would come to a final parting in such an unearthly setting, so far from the living planet whose verdant hills and flowing water they had both revered? *May your turbulent spirit find peace at last, my friend,* she prayed silently.

"He was a tough sunovagun, I'll say that for him," the Hulk said with surprising solemnity. His gigantic presence took up a full three seats at the rear of the passenger compartment, having supplanted Dr. Banner during their tumultuous engagement with the Skrull spacecraft. The Hulk's brutish visage held a look of genuine regret. "A real scrapper. He always put up a good fight."

High praise from such as the Hulk, Storm acknowledged. Wolverine's combative rivalry with the Hulk, she recalled, predated Logan's involvement with the X-Men; for all his coarseness and ill temper, the mighty ogre had known their fallen comrade even longer than she had. Ororo found herself strangely moved by the Hulk's unsolicited tribute to Wolverine. Perhaps there was more to the barbarous creature than unreasoning violence and hostility?

"He lived a full life," Captain America added, "and a long one. From the time I first met him, in Madripoor back during the War, I knew that Logan was a man of uncommon courage and heroism. I'm proud to have fought beside him."

Cyclops placed a comforting hand on Storm's arm. "We didn't always get along," he admitted, "but he was a real credit to the X-Men. He gave as much for the Professor's dream as any of us. Maybe more."

A funereal dolor hung over the interior of the quinjet, illuminated by the chill and sterile radiance of the moon. "If there had been any other way," Iron Man said uncomfortably, "you know I wouldn't have placed Wolverine's life in jeopardy."

Storm nodded. "Do not reproach yourself, Iron Man. You did what was necessary. Logan would have understood." Her eyes ached with unshed tears, but there would be time enough for mourning later. Although Logan had been lost to them, Rogue and the Scarlet Witch remained in danger. "He would also want us to continue our mission with undiminished resolve." She held her chin high, her determined gaze fixed on the shadowy recesses of the Tycho crater as Iron Man piloted the quinjet down toward the lunar surface. "It is the Leader and his alien allies who are the true architects of Wolverine's harsh passing. Let us take our just and righteous anger and deliver it to our adversaries' doorstep."

"Sounds like a plan to me," the Hulk grunted in approval. Banner's sweater hung in rags from his freakishly large shoulders. "I'll make sure the Leader gets what's comin' to him. The rest of you can handle those stinkin' Skrulls."

Captain America provided a note of forbearance. "We all want to see justice done, people, but let's not forget that our top priority is to secure the safe return of Wanda and Rogue. No matter how hurt and angry we are, we've got to see to the living first, and avenge our honored dead later."

Storm found it ironic that it was the leader of the melodramatically-named Avengers who spoke out for rescue over revenge, but his point was well-taken. "Of course, Captain," she assured him. "You are quite correct. The deliverance of our stolen comrades remains our utmost concern."

"We'll see about that," the Hulk muttered ominously, dispelling much of the good will Storm had granted him after his gruff testimonial to Wolverine moments before. Not for the first time, she questioned the wisdom of including such an explosive and unpredictable entity in their mission. That the Hulk added an incalculable amount of raw power to their forces was undeniable, but was that extra strength worth the risk of the undisciplined giant running amuck? She could not forget the appalling injuries the Hulk had inflicted upon the android Vision in a moment of savage pique; that those injuries had been easily repaired by Iron Man's technological expertise did little to alleviate her fears about the monster in their midst.

"Check your seatbelts, everyone," Iron Man announced from the cockpit. "We're heading in for a landing."

Through the wide front windshield, the Leader's moonbase was now easily visible: an opaque white dome nestled in a rugged, barren landscape that looked much less flattened than the sandblasted plains seen elsewhere upon the moon. Jagged boulders thrust toward the sky above overlapping ridges of long-hardened lava. Judging from its rough appearance, Storm guessed that Tycho was a young crater, geologically speaking, less weathered by time and the gradual rain of spaceborne debris. Smaller craters, ranging from inches to miles in diameter, testified to the impact of those meteors that had slammed into Tycho's floor.

Unlike her beloved Earth, this was a dead world, inhospitable to life. Storm repressed a shudder at the sight of the stark and arid moonscape below. How could any thinking being, no matter how depraved, willingly choose to live here? Even the great Kalahari desert, which she had crossed in her youth, was more welcoming than this lifeless crater.

"You see anything that looks like a docking port?" Iron Man asked the Vision.

"Negative," the android replied. "The surface of the dome is uniformly seamless in appearance."

"Don't worry," Iceman said. "You get us close enough, I'll make us a tunnel."

Without any atmospheric moisture to draw upon? Storm wondered and worried. "You realize, Bobby, there is no air or water below." Her own powers, too, would be of limited use on a world without weather. At least outside the dome.

"Hey, I didn't say it would be easy," Iceman retorted. "But if Iron Man can park right up close to the dome, I should be able to provide door-to-door service."

"We may take you up on that," Iron Man told him. He kept his gaze on the bottom of the great crater, no doubt seeking out the best landing site. "The ground looks pretty uneven below," he called out. "Brace for a bumpy landing, everyone."

Unlike conventional aircraft, including NASA's famed space shuttle, the quinjet required no runway to touch down. With a skill born of long experience, Iron Man employed the vessel's VTOL—Verticle Take-Off and Landing—capacity to bring the quinjet to rest upon the rocky terrain. An unnerving jolt rattled Storm's bones when the quinjet's landing gear first came into contact with the basaltic floor of the crater, but the ship maintained a solid footing upon the moon, declining either to topple over or crash nosefirst into the unforgiving ground. *Praise the Goddess,* she devoutly gave thanks, before unfastening her seatbelt and stretching her weary legs. After so many hours sitting in one place, it felt good to stand once more, even if the gravity was palpably lighter than she was accustomed to.

"Whoa there!" Iceman blurted, rising too fast from his seat. His head bumped into the ceiling as his momentum carried him higher than he intended. Unable to find purchase, his boots kicked uselessly above the floor.

"A little less impetuousness," the Beast advised, helpfully tugging his longtime friend and teammate down from the ceiling. "It behooves us to remember that, regardless of the gravity of the situation, actual gravity is in rather short supply."

As always, Storm was both impressed and mildly baffled by the Beast's propensity for joking even in the most dire of circumstances. Perhaps it was a mutant trait of a sort uncatalogued by Cerebro? In any event, she appreciated his attempt to lighten the doleful atmosphere brought on by Wolverine's tragic fate.

Staring out over Iron Man's burnished shoulderpieces, she saw the outer wall of the crater rising in the distance, higher than many earthly mountains. Night had fallen over the scene, which was lit only by the eerie blue glow of the Earth. Given the moon's slow rotation, it was possible that the night had already lasted for several days by Earth's reckoning, and might well endure another week or so. Storm felt very distant from the planet that sustained her.

"The dome's to starboard," Iron Man explained, "right outside the exit." Still linked to the quinjet's instrumentation via his gauntlets, he released the lock by remote control. A metal door swung outward, only a few feet away from Storm. "You don't need to hold your breath," he assured them. "An electrostatic force field will hold the ship's atmosphere in place for the time being."

As promised, the featureless exterior of the dome could be seen through the open doorway. Only a few yards of earthlit moonscape, littered with motionless powder and chips of rock, separated the quinjet from the Leader's lair, but traversing that distance, devoid of oxygen or warmth, was no small matter. Blue shadows were draped over a scene of utter stillness.

"All right, popsicle," the Hulk grumbled. Even though the quinjet had been designed to accommodate the likes of Hercules and Thor, he still had to hunch over to avoid smashing his head through the roof. "Show us what you've got."

Bobby squeezed past Storm to take a place directly in front of the exit. "Here goes," he said, taking a deep breath. A frosty glaze rushed over his body as he transformed ordinary flesh and blood into living ice. Within an instant, the brown-haired, pink-skinned youth became an arctic sculpture composed of translucent blue ice. Even his uniform, composed of unstable molecules, took on a frozen sheen. "Give me just a second to get ready," he asked. His voice had transformed along with the rest of him, acquiring a crystalline ring. "Er, this might get kind of uncomfortable for a couple minutes."

He wasn't kidding. Almost immediately, Storm felt Iceman sucking the moisture from the air, turning it dry as bone. The dehydrated air seemed to leech precious moisture from her own body, leaving her throat parched and thirsty. She swallowed hard, but no saliva came; her mouth was dry. A trickle of blood seeped from her nose as the air within the quinjet grew more arid still. Looking about her, she saw her fellow passengers looking equally distressed. Only Iron Man, his human frailties concealed by his all-encompassing armor, and his android co-pilot did not display the early symptoms of dehydration.

Except for Iceman, that is. He gained in size and stature as he gathered up every last drop of ambient moisture. Icy limbs thickened noticeably and a dense mane of glittering icicles formed around his resolute face. "Okay," he said, unwilling to prolong his companions' discomfort an instant longer than necessary. "That should do it. Drop the field, Iron Man."

A crackle of discharged energy signalled the removal of the electrostatic barrier. At the same time, Iceman threw himself forward, the frigid contours of his body flowing and changing as he did so. With no atmosphere outside to provide him with raw material, he formed a tunnel to the Leader's sanctuary out of his own transmuted substance, stretching all the way to the wall of the dome.

Storm was impressed by Iceman's feat. Bobby had come a long way over the last few years when it came to mastering his mutant gift; ironically, it had required an episode of psychic possession by a ruthless telepath to awaken Iceman to the full potential of his unique abilities. Strange to realize they had Emma Frost, the infamous White Queen, to thank for Iceman's increased versatility.

"C'mon, gang!" he hollered to them, his face looking down from the ceiling of the tunnel like a decorative bas-relief. Clearly, the atmosphere within the quinjet had flowed out into the newly-formed passageway, providing a medium through which Iceman's chime-like voice could propagate itself. "I can't keep this up forever."

"Good work!" Cyclops praised their teammate. Confident in Iceman's ability to keep the vacuum at bay, he ran into the tunnel Bobby Drake had become. Golden boots pounded the lunar soil, throwing up clouds of gritty powder, until his way was blocked by the sloping wall of the dome. Without missing a step, Cyclops raised the lens of his visor. . . .

Neither a scientist nor an engineer, Storm had no idea what substance the Leader's dome was composed of, but it proved no match for the unleashed power of Cyclops's eyebeams. A crimson burst of extradimensional force hit the dome like a battering ram, smashing open a new entrance to the dome's interior, which he ran through unafraid, sweeping what lay beyond with a continuous surge of ocular energy. Any foe lying in wait inside the dome would have to contend with Cyclops's eyebeams before springing their trap.

"The way is clear!" Storm announced to the others. She hurried after Cyclops with the rest of the rescue team piling into the tunnel to follow her to the perforated dome. It was a tight squeeze for the Hulk, but he managed to creep through to the other side, his deep footprints all but swallowing those left by the preceding X-Men and Avengers. In his haste, the intangible Vision literally passed through the slower-moving Hulk, reaching the end of the tunnel seconds before the immense brute who had been in his way. Iron Man was the last to exit the quinjet, closing and locking the aircraft's door before joining his allies inside the dome.

His task complete, Iceman withdrew the tunnel from the quinjet, swiftly resuming his usual shape and proportions. Stepping briskly through the gap Cyclops had carved with his eyebeams, the frozen mutant used the excess ice to seal the breach in the wall, then paused along with the other heroes to take stock of their new surroundings.

For a terrifying moment, Storm thought that they had somehow ended up outside after all, exposed to the deadly lunar environment. Then she realized that the towering dome was only opaque on the outside; from within, the outer wall permitted a clear view of the surrounding moonscape. She marveled that anyone could find such desolate scenery appealing, but who knew what sort of alien aesthetic the inhuman Skrulls subscribed to? It was possible, she speculated, that they found beauty in lifelessness.

Or perhaps the forbidding panorama was simply intended to discourage escape attempts on the part of the dome's captives. Tycho made an excellent prison, she conceded; even if runaway hostages secured the means to survive the freezing vacuum outside, the miles-high wall of the crater posed a considerable obstacle to any desperate trek to freedom. *How far could Rogue and the Scarlet Witch get before being recaptured?* she wondered. *Probably not far at all.*

"Weird," Iceman commented. "What sort of place is this anyway?"

They found themselves on a wide, curved track that

appeared to circle a large cylindrical structure at the center of the dome. From its vast dimensions, Storm guessed that the cylinder held most of the Leader's lunar habitat. Stenciled markings, penned in an alien script, labeled various portions of inner wall. A three-wheeled vehicle, perhaps intended for a Skrull maintenance crew, was parked on the pavement not far from where Cyclops had forcibly entered the dome. "Anyone here read Skrull?" the Beast inquired, examining the unearthly signage upon the wall. "Alas, I feared as much," he admitted when no one stepped forward to translate the indecipherable markings. "Extraterrestrial languages are a neglected field of study, it seems."

"Look sharp, people," Captain America cautioned, holding his shield before his chest. "We have to assume the Leader and his Skrull associates know we're here, especially after what happened to their saucer."

Storm winced at the memory of that fatal conflagration. She took a deep breath of the humidified air within the dome, which came as a relief after the desiccated environment Iceman had created aboard the quinjet. The atmosphere indoors was surprisingly warm, probably eighty degrees or so; a concession, she suspected, to the Skrulls' reptilian metabolisms. And was that music she heard, playing gently in the background?

Iceman noticed the lilting refrain as well. "Hey, since when did super-villain hang-outs come complete with elevator music?" he asked. A frown rearranged the icy planes of his face; apparently, he didn't think much of their adversaries' taste in music.

"Mendelssohn's 'Italian Symphony,' Op. 10, to be precise," the Beast supplied. "The original London recordings, I believe."

The Hulk snorted disdainfully. "Sounds snobby enough for the Leader." He glanced around impatiently. "So where's the welcoming committee?" Shaking his fists, he bellowed loud enough to be heard all across the dome. "I know you're watching, Sterns!" he shouted, addressing the self-styled Leader by his actual name. "Come on out and play, before I tear this place apart!"

So much for stealth, Storm concluded reluctantly. Captain America was doubtless correct, though; their coming had surely been noted since the Skrull saucer was first dispatched to assail the quinjet. *Perhaps the Hulk has the right approach, for once. Let us confront our enemies without delay.* Rogue and the Scarlet Witch had been incarcerated long enough.

Unwilling to search for an entrance into the cylinder, the Hulk stomped over to the concrete wall and drew back his fist. Before he could deliver a typically earth-shattering blow, however, concealed vents opened above their heads and began spraying a fine pink powder onto the pavement below. "What in the Goddess's name?" Storm exclaimed. Holding one hand over her mouth to avoid inhaling the pink dust, she brushed the clingy sediment from her arms and uniform. It felt dry and spongy to the touch.

Iceman and Cyclops looked as perplexed as she, but the unruly Hulk merely scowled in recognition. "Oh geeze," he muttered, "this stupid stuff again." He kicked a heap of powder away from him. The loose particles wafted down the track before settling once more onto the pavement. "I know what this means: Humanoids!"

Storm started to ask the Hulk what he meant, but the shifting sands preempted her query, providing their own shocking answer. As if of their own volition, the spreading powder began to clump together, forming rudimentary bodies that seemed possessed of animation and purpose. Even as she gasped in astonishment, a legion of synthetic beings rose from the mysterious pink dust, like mythological warriors sprung from the dragon's teeth.

"Plasticform humanoids," Iron Man explained quickly. Evidently, both the Hulk and the Avengers had faced these soulless creations before. "The Leader's preferred form of mass-produced minions. They have no will of their own, are incapable of pain or fear, and they never stop coming."

So it appeared. Already the multiplying humanoids outnumbered them by many dozens. Their sexless, identical bodies squeaked like rubber as they jostled against each other, surrounding Storm and her confederates in a sea of smooth, pink figures. The humanoids lacked faces, she noted, having only blank white patches where their eyes should have been. Their heads were pail-shaped, sitting atop immaculate torsos devoid of hair or individuality. They seemed an obscene mockery of humanity as she knew it. Unlike the Vision, or the techno-organic entity the X-Men knew and trusted as Douglock, Storm sensed no true life or personality in these unthinking puppets.

"Holy homunculi!" the Beast exclaimed, suggesting to Storm that Hank McCoy's long stint among the Avengers had not included any previous encounters with these bizarre creations. Like her, he was witnessing the birth of the humanoids for the first time. "Freeze-dried flunkies! What will they think of next?"

Perhaps it was not too late, Storm thought, to dispel

the remaining powder before more humanoids could take form? She let her mind reach out to the artificial atmosphere of the Leader's moonbase. The connection was not as strong and pure as that which she felt to the unfettered wind and water of the Earth, but she had raised tempests in controlled, air-conditioned environments before. Kneading the air with her will, subtly manipulating minute differences in temperature and pressure, she summoned a powerful wind that sent a cloud of dust, plus a few semi-formed limbs and bodies, blowing around the curve of the cylinder and out of sight. Even the completed humanoids, standing erect upon the pavement, swayed before her obedient gale.

"Feel the power of the wind!" she declared proudly. If the Leader was indeed observing them, as the Hulk surmised, let him know that she would not be intimidated by his unliving horde. "Just as this zephyr scatters the makings of these creatures, so shall the wind of freedom blow away all obstacles that come between us and our imprisoned friends."

"Good try," Iron Man whispered to her in a low voice, "but the Leader's not going to run out of humanoids anytime soon." He pointed an armored finger at the vents overhead, from which still more powder spewed in large quantities. The dust, the prime constituent of the thronging humanoids, seemed to fall even faster than she could blow it away. Each new handful only added to the creatures' numbers. "Here they come," the Golden Avenger warned prophetically.

Responding to a single silent signal, the humanoids surged forward, advancing on the hemmed-in heroes, who fought back against the synthetic multitude reaching out for them with plastic hands and fingers. "Avengers

Assemble!'' Captain America shouted as he led his teammates into battle, hurling his trusty shield like a discus at the advancing horde.

''Ah, how I've missed that classic clarion call,'' the Beast remarked. Exchanging a whimsical look with Storm, he shrugged his broad, beastly shoulders. ''Somehow 'X-Men Exacerbate' doesn't have quite the same ring to it.''

Then the glut of humanoids was upon them, providing no further opportunity for humorous asides. Storm flung a lightning bolt at the nearest clump of humanoids, but, even at such close range, the thunderbolt had little effect on her targets; the rubbery substance of their bodies appeared to provide excellent insulation against electrical attacks. To her distress, she saw that the pink synthetic flesh of the humanoids was not even scorched. Glancing quickly around her, she saw that the other heroes found their efforts similarly thwarted.

Captain America's famous shield rebounded harmlessly off the elastic anatomies of the humanoids, who seemed to be even more resilient than the X-Men's old foe, the Blob. Like that corpulent mutant, the humanoids blithely absorbed whatever force was directed against them, then sprang back unharmed, ready for more. The star-spangled Avenger retrieved his shield easily, the ricocheting disk sliding back into his outstretched hand in one smooth, unbroken motion, but there seemed little point in pitching it at the undaunted humanoids once more, even if the crush of plastic bodies left him any room in which to throw the shield, which was hardly the case. Captain America was forced to fight hand-to-hand with the humanoids assailing him, combining solid punches with expert kickboxing to keep the artificial creatures from overpowering him, despite their staggering numerical advantage.

Nor were the humanoids deterred by Cyclops's inexhaustible eyebeams, even though the concussive force of his beams stretched their malleable bodies like taffy. Storm wondered if Cyclops was reminded of the Blob as well; the best Scott could accomplish was to keep a steadily-shrinking swath of crimson energy between himself and the swarming humanoids. No matter how extensively his beams distorted the creatures' anthropomorphic contours, turning humanoid midsections into elongated rubber bands, the Leader's inhuman servitors refused to retreat. "And I thought Sentinels didn't know when to give up!" he muttered darkly, frustration tingeing his voice. "At least Sentinels come apart if you hit them hard enough!"

Iron Man's repulsor rays proved equally ineffectual. Like Captain America, he quickly abandoned his specialized armaments to toss the humanoids aside with his mechanically-enhanced muscles. But for every humanoid he sent flying, several more spilled forward, heedlessly throwing themselves against his armored might. "Remind me to remind Mr. Stark," he asked out loud, "to figure out just what these stooges are made of sometime, and to come up with a solvent to dissolve them!"

"We are sorely in need of just such an efficacious emollient," the Beast agreed, "the better to rid ourselves of the Leader's manufactured myrmidons." The acrobatically-gifted X-Man had thus far managed to evade the humanoids' grasp by bouncing nimbly atop their clustered heads and shoulders, a workable defensive strategy that nevertheless failed to immobilize even one of their teeming antagonists. "I don't suppose your amply-accoladed employer could fax us a few experimental formulae with all deliberate speed?''

"I think he's kind of busy at the moment," Iron Man grunted through his helmet. A transistorized punch buried his right arm elbow-deep in the gummy chest of uncaring humanoid, who, along with his innumerable cohorts, battered its own plasticform fists against the Avenger's gleaming armor. Storm could barely catch a glimpse of Iron Man, so dense was the mob of humanoids engulfing him. Only his gilded helmet could be seen above the profusion of identical pink bodies. "But I'll send him a memo if we ever get out of here."

"Fascinating," the Vision observed with characteristic aloofness. As intangible as he was artificial, the android thrust a vaporous hand into a plastic skull. "The humanoids' internal structure appears to be completely undifferentiated. I can detect no organs or controlling mechanisms to disrupt." He levitated above the fray, coolly looking down upon the synthetic drones, whose utter mindlessness made his own dispassionate attitude seem positively effusive. Thermoscopic beams radiated from his amber eyes, yet the humanoids neither blistered nor burned. They climbed atop each other trying to reach the hovering Vision, persistently clawing at him no matter how many times their hands passed through the Avenger's immaterial form. The Vision's untouchability inevitably reminded Storm of Shadowcat's phasing power, even though the stoic android was otherwise very different from Kitty Pryde. Ororo felt relieved, for Kitty's sake, that the young woman was safely back on Earth, not adrift in a sea of hostile humanoids.

The faceless creatures clung like leeches to the Hulk's gargantuan frame, which rose above the plethora of humanoids like a green, grassy mountain rising from the ocean. "This is getting real old," he grumbled. "How many times do I have to wade through you plastic punching bags?" He shook over a dozen humanoids from his head and shoulders, like a wet dog ridding himself of stray water. A stomp of seismic proportions sent still more pink bodies flying through the air. The flung humanoids made a rubbery, slapping sound as they smacked against the walls and floor; that was the only noise the mouthless creatures were capable of making. Storm found the deathly silence of the humanoids' attack more disturbing than any angry threats or ultimatums could have been.

"Guess these guys don't worry much about frostbite," Iceman complained. The unfeeling mannequins appeared immune to cold, although he trapped a coterie of humanoids by creating an icy carpet, at least a foot deep, that locked the drones' legs in place. The shackled humanoids stretched their lower limbs out of shape trying to yank them free of the ice, but, before they could succeed in extricating themselves, another cascade of humanoids clambered over their immobilized twins, anxious to apprehend the refrigerated mutant, who fended them off with flash-frozen snowballs. Crystalline spikes sprouted from his shoulders and arms, so that Iceman resembled a human porcupine, but the persistent humanoids fearlessly impaled themselves upon his icy carapace, the points of his spikes blunted by the creatures' gummy consistency.

Transforming his right hand into a serrated ice-scimitar, Iceman sliced off a humanoid's arm just above the elbow. A drastic measure, Storm thought, swiftly reminding herself that the maimed humanoid was not truly alive. Iceman's other hand assumed the shape of an axe blade, which cleanly decapitated another humanoid. Impressed by the effectiveness of his newly-honed sharp edges, the frigid X-Man began slashing away at the myriad humanoids with a ferocity worthy of Wolverine. Humanoid heads and limbs were scattered like chaff, falling bloodlessly onto the pavement. "Yahoo!" Iceman crowed excitedly. "Just call me Bobby, the Humanoid Slayer!"

His triumph was short-lived, however. To his chagrin, the butchered humanoids rapidly regenerated their missing pieces. New arms grew from truncated stumps. Fresh craniums sprang from headless shoulders. Even the discarded scraps speedily rejoined the struggle, wriggling across the floor to link up with other amputated segments to form new, composite humanoids. Each and every stray fragment of pink plastic flesh seemed to possess the knowledge and the will to build another humanoid from scratch. Iceman soon found himself swamped by the same faceless monstrosities he had sliced to pieces moments before. "This is crazy!" he protested, flailing away the neverending horde. "We're getting creamed by Silly Putty!"

Storm had no idea what Silly Putty was, but she shared Bobby's anxiety. Wave after unrelenting wave of determined humanoids descended upon them, the oppressive crush of their ductile bodies triggering a sense of claustrophobic panic in the mutant weather goddess. The humanoids were all around her, smothering her, cutting her off from the world! Desperate to escape the ceaseless flood of synthetic lackeys, she tried to take to the air; in the diminished gravity, it required only the barest of breezes to carry her aloft. *Free!* she thought, her heart pounding in her chest. *I must be free!*

But she could not rise fast enough to elude the eager clutches of the humanoid mob. Multiple plastic fingers, slick and clammy in texture, wrapped around her calves and ankles, intent on dragging her down into the serried, suffocating swarm she sought so fervently to break free from. "No!" she commanded. "Let me go!" Fanned by her aroused emotions, a swelling wind lifted the latex wings beneath her arms, yet the stubborn, single-minded humanoids would not release her. Her captured legs felt like they were being pulled from their sockets; unlike the extraordinarily flexible humanoids, she could not be stretched so without pain or injury. Any agony was preferable, though, to the thought of being pulled once more into the tightly-packed mass of humanoid bodies, to being buried alive beneath that unliving multitude. "Gods of earth and air," she pleaded, "let me be free!"

Caught up in her increasingly frantic struggle to shed the humanoids weighing her down, she barely heard Captain America call out to his fellow Avengers. "Iron Man!" he shouted urgently. The edge of his shield divided a humanoid in twain, but the divided halves reconnected immediately without missing a step. "Remember the last time we fought these things? Outside the Leader's space station?" He used a judo hold to flip the reconstituted humanoid over his shoulder, where it smacked against its identical counterparts. "Captain Marvel used a burst of infrared heat to sear away the humanoids' outer membranes, leaving them vulnerable to the cold of space!"

"Right!" Iron Man recalled. Armored knuckles left a temporary impression on the blank face of a humanoid. "I'm on it." Igniting his boot jets, he blasted off toward the ceiling, dragging several humanoid hangers-on with him. A repulsor blast from his chest projector cleared away the humanoids adhering to the front of his armor, and sent the dislodged creatures raining onto the heads of their invulnerable brothers. With his chestplate momentarily exposed, Iron Man used its central lens to direct a wide-angle heat beam on the combatants below. Storm felt a sudden warmth rush over her. The humanoids' grip on her ankles loosened for an instant and she kicked her feet from the confines of her boots. *A small sacrifice,* she thought, *to pay for my freedom.* Liberated from the humanoids' hold, she ascended to join Iron Man and the Vision above the heads of their attackers.

"Iceman!" the Golden Avenger called to Bobby. "The ball's in your court now. Give them the freeze treatment."

"If you say so," the X-Man replied dubiously. He rose from the floor of the track atop a rapidly-forming column of glistening ice. Humanoids tried to climb after him, but their hands and feet slipped upon the slick, frozen sides of the pillar. Having gained a moment to concentrate, Iceman stretched out his clear blue arms and closed his eyes. "Get ready for goosebumps," he warned.

At once the temperature plummeted, descending to arctic lows. Storm's breath misted before her lips and, shivering, she hugged herself tightly, trying to hold on to every last degree of bodily warmth. A spreading layer of frost clouded the transparent walls of the dome, obscuring her view of the lunar vista outdoors. Goose pimples indeed erupted along her exposed arms and legs. "Hold on," Iron Man said, noting her discomfort. He turned the welcome heat of his chest-beam upon her, dispelling the worst of the chill, much to Storm's gratitude. The golden radiance warmed her like the African sun at mid-day.

The effect of the extreme cold on the humanoids was less readily apparent—until Captain America struck an inhuman figure soundly with his shield, and the humanoid shattered with a loud crack that sounded like music to Storm's ears. The Hulk achieved equally heartening results by slamming two gigantic handfuls of humanoids together, reducing them to a pile of broken chips and flakes that showed no sign of regenerating. The beam from Cyclops's visor no longer harmlessly prodded the humanoids; instead the potent force beam caused the artificial creatures to crack and crumble on impact.

Even the Beast got into the act. The agile X-Man vaulted into the driver's seat of the small tri-wheeled vehicle, and began running the suddenly vulnerable humanoids down with abandon. Humanoids splintered beneath his wheels or broke apart against the vehicle's front chassis. "Eat my dust!" he whooped merrily. "Pink humanoid dust, that is." The tri-wheeler skidded sideways across a convenient patch of ice, sending now-fragile humanoids scattering into smithereens like so many porcelain bowling pins. "Who might have imagined that vehicular mayhem could be so invigorating?"

Storm's heart leaped at the bloodless carnage below. Captain America's plan had worked! Without the protective membrane he'd mentioned, eliminated by Iron Man's admirably adaptable armor, the gummy humanoids had become hard and brittle in the cold. No longer capable of absorbing an infinite amount of punishment without visible harm, the Leader's unnatural creations were now thoroughly breakable. "Just like those O-rings on the Challenger space shuttle," Iron Man observed, referring to the frozen rubber components that had doomed that ill-fated space shuttle. Storm was no engineer, but she understood the comparison. The more unbending the sapling, the more vulnerable it became to the force of an angry wind.

What had been an inescapable morass became a massacre. From her vantage point high above the circular track, Storm commanded powerful winds to toss scores of humanoids against the concrete wall of the moonbase's inner cylinder. The howl of the maddened winds, followed by the loud snapping of humanoid limbs, drowned out the melodic refrains of the Leader's muzak. Pink whirlwinds scattered the crumbling detritus all along the track.

Swooping silently from above, his saffron cloak billowing in his wake, the Vision passed like a wraith into the clustered bodies of the humanoid host, then instantaneously increased the density of his android form to diamond-hardness while he still occupied the same space as his humanoid targets. An entire row of brittle humanoids exploded as a result, showering their uncomprehending neighbors with shards of pink plastic. "My congratulations, Iron Man," the Vision intoned. "Your infrared radiation has yielded demonstrably better results than my own thermoscopic beams."

"It's all in the wavelength," Iron Man confided, like a craftsman sharing a trade secret. His repulsors could now wreak havoc on the hardened humanoids, blasting them to bits. "I just mimicked what Captain Marvel did a few years ago, back before she changed her name to Photon."

"There's no substitute for experience," Captain America declared, "not to mention effective teamwork." His shield careened through the air, ricocheting from humanoid to humanoid, and fracturing a half dozen opponents with a single throw. "This just proves our two teams *can* work well together; we couldn't have succeeded without Iceman."

"Whatever," the Hulk rumbled. His cudgel-like fists hammered one humanoid after another. They disintegrated to dust beneath his catastrophic blows, leaving him ankle-deep in powdered humanoid. The swirling particles irritated his nose and he sneezed with volcanic force, dispersing the accumulated residue over several yards. "Just so they stay down when I hit them," he muttered irritably.

Storm was not surprised by the man-brute's lack of gratitude; by now, she expected nothing more from him. "Well done, my friends!" she said warmly, bestowing her thanks on her valiant comrades. A zealous wind carried her over the one-sided conflict below, side-by-side with Iron Man, who continued to decimate their foes with well-aimed repulsor rays. A fresh bolt of lightning proved more puissant than before, cracking an unlucky humanoid straight down the middle. "Never doubt that we shall prevail!"

Victory was clearly theirs, even though the remaining humanoids appeared incapable of recognizing that the tide of battle had turned. Evidently, the Leader considered his homegrown henchmen expendable; despite abundant casualties, the mindless entities kept on throwing themselves against the heroes. Greatly outnumbered at the onset of the melee, the combined efforts of the X-Men, the Avengers, and the Hulk made short work of the remaining humanoid legions now that their uncanny resilience had been neutralized. Catching a glance at the elevated vents in the wall, Storm noted that the stream of pink dust had run dry. The Leader knew his soulless soldiers had failed, it seemed, even if the surviving humanoids did not.

The Hulk disposed of the last few stragglers by clapping his great hands together with deafening force. The resulting shock wave struck the indefatigable humanoids like a typhoon, peeling away bits and pieces of their fragile substance until only shreds remained. With the enemy annihilated, Storm half-expected the Hulk to beat his chest in triumph, but the pugnacious giant merely inspected his destructive handiwork with a sullen expression upon his rough-hewn features. "Now then, where was I?" he asked himself ominously. "Oh yeah, I remember."

Without further ado, he stomped over to the concrete cylinder and smashed a hole in it with his fist. The rest of his titanic frame followed his fist in short order, crashing through the wall like a bipedal bulldozer. Pulverized cement dusting his head and shoulders, he glanced back at the other heroes, sneering. "So, you losers comin' or not?"

"After you," Captain America said unflappably. His shield upon his arm, he led the way, deftly stepping over and around the chunks of debris left behind by the Hulk's passage. "Keep your eyes open, people," he warned. "We don't know what the Leader's likely to pull next."

Intangible once more, the Vision glided through the solid concrete above Captain America while the rest of the rescue team hurried toward the Hulk-wrought gap in the wall. Iceman skated down from his frozen pedestal while the Beast abandoned his borrowed vehicle. Flying away from Iron Man, Storm spotted her discarded boots lying amidst a heap of pink plastic splinters. A deliberate gust of wind reclaimed her unharmed footwear, carrying them into her arms. Quickly tugging her boots back on, she landed on the pavement in front of the Hulk's impromptu entrance and stepped into line behind the Beast and Cyclops. The breach was large enough that the sundry X-Men and Avengers were able to pass through two at a time. Ready to hurl a thunderbolt at the first evidence of another attack, Storm's fingertips tingled with electrical potential.

With her colleagues, she stepped into a sterile white corridor lined with vertical tanks capable of holding many gallons of gas or liquid. Pipes and gauges filled the wallspace between the high-volume tanks. The muffled sound of steady pumping competed with the classical music coming from overhead. "Life-support systems," Iron Man guessed, peering at one of the many gauges attached to the tanks. As before, the equipment was inscribed with characters from an alien alphabet or number system. "Probably water or air or both."

Storm recalled that the Skrulls, like their Shi'ar rivals, breathed oxygen just as Terrans did. The basic principles of respiration and metabolism seemed more or less constant throughout the inhabited worlds of the universe; even the loathsome Brood and the extraterrestrially-diverse Starjammers all thrived within an Earth-like atmosphere. *Thank you, Bright Lady, for this small mercy,* Storm thought, grateful that she need not be confined within an enclosed spacesuit. This corridor, in fact, was warmer and more comfortable than the track they had just departed; now that there were no more humanoids to freeze, Iceman no longer needed to freeze the very air around them. Storm savored the rise in temperature.

The Leader's moonbase appeared to be laid out in a series of concentric circles. Like the ring of pavement where they'd just fought the humanoids, the tank-lined corridor seemed to circle yet another cylinder, this one smaller than the one before. *Not unlike the Russian dolls poor Illyana used to play with as a toddler,* Storm reflected sadly, *before we lost her to Limbo and the Legacy Virus.*

The corridor was distinctly unpopulated. Aside from a few scuff marks upon the tile floor, she detected no evidence of the Leader or any Skrulls, let alone their missing teammates. Was the moonbase inhabited at all, she wondered, or had all their foes perished when the Skrull saucer exploded in space? She supposed it was possible that some automated defense system had released the humanoids when the rescue team broke into the dome, but what then had become of Rogue and the Scarlet Witch? Had they also been aboard the saucer when it met its fiery end, or were they still trapped somewhere inside the moonbase?

The hermetic environment of the dome had not permitted her claustrophobia to subside entirely. The circumscribed nature of the Leader's domicile weighed heavily upon her, as did her prolonged separation from the Earth. She could not help recalling the Danger Room scenario she and her teammates had played out less than forty-eight hours before, perhaps at the very moment that Rogue and the Witch had first run afoul of the disguised Skrulls. In that exercise, set aboard a collapsing Shi'ar space station, they had attempted to escape in an available space shuttle, only to "die" in the attempt. *May the Goddess grant that this real-life excursion into space ends more happily!*

The Hulk looked disappointed that they had found no foes to fight. "I say we keep smashing our way toward the center of this circular rathole. *Unless,*" he added pointedly, glaring up at the ceiling, "you want to show your skinny face, Sterns, and save us all a lot of time!" He punctuated his challenge by ripping one of the multi-gallon tanks from the wall. Compressed vapor hissed from the severed pipes and sundered tank, which the Hulk compressed into a squat ball of crumpled metal, then drop-kicked down the hall.

"That's pure oxygen," Captain America cautioned, sniffing the released gases. "Nobody light a match, got that?"

Despite his warning, a blinding flash startled Storm and the others. Instinctively, she raised her hand to shield her eyes from the unexpected viridescent glare. Bright green spots danced before her eyes and she blinked to clear her vision. As the intense glow quickly faded, she discovered that they were no longer alone in the corridor.

Samuel Sterns, alias the Leader, looked just as he had been described to her: a freakish figure notable for his pale green skin and enormous brain. He wore a utilitarian orange jumpsuit, plus black wristbands equipped with electronic controls of some sort. Although his flesh bore the greenish hue characteristic of gamma mutation, the Leader's complexion was several shades grayer and more sickly than the Hulk's vibrant chartreuse skin. Curiously, the villain's bulbous green skull reminded her somewhat of Leech, the young Morlock child currently residing at Professor Xavier's School for Gifted Youngsters. Would Leech look like the Leader when he grew up? Storm hoped that, if nothing else, the orphaned Morlock would acquire a far less sinister mien than the smirking fiend who now stood before them.

"Please, Hulk, spare me any further vandalism," he said sardonically. His falsetto voice was the polar opposite of the Hulk's cavernous rumbling. "You might actually damage something important in your testosterone-fueled histrionics."

For a wanted criminal, he seemed remarkably unruffled by the sight of nine invading super heroes. "We have come for our friends," Storm proclaimed, offended by the Leader's arrogant nonchalance. "Return Rogue and the Scarlet Witch to us at once." The Leader did not bother to deny any knowledge of the abductees.

"And if I give you back your misplaced colleagues, hypothetically speaking, will you then depart in peace, leaving me to the privacy of my tranquil lunar retreat?"

"Not a chance," Captain America stated sternly. "You're already wanted for numerous crimes against humanity. We're not about to leave you free to commit future atrocities."

Speaking for the X-Men, Cyclops seconded the Avengers' leader. "Not even Magneto ever nuked an innocent American city the way you did to that town in Arizona. Captain America is right; you have to face justice for your crimes"

"Perhaps," the Leader said. "Perhaps not." He strolled over to the compacted metal sphere the Hulk had created from one of the base's oxygen tanks. "Tsk-tsk," he clucked, shaking his head wearily. "Must you make a mess wherever you go, Hulk?"

"I'm just warming up," the Hulk promised grimly.

He peered at his longtime nemesis through wary eyes. Obviously, he didn't expect the Leader to surrender easily.

Captain America looked past the Leader at the empty corridor curving away to the right. "Where are your Skrull allies?" he demanded. "If it turns out you've been conspiring with an alien empire to conquer the Earth, that's high treason in my book, mister."

"Please!" The Leader rolled his beady eyes, unimpressed by the living legend's accusation. "I lost interest in Earth years ago, Captain. Feeble-minded humanity has already turned my native planet into a global garbage heap: holes in the ozone, toxic waste everywhere, a greenhouse effect galloping out of control, not to mention an ever-growing excess of unruly and ungovernable human vermin. Just thinning the world's population down to a manageable level would be a full-time job, one unworthy of my transcendent intellect and vision."

"Transcend this!" the Hulk roared, stalking forward, his enormous fists raised above his head. Murder blazed in his emerald eyes.

Captain America courageously held out his hand to halt the lumbering giant. "Not yet," he ordered. "Let him talk."

Storm assumed that Captain America hoped to learn more about the hostages' whereabouts before another battle royal broke out. To her surprise, the Hulk assented to the Avenger's request, grudgingly stepping backwards and lowering his fists. Storm's respect for the legendary American hero increased; not many people had the authority and confidence to command the Hulk. "You were saying?" Captain America prompted the Leader.

"My alien partner, along with his subordinates, comes

from a considerably older and more advanced civilization than the one you so-called heroes constantly seek to
defend," the Leader explained pedantically. "They have
promised me a new world of my own, to reshape from
the ground up according to my own superlative design.
I intend to create a new race of gamma-spawned beings
to inhabit my world, incorporating, incidentally, some of
the intriguing mutations I've had occasion to study in
my recent guests."

"Guests?" Storm echoed indignantly. "You mean
prisoners, of course, taken by force against their wills."
She confronted the Leader, her stony voice full of controlled anger. "Do not play games with us, kidnapper.
Where are our friends? Bring us to them now."

The Leader's enlarged cranium rocked slightly as he
shrugged his shoulders. "If you say so." He pressed one
of the touchpads upon his wrist and the green glow returned, even brighter than before. Blinking against the
sudden radiance, Storm feared that the Leader had teleported to safety, but, as she wiped the tears from her
eyes, she saw that he had merely beamed three more
figures onto the scene.

Her spirits soared at the sight of Rogue and another
woman standing behind the Leader. Even greater was
her joy at the discovery that Wolverine, alive and well,
stood between the two women. Then Logan had not perished aboard the saucer after all! She could only assume
that he had been teleported over to the Leader's moonbase sometime before the alien spacecraft exploded.
Blessed be the Goddess! she thought ardently. Their beloved friend and comrade still lived!

As her initial elation waned, however, she observed
that all was not right with the Leader's supposed guests.

Clad in matching orange jumpsuits, the abducted heroes displayed no sign of relief or recognition upon their faces. Rogue and the other woman, whom Storm now recognized as Wanda Maximoff, without her distinctive scarlet uniform, stared ahead blankly, their eyes glassy and unfocussed. Logan's bronze eyes, by contrast, were bloodshot and crazed, retaining their usual feral gleam, but lacking any semblance of sanity or civilization. Flecks of foam dotted the corners of his mouth. He looked like a rabid animal, barely held at leash.

"Logan?" Storm asked uncertainly. "Rogue?"

"Wanda?" the Vision added. For the first time, his saturnine voice held a trace of human emotion. Storm recalled that the android had once been married to the Scarlet Witch. The levitating Vision descended to the floor, as if weighed down by mortal concerns. "Are you well? Wanda?"

The Leader smiled evilly. "I'm afraid they don't respond to those appellations anymore, or to anything else you might care to say." He snapped his fingers and the three stolen heroes fanned out in front of the Leader, defending him. Claws popped out of Wolverine's hands, the Scarlet Witch extended her fingers in a mystical configuration, and Rogue peeled off a pair of orange surgical gloves. There was no mistaking the menace inherent in their actions.

"That can't be them!" Iceman chimed. "Those are just Skrulls in disguise."

"Nah," the Hulk spat in disgust. "He's got them brainwashed. I've seen it before. All he has to do is touch you and he's got you under his control." He glowered at the Leader, emerald eyes burning balefully beneath his sloping brows. "But your mind-tricks don't work on me, do they, Sterns? Tell them that, why don't you?"

"Why should I," the Leader asked, "when you've so helpfully updated them on my mental manipulation and its limitations? Not that it matters. My psychic influence worked well enough on your former colleagues, as you can see." His smug smile stretched even wider. The intricate convolutions of his swollen cerebellum pulsated like a malignant heartbeat. "Specimen #s 1 through 3, destroy the intruders!"

As the entranced mutants charged at their would-be rescuers, Storm refused to despair. There had to be a way, she knew, to free their teammates from the Leader's insidious mind control; the X-Men had often overcome foes with similar hypnotic powers: Mesmero, Sauron, the Shadow King, even Dracula, the bloodthirsty Lord of the Undead. Storm had no doubt that, given the opportunity, Professor X could release the Leader's hold on his victims' minds, but first she and the others had to defend themselves against their own dear friends, without bringing permanent harm to those they had come to rescue.

That, she realized, *is going to be the difficult part.* . . .

The antiseptic white corridor, reminiscent of something from Kubrick's *2001,* became a battleground. Intent on the Leader, the Hulk bounded at his perennial nemesis, only to be blocked by Wolverine's flashing claws. Slashing and biting, Logan launched himself at his frequent sparring partner, the force and ferocity of his attack proving sufficient to keep the Hulk, at least for an interval, away from the Leader.

What an irrefutably distressing turn of events, the Beast thought, shaking his shaggy head at Wolverine's misdirected energy and aggression; given a choice, the Beast vastly preferred to have Logan's innate bellicosity on his side, not dispatched against him. *I certainly never anticipated rooting for the Hulk in he and Wolverine's latest grudge match!*

Deploying along party lines, the rest of the heroes attempted to subdue their brainwashed brethren. Iron Man and the other Avengers converged on the Scarlet Witch, while Cyclops led the X-Men against Rogue. Torn by conflicting loyalties, the Beast briefly hesitated before joining the conflict, then hopped after Captain America. An honest appraisal of his abilities led the Beast to suspect that his preternatural agility might come in handier against the Scarlet Witch than pitted against Rogue's superior strength and invulnerability. Moreover, as the most minimally-clothed of the various X-Men and Avengers present, the fur-covered mutant realized that he presented a large, indigo target for Rogue's parasitic touch. *Best to keep a safe distance from those voracious fingers,* he judged, *lest I prematurely find myself in a comatose state.*

Perhaps the most powerful Avenger present, Iron Man was also the first to fall victim to the Scarlet Witch's hex power. In response to her arcane gestures, a sphere of incarnadine light surrounded the Golden Avenger, triggering a highly improbable series of malfunctions in his ordinarily infallible armor. His left boot jet misfired, tossing him sideways into a tank of oxygen. Unwanted bursts of plasma erupted from his gauntlets, carving out an enormous pit beneath him, into which the dazed Avenger began to slide. His steel-sheathed hands grabbed onto the edge of the pit, leaving Iron Man literally hanging by his fingertips above the moon's newest crater. "My armor!" he shouted, his voice no longer sounding electronically amplified or disguised. "It's gone dead. There's no more power!"

Following close behind Iron Man, Captain America almost ran headlong into the gaping pit, but his combat-honed reflexes spared him from the plunge. Taking advantage of the moon's lesser gravity, he cleared the crater in a single leap. "Beast!" he called out in mid-air. "See to Iron Man." His spinning shield flew from his hand before his boots hit the floor, whooshing down the corridor to strike the Scarlet Witch in the stomach, knocking her off her feet. Even though he recognized the necessity of Captain America's action, the Beast still winced in sympathy for his former teammate. *If I know Cap*, he assured himself, *he didn't throw his shield hard enough to really hurt Wanda, just enough to pound the wind out of her.*

"Vision!" Cap barked. His shield bounced back into his grip as though connected to his glove by an elastic band. "Put her out while she's down. This is our chance!"

"Understood," the Vision answered, sounding even more somber than usual as he glided toward his estranged wife. Spectral fingers stretched out for the Scarlet Witch's head, hovering momentarily over her tumbled auburn curls. All he needed to do was insert those insubstantial digits into the downed Witch's brow, then solidify them partially, and the resulting shock to her system would render the ensorcelled sorceress out like the proverbial light. "Forgive me, Wanda," he said in a dour monotone, pausing a second before delivering the incapacitating blow.

"Now, Vision!" Captain America urged, running across the tile floor toward the poignant-yet-suspenseful tableau. "On the double!"

His hesitation cost the synthezoid dearly. Before his immaterial fingers could insinuate themselves into the Scarlet Witch's brainpan, her own fingers twitched and a luminescent scarlet orb enclosed the Vision. His outstretched hand poked against her pale forehead, but went no further; the Witch's occult sphere had made him tangible once more. A backhanded swipe from his former wife sent the Vision reeling, giving the Scarlet Witch a chance to scramble to her feet.

"Dear me!" the Beast exclaimed, looking over his shoulder at the debacle as he struggled to pull Iron Man from the brink of his inadvertently-created precipice. Although many pounds lighter than it would have been on Earth, the Golden Avenger's armor retained all of its considerable mass. Tawny muscles bulged along the Beast's simian arms as he yanked on his colleague's iron-clad arm. "I can't say I approve of the way this particular skirmish is proceeding."

"You can say that again," Iron Man grunted, dangling. With the Beast's help, he hoisted his armored elbows over the ledge of the chasm. "We need Storm, pronto!"

"Rogue! It's me, Bobby! Snap out of it!"

Iceman didn't care how smart or how powerful the Leader was supposed to be. He couldn't resist trying to get through to Rogue, to reach the strong, spirited woman beneath the brainwashing. He and Rogue had run off together several months back; things hadn't worked out, but he felt that he knew the real Rogue, the one no sneaky mind games could keep down for long. "Fight it!" he urged, sliding toward her on a freshly-generated track of frozen moisture. "You can do it! I know you can!"

Her feet lifted from the floor and she flew at him, fists forward. His track angled up to intercept her, on a collision course that brought them barrelling toward each other at top speed. He kept expecting her to come to her senses, swerve away and maybe go after the Leader instead, but, to his dismay, she kept on coming. At the last minute, he threw up an ice shield to protect him from her incoming fists; she smashed right through it like it was made out of sugar cubes. Chunks of frozen shrapnel went flying off in all directions, and Iceman toppled over, sliding backwards down his track.

Flat on his back, he coasted to a halt at the bottom of the ramp. His spill left him in a poor position to defend himself as Rogue dived at him. Would her super-strength turn him into a pile of crushed ice before she absorbed his powers? It looked like he was about to find out—until a very familiar red beam came from out of nowhere, blindsiding Rogue and driving her away from the downed Iceman. "Way to go, Cyke!" Iceman cheered his rescuer, grateful for the save. "Perfect timing as usual!"

Cyclops kept his eyebeams focused on Rogue, pounding her with the full force of his optic blast. "Iceman," he shouted as he kept Rogue at bay, "take care of those gas links so Storm can use her lightning."

That's Cyke, always thinking, Iceman thought, back on his frigid feet and heading for the ruptured pipes.

Bobby hadn't even realized until now that pure oxygen and Ororo's super-sized sparks made a dangerously bad combination. *Guess that's why he's the leader guy, and I'm just a frozen dessert.*

Following Cyclops's instructions, Iceman sealed the broken pipes with a couple of improvised ice-plugs. The hiss of escaping gas fell silent and Storm diluted the concentrated oxygen in the air by blowing it away with an emphatic gust of wind. "That's better," she stated simply, nodding at Iceman. Electricity crackled around her, lifting her long white hair so that it framed her elegant features like a halo. She looked to where Rogue and Cyclops now contended, and lifted her hands to intervene, but a compelling cry from Iron Man seized her attention.

"Storm!" he shouted from across the hall, while the Beast waved his long arms to attract her notice. "I could use a recharge over here." The armored Avenger knelt near the brink of a deep cavity in the floor, his batteries apparently drained of juice. Iceman guessed that the Scarlet Witch had something to do with Iron Man's personal energy crisis; he remembered the sort of stunts she used to pull back when she still worked for Magneto. "Anytime you're ready!" Iron Man called out to Ororo.

"Gladly!" she replied, soaring toward the pit and away from Iceman, who checked to see how Cyclops was doing. *Between the two of us,* he thought, *we should be able to slow down a mixed-up Rogue. I hope.*

Against anyone less durable than Rogue, Cyclops's eyebeams would have already pummelled her into unconsciousness, if not into a pulp. Even Wolverine might be black-and-blue after such treatment; unfortunately, Cyke's force beams only seemed to make Rogue mad.

A look of major annoyance showed through the zombified glaze in her eyes as she advanced against Cyclops's eyebeams like a salmon fighting its way upstream. Crimson energy broke upon her orange-clad physique and her fists swung repeatedly at the steadily-shrinking swath of red light between her and Cyclops, pounding away at the incandescent ray as if it was a physical impediment.

Iceman's crystalline jaw dropped open. He'd known Rogue was a powerhouse, but he'd never guessed that she could shrug off Cyke's eyebeams like that. A suit of icy armor, separate and distinct from the organic blue ice that his body was composed of, flowed over Iceman from head to foot. A transparent mace and matching shield formed in his hands. Figuring he was now protected against Rogue's vampiric touch, he circled around her, hoping to club her from behind while she was preoccupied with Cyclops's eyebeams. The tricky part was going to be *not* pulling his punch just because it was Rogue. *Sorry, babe,* he thought, wondering how hard was too hard for someone as tough as the X-Men's favorite steel magnolia, *I hate to say it, but I hope this hurts you more than it does me!*

Carried forward by a moving sheet of ice, he swung the mace at her broad-striped scalp. Just then, however, Rogue put on a burst of speed, pulling away from Iceman and breaking past Cyclops's force beam. Before either X-Man realized what was happening, Rogue's bare fingers splayed across Cyke's face, touching his exposed mouth and jaw.

The effect was immediate—and alarming. Cyclops's nonstop eyebeams conked out like someone had flipped a switch; Iceman caught a rare glimpse of Scott Summers's brown eyes before Cyclops collapsed, out cold, onto the floor. At the same instant, identical eyebeams burst from Rogue's green orbs, slamming into everything she turned her gaze upon.

Without the ruby quartz lens in Cyke's visor, Rogue had no way to control her newly-acquired eyebeams. Not that this seemed to worry her much; inexhaustible amounts of energy pouring from her transformed peepers, she swung her head around and zapped the Vision from a half-dozen yards away. Watching anxiously, Iceman expected the beams to pass right through the android, perhaps hitting the Scarlet Witch by mistake, but something must have happened to the Vision's powers because the beams struck him squarely in the back. He let out a surprisingly human cry of shock and pain before falling facefirst onto the clean white tiles.

That's two down, Iceman thought, gulping ice water, *and we haven't even got to the Leader yet.*

Rogue's power-packed eyes found Captain America next. . . .

Thunder boomed inside the moonbase for possibly the very first time. A sizzling bolt of lightning lit up the circular corridor. *This is more inclement weather,* the Beast reflected, *than Tycho has likely seen in over three billion years.*

Storm's handmade thunderbolt, striking Iron Man directly against his chestplate, had the desired effect. Newly-energized, Iron Man flexed his armored limbs and waited for his computerized hardware to reboot. Signal lights flashed along the top of his crimson-and-gold helmet. The disk-shaped lens in his chestplate lighted up. ''Ah, that's more like it,'' the Golden Avenger declared, his voice once more possessed of its unique electronic timbre. He tilted his faceplate up toward Storm, who was floating several feet about the steep chasm. "You're going to have to send me a power bill sometime." This was twice, or so the Beast had heard, that Storm's galvanic prowess had revitalized Iron Man's trademarked exoskeleton.

"Thank me by restraining Rogue," she instructed. "Your armor should shield you from her touch, but be on guard. Her strength and speed are comparable to your own."

"You don't need to remind me of that," Iron Man said. "I've fought her before, back during that brawl on Ryker's Island a couple years ago." His boot jets lifted him off the ground and he spotted Rogue grabbing Cyclops's face despite the formidable force beam emanating from the X-Man's eyes. "Leave her to me."

Good luck, the Beast thought. Then he caught a scarlet flash out of the corner of his eye and cartwheeled away instinctively. An instant later, a hex bolt struck exactly where he'd been standing, causing an entire section of the floor to cave in, sliding like a miniature avalanche into the open pit. He counted at least five seconds before the falling rubble hit the bottom of the chasm. Even allowing for the fractional gravity involved, that was a long way down.

The Beast found firmer footing ten feet back from the expanding edge of the crater. *That was an exceedingly unwelcome blast from the past,* he thought. Not counting the occasional practice run at Avengers HQ, it had been many years since he had last squared off against the Scarlet Witch in pitched combat—not since those halcyon days of yore when the original X-Men, still a tad green and inexperienced, had often opposed Magneto's newly-forged Brotherhood of Evil Mutants, including a young mutant sorceress named Wanda Maximoff, who had not yet found a more socially-acceptable and altruistic outlet for her eldritch abilities. *Just like old times, alas,* the Beast mused.

The Vision, his own powers disrupted by some singularly scarlet witchcraft, remained the nearest to Wanda, although Captain America, shield in hand, was reducing the distance between himself and the enslaved enchantress. The synthezoid, looking as though his positronic synapses had been slightly scrambled along with his powers, was caught offguard by another blow to the head delivered by his former spouse. The Beast expected his computerized confederate to recover quickly, but that hope was unequivocally dashed when a crimson ray streaked across his view to drop the stricken Vision like a bolt from the blue.

Cyke? The Beast was baffled fleetingly, but his understandable confusion evaporated as his deductive faculties quickly reconstructed what must have transpired. Risking a glance behind him, he saw that, verily, Rogue had indeed taken custody of Cyclops's estimable optic beams. *Sans* visor, to say nothing of free will, their rambunctious Southern belle showed no compunction against turning those beams upon those who strove to emancipate her from physical and mental incarceration. "Cap, heads up!" he forewarned as the shanghaied eye-beams zeroed in on the star-spangled Avenger.

Rogue's ocular attack, plus a hex bolt from the Scarlet Witch, struck Cap's shield at the same moment. Crimson and scarlet energies merged, and the combined beam bounced off the shield, ricocheting straight at the Beast, who somersaulted out of the way with only a heartbeat to spare. The beam struck an oxygen tank instead, denting it on one side. "Lordy, lordy!" the Beast exclaimed, "that was a closer shave than my naturally hirsute hide has seen in years!"

The Beast's escape still left Captain America under fire by both possessed super-heroines. His impervious shield expertly warded off beams and bolts long enough for Iron Man to intercede on his behalf. The Golden Avenger parried Rogue's purloined eyebeams with his own repulsor rays, deflecting the beams away from Captain America and the Beast. Rogue turned her destructive gaze on Iron Man, but the refractive coating of his armor shielded him from the worst of its effect. "Seems to me, I remember you punching me through a jailhouse wall a few years back," he said. "Maybe it's time to return the favor. For your own good, of course."

Swooping in under Rogue's unregulated fusillade of eyebeams, he socked her in the jaw with his state-of-the-art iron knuckles. The transistorized power of his punch sent Rogue zooming backwards over the heads of all concerned, with Iron Man flying in hot pursuit. *Go get her!* the Beast cheered him on as they rocketed out of sight.

With Rogue otherwise occupied, that left the Scarlet Witch on her own against the Beast, Captain America, and Storm. Forced to go on the defensive, Wanda swept her arm in a circle, forming a shimmering scarlet sphere all around her, thereby creating, as the Beast grasped at once, a buffer zone in which the odds were very literally on her side. *Double, double toil and trouble,* he thought, *it's going to be hard to get past that bubble!*

The Witch's strategy demonstrated its utility almost immediately. Thrown like javelins at the enthralled

Avenger, Storm's lightning fizzled out at the periphery of the glowing sphere, while hurricane-strength blasts of wind consistently detoured around the globe's borders. Most improbable of all, Captain America threw his shield at the Scarlet Witch—and missed! Defying conventional aerodynamics, the speeding shield arced upward to bounce off Storm's mahogany brow by mistake. "Holy cow!" the Beast gasped, taken aback by the sight of Cap's shield gone astray. "That never happens to Xena!"

No student of nineties pop culture, Cap missed the allusion. "Thena?" he said, sounding puzzled. "Of the Eternals?"

There was no time to explain. Dazed by the unexpected blow, Storm plummeted toward the pit. The Beast vaulted to her rescue, catching Ororo in his broad arms as he leaped across the beckoning crater. An ugly purple bruise upon her forehead, Storm appeared to be down for the count. *And then there were five,* the Beast thought, *with apologies to Agatha Christie. . . .*

He laid her gently upon the floor, using her stiff headdress to cushion her battered skull. A gold-plated earring shaped like a thunderbolt came loose and he tucked the dislodged jewelry into her boot for safekeeping. Then, convinced that the unconscious Ororo was as safe as could be under the circumstances, he redirected his intellect to the thorny problem of how to beat the Scarlet Witch's supernaturally-enhanced good fortune. *Luck be a lady indeed,* he thought, *at least where Wanda's concerned.*

To his chagrin, the Leader's mind-numbing sway over her did not appear to have impaired her natural instincts and skill; furthermore, the Beast could only assume that the Scarlet Witch was considerably more proficient a combatant now than she had been back in the good old days of the X-Men versus the Brotherhood. *Then again, I've improved with age as well,* he considered. He was quantitatively more spry, not to mention extensively hairier, than he'd been when last they'd found each other on opposite sides of a fracas.

The key, he realized, was to trick Wanda into lowering her protective hex sphere long enough to get to the mortal sorceress inside the magic bubble. "Oh, Glinda!" he called out to her, with an eye to drawing her fire. Indeed, cocooned in her spherical nimbus, Wanda did somewhat resemble Billy Burke arriving to greet Dorothy. "Are you a good witch or a bad witch?"

She didn't take his bait right away, so he resolved to make himself into a more tempting target. Spying Captain America's shield lying on the floor behind Wanda, a few feet beyond the borders of the probability-warping sphere, he galloped straight for the shimmering globe, hooting too loud to possibly be ignored. "Choo-choo-choo!" he shouted gleefully at the Scarlet Witch. "Beast Express, coming through!"

He waited until he was only inches away from the radiant scarlet globe, then went into a handspring that sent him up and over the sphere. "Allez oop!" The reduced gravity made it child's play to clear the top of the orb with room to spare, but, as he had hoped, Wanda could not resist firing a hex bolt at the Beast as he passed over her head. A peculiar sensation, like being rubbed the wrong way, ruffled the fur at the back of his neck as the loosed hex bolt grazed his pelt as it shot past the swiftly-springing X-Man, causing a spidery network of cracks to spread through the ceiling where it ultimately struck home.

Voila! the Beast thought jubilantly as his sasquatch-sized feet smacked down on the tiles behind the Witch. In order to unleash her ire at the buoyant Beast, the brainwashed Avenger had been compelled to let her defensive sphere dissolve into thin air. *Now is the time,* he realized, *for all good Beasts to come to the aid of their country . . . !*

Snatching the wayward shield by his toes, he chucked it back at the momentarily vulnerable Witch, catching her right behind her knees. Legs buckling, she toppled forward, throwing out her hands to break her fall. The Beast spun around and pounced on his faltering foe, landing his ape-like body squarely astride her back. Wanda gasped out loud as his sudden weight squeezed the air from her lungs. Large blue feet descended upon her hands, pinning them to the floor, while he clasped equally larger-than-life hands over her eyes. Suddenly, and in more ways than one, the Scarlet Witch was in no position to cast any more spells.

"Please pardon this immoderate imposition," he asked the pinioned Witch. "Providence willing, we'll look back at this someday and laugh."

Or so he hoped.

"Listen, short stuff, cuz I'm only going to say this once: TAKE ME TO YOUR LEADER!"

The Hulk's bellow echoed down the sterile corridor, but Wolverine gave no sign of acceding to the Hulk's thunderous demand. The mind-controlled mutant tore into the jade giant with a vengeance, his flashing claws trying their best to cut the Hulk down to size. Unfortunately for the feral X-Man, the Hulk's gamma-irradiated muscle grew back faster than Wolverine could shred it, so that to a casual observer it might have looked as if the adamantium claws had little or no effect on the indestructible green behemoth.

That didn't mean it didn't hurt like blazes.

"Get outta my way!" the Hulk roared, swinging his fists at Wolverine, who managed to keep ahead of the monstrous paws by weaving and ducking under the Hulk's earth-shattering blows. Ordinarily, the Hulk would welcome another go-round with the feisty Canadian, but not while the Leader stood by, smirking while the rest of them took their lumps. *That's just like him,* the Hulk raged silently. *Keeping his scrawny hands clean while everyone else gets stuck cleaning up his messes. Well, not this time!* "You can't hide from me forever, Sterns!" he promised, even as Wolverine drove his claws into the Hulk's side all the way up to the X-Man's knuckles. The Hulk grunted in pain, then knocked Wolverine away with a cyclonic slap that sent the mutant flying into the nearest wall hard enough to shatter most anyone else's bones. Sticky traces of emerald blood clung to Wolverine's silver claws as they were yanked free of the Hulk's flesh. "Do you hear me, Sterns? I don't care how many hypnotized do-gooders you throw at me. You're mine!"

But Wolverine, in the full throes of a bloodthirsty frenzy, could not be readily swept aside. Unbroken and undeterred by his jarring collision with the wall, he came at the Hulk again. Wild, reddened eyes blazed with primordial savagery. His lips were curled back, exposing clenched and jagged teeth. Seemingly incapable of civilized speech, Wolverine growled like an animal as he launched himself at the Hulk with all the untamed aggression of his predatory namesake. The Hulk caught only a glimpse of the Leader's smug, self-satisfied features before the crazed X-Man lunged once more into his field of vision, hacking away at the Hulk's colossal magnitude. The Hulk felt dozens of fleeting incisions stab at his chest. Wolverine's teeth sank into his throat, breaking the skin.

Enough of this garbage! he thought, his irritation at the berserk X-Man almost surpassing his overwhelming hatred of the Leader. With a snarl of his own, he twisted his thick neck free from Wolverine's deadly jaws and batted the raging mutant away. The Hulk clapped his hands together loudly, producing a deafening boom that left Wolverine clutching his ears in agony. *Ha!* the Hulk gloated pitilessly. *Bet that did a number on your supersensitive hearing!*

The pain only inflamed the X-Man's volcanic bloodlust. Foaming at the mouth, Wolverine howled in defiance and leaped at his towering adversary. The Hulk braced himself for Wolverine's assault, then blinked in surprise as, suddenly, there were *five* more Wolverines attacking him. Without warning or explanation, he became surrounded by identical, pint-sized mutants with matching sets of razor-sharp claws. Half a dozen Wolverines laid into him tooth and nail, slashing and biting from all directions. The Hulk flailed about wildly, trying to smash every one of the savage sextuplets to kingdom come, but there were too many flashing blades and darting figures to keep track of; he couldn't tell if he was slugging all of the Wolverines or just the same one over and over. Meanwhile, the claws kept coming, subjecting him to the death of a hundred thousand cuts. But why was this happening? Where had all the extra Wolverines come from?

This is the Leader's fault, he realized. A clump of matted green hair went flying as a set of claws scraped against the Hulk's lumpish skull. *This is some crummy illusion he's projecting into my head to mess me up!* Adamantium claws gouged his face. A deep gash across his forehead leaked a trickle of green blood into his eyes, blinding him. *It's working, too.*

No matter how accurate, his brilliant deduction didn't do him much good in the short term. How could he tell which Wolverine was real? He wiped the blood from his eyes with the back of his hand, but the multiple Wolverines remained. In theory, he only needed to watch out for the actual, flesh-and-blood X-Man, but he couldn't begin to distinguish the illusions from genuine article. Every slice and stab felt like the real thing.

He stomped the floor with deliberate *oomph,* hoping that only the authentic Wolverine would be thrown for a loop by the cataclysmic tremor. No such luck; all six Wolverines shook in unison, gnashing their teeth while flaunting a total of thirty-six lethal claws. Once the quake subsided, they descended upon him like a pack of rabid wolves. The Hulk fought back furiously, but for all he knew he was swinging at empty air. An endless onslaught of silver blades jabbed and carved and cleaved and cut. Before he knew it, they had dragged him to the floor. He tried to yell angrily, but sharpened adamantium sliced through his larynx, which took a second to grow back. Unable to free his hands from the spikes nailing them to the floor, he could only watch in rage and alarm as yet another set of shining metal spears came at his eyes. *This is gonna hurt,* he thought. *Big time.*

A muffled clang caught him by surprise, and the on-rushing claws fell away, along with the Wolverine who had been on the verge of blinding him. Then he saw Captain America standing behind the downed X-Man, holding his shield in both hands. *Figures,* the Hulk thought, putting together two and two, *that blasted shield's probably the only thing on Earth harder than Wolverine's head.* "Are you all right, Hulk?" Cap asked solicitously. "What's the matter? Is something holding you down?"

Obviously, Cap had clobbered one Wolverine—and couldn't even see the rest of them, making it pretty clear whom the illusions were. The Hulk could still see the other Wolverines, feel their claws dissecting him, but that didn't matter anymore; his seething vexation at being rescued by Captain America—of all people!—made him mad enough and strong enough to ignore the Leader's murderous mirages. "I DIDN'T NEED ANY HELP!" he boomed, shrugging the phantom Wolverines aside and climbing back onto his feet, so that he loomed over Captain America and the stunned Wolverine, whose prone body was already starting to stir.

"That's what teamwork's all about," Cap lectured, alert to Wolverine's signs of life. Like the unstoppable killer at the end of hundreds of low-budget slasher movies, the revitalized X-Man abruptly sprang back into action. Cap deftly blocked Wolverine's claws with his shield while continuing to scold the Hulk. "You ought to learn to appreciate the value of a helping hand."

"Like that's going to happen," the Hulk snorted in derision. He barged in between Cap and Wolverine, heedless of the invincible shield and raking claws. *The Leader can wait,* he decided. Right now he had to prove to Captain America, that self-righteous, pontificating yankee doodle, that he could beat Wolverine on his own—or die trying. "Save some of that for me, half-pint!" he challenged the growling X-Man and his adamantium ginsu knives. "I'm goin' to demolish you fair and square!"

Even with her will sapped by the Leader's psychic mesmerism, Rogue was just as strong as Iron Man remembered. *As strong as Ms. Marvel used to be,* he recalled, before a younger Rogue stole the other super-heroine's powers for good, nearly ruining an Avenger's life. Tony Stark scowled behind his golden faceplate at the thought of everything poor Carol Danvers had endured ever since Rogue ambushed her years ago, setting Carol off on a downward spiral from which she still hadn't fully recovered. Iron Man's anger showed through the ductile metal of his iron mask as he fought Rogue high above the floor of the corridor.

Ruby-red eyebeams slammed into his torso, bruising his ribs even through several layers of armor and padding. Iron Man retaliated with a volley of repulsor rays that raced from his gauntlets to strike Rogue in her side, provoking a pained groan but doing little else to bring down the high-flying X-Man. She wasn't just strong, she was invulnerable, too. *Just my luck,* he thought.

Even allowing for the high ceiling, the interior of the moonbase provided cramped conditions for an aerial dogfight. Iron Man had to follow the curve of the corridor to keep from smashing through either the inner or outer wall. The engineer in him couldn't help taking notes on the design of the Leader's lunar habitat, especially since he hoped to build one of his own someday.

He fully intended for Stark Solutions to be at the forefront of lunar colonization as soon as the prospect became economically feasible. The idea of having a branch office on the moon appealed to him immensely. *I wonder if it's too early to claim salvage rights on this base?* he wondered, making himself a mental note to negotiate a deal with S.H.I.E.L.D. once the Leader was defeated.

Defensive sensors and software alerted him to another strafing run by Rogue as she tried to catch him with her eyebeams again. Iron Man banked sharply to the left to dodge the crimson rays, then went into a barrel roll that brought Rogue within range of his chest-projector. A luminous purple tractor beam seized onto the iron in her blood and body, slowing her down for a few seconds, but she broke free of the magnetic ray before he could gain more than a foot on her. Looking back over her shoulder, she sprayed a nonstop stream of destructive energy behind her to discourage pursuit, forcing Iron Man to angle upward above the plane of her attack. The back of his armor scraped against the ceiling as he chased her round the bend of the corridor.

How long can she hang on to Cyclops's mutant power? he wondered. *Indefinitely, like the Super-Adaptoid, or is there a time limit?* They had already completed two circuits of the circular hallway; he estimated that Rogue had been in possession of Cyclops's eyebeams for close to five minutes now. *Long enough for them to start wearing off?* He wasn't sure, but it looked as though her incandescent firepower was already weakening in intensity. The ruby effulgence gushing from her eyes seemed dimmer, less brilliant than before. *Good news for everybody,* he thought, *except maybe the Leader.*

Iron Man decided to test her by going in closer, until he was flying right above her heels. She tracked his progress with her eyes, but the beams radiating from her eyes flickered and dissipated before they even came close to the magnetic force field shielding his armor. Her eyes glowed crimson for a few heartbeats more, then returned to their previous sea-green shade. "Easy come, easy go," he taunted her, unleashing a blast of concentrated repulsor rays along her spine. *Careful,* he reminded himself. Despite her dubious past, he didn't want to injure her permanently. *She's not responsible for her actions right now.*

Rogue slowed down suddenly, causing Iron Man to shoot past her before he could reduce his own speed. Accelerating once more, she climbed steeply toward him, turning the beam-projector on his chest into a bull's-eye. A pair of super-strong fists crashed into his chestplate, shattering the lens of its central beam projector. Fiery blue sparks erupted from the chest-unit, without burning a single hair of Rogue's unprotected hands. Her powerful blow did not smash all the way through his armor to the man inside, but it made mincemeat out of the layers of intricate circuitry beneath the crystallized iron and high-temperature enamel. Reports of system failures and major malfunctions flashed before his eyes, dutifully reported by his armor's diagnostic programs. VARI-BEAM CAPACITY OFF-LINE, a lighted display announced. *No kidding,* he thought sarcastically.

The obvious moral: Eyebeams or no eyebeams, he underestimated Rogue at his own risk. She was a handful even without any extra powers.

He expected her to follow up her brutally effective sortie with further attacks, but instead Rogue pulled away from him, zipping ahead at top speed, so that all he could see were the soles of her bare feet as she left him in her slipstream. The strong breeze generated by her breakneck flight blew against Iron Man's armor as he put on a boost of speed in hopes of catching up with her. *Where's she going in such a hurry?* he worried. *Where's the fire?*

Activating the telescopic lenses in his eyepieces, he scanned the corridor ahead of Rogue, spotting a confusion of colorful costumes just before the next bend. Jagged streaks of lightning, accompanied by scarlet flashes, tipped him off; he realized that he and Rogue's airborne battle had once more brought them full circle to where the rescue team had first confronted the Leader and his thralls. His audio receptors picked up the sound of booming thunder, crashing ice, and bestial howls.

A chill ran down his spine as he hurriedly deduced what Rogue had in mind. *Good Lord,* he thought, *she's going shopping for some new super-powers!*

It wasn't hard to guess who she'd go for first, and, sure enough, she made a bee-line for the Hulk. *All that exposed green skin,* Iron Man realized, shuddering at the prospect of the Hulk's awesome strength being forcibly shifted from their side to the Leader's; if Rogue got her hands on the Hulk, she'd simultaneously take out their most unstoppable ally while increasing her own strength and endurance to an unimaginable level. *I can't let that happen!*

Rogue had too much of a head start on him, though. There was no way he could overtake her before she laid her eager fingers on the Hulk's chartreuse epidermis. Fortunately, he didn't have to; with a cybernetic command, he released his gauntlet's exo-units, turning the metal gloves into a set of long-range grapples connected to his wrists by thin tungsten cables. Propelled by miniature explosive charges, the detached gauntlets sped forward and grabbed onto Rogue's fleeing ankles, hauling her up short only a few feet away from the Hulk's unbelievably broad shoulders. As she strained to reach the unsuspecting giant, who was busy coping with Wolverine's animal fury, Iron Man felt like an angler with a catch of Moby Dick proportions on his line.

Inner gloves of flexible gold foil covered his hands as he reeled Rogue in. She fought back at first, testing the steel cables to their limits, but he had designed his grappling system to stand up to stress of several orders of magnitude. He diverted the bulk of his power reserves, freshly replenished by Storm, into the high-speed motors rewinding the cables. Despite Rogue's strenuous exertions, Iron Man pulled her all the way back until, the tungsten lines completely retracted, his gauntlets clicked back into place upon his hands. He immediately added his own muscles to the grapples' grip.

Her invulnerable limbs strong enough to withstand his iron grip. Rogue pulled one foot free from his gauntlet, even though she had to leave a layer of skin behind. Ugly red abrasions upon her right ankle, she twisted in the air so that she was facing Iron Man. She clawed incessantly at his helmet, her prying fingers digging into his eye and mouth slits, determined to get through to the vulnerable human tissue inside. Her nails scratched the reinforced plexiglass lenses shielding his eyes, yet she still couldn't employ her vampiric touch against the human being inside the iron suit.

Trust me, he thought with bitter humor, *you're not missing anything. The best you could absorb from me would be a bad heart.* Committed to keeping Rogue away from the other X-Men and Avengers, Iron Man altered his trajectory to send them both, locked together like binary stars, through the ad-hoc entrance the Hulk had hammered out with his fists. Glimpses of the desolate lunar landscape, visible through the transparent wall of the dome, poked their way past the pale white fingers probing his eye slits. *I should* let *her steal my natural strengths and weaknesses,* he thought. *It would serve her right. . . .*

The whoosh of powerful jet engines roared in Iceman's ears as the tussling figures of Rogue and Iron Man raced by overhead. Several yards away, the Hulk and Wolverine competed to see who could growl the loudest and the most savagely, while Captain America and the Beast used all their athletic prowess to stay one leap ahead of the Scarlet Witch's unpredictable hex bolts. With all of the Leader's brainwashed pawns caught up in the chaotic free-for-all, Iceman realized with a start that he had a clear shot at the big-brained baddie himself!

Like a frozen flying carpet, a self-generated glacier bore him down the corridor toward the Leader, bridging the yawning chasm separating him from the criminal genius responsible for all this violence and suffering. "I'm coming for you, mister!" he threatened. He gripped his ice-mace in one hand and a clear blue shield in the other. "Get ready to get put on ice!"

According to the Hulk, the Leader had to touch someone to take over their mind, so Iceman figured he was safe inside the icy armor he had crafted over his physical body. For a second he wondered how the heck the Leader had managed to touch Rogue without getting drained of all his smarts, but then a wall of emerald flame erupted between Iceman and his sneering target, forcing the refrigerated X-Man to put on the brakes to keep from skating right into the inferno. ''What?!'' he gasped, his crystalline jaw dropping in surprise. *Where in the world—or the moon—did that come from?*

Waves of scorching heat poured from the blaze, melting the weapons in his hands to ice water. Crackling tongues of green flame licked the ceiling; through the fire, the Leader's sinister visage seemed to ripple like a mirage. Iceman backed away from the terrifying conflagration. He could feel the awful heat liquefying his armor, stripping away his defenses and threatening the very integrity of his frozen body. *Must be a couple hundred degrees Fahrenheit,* he thought in amazement. *If I get any closer, I'll be nothing but a puddle myself!*

A firm, resolute voice called out to him. ''Iceman!'' Captain America shouted. He sounded like he was still back where the Beast and the Scarlet Witch were. ''What are you waiting for? Stop the Leader!''

Iceman was confused. Couldn't Cap see the flames? ''I can't!'' he blurted. His armor was totally gone now, the melted ice streaming down the surface of his body. He watched in horror as his fingers and toes succumbed to the terrible heat, his hands and feet dissolving into icy stumps. ''The fire—it's too hot!''

''Listen to me, Iceman,'' Cap insisted. ''I don't know what you're seeing, but there's nothing there. The Leader can project illusions with his mind.'' The patriotic Avenger sounded reassuringly confident and certain. ''You can do it, man. Don't let the Leader fool you with his tricks!''

Illusions, huh? Iceman squinted skeptically at the

towering wall of fire. The dancing flames looked and felt convincing enough, but Iceman knew just how believable a good illusion could be. *Mastermind used to try to fake me out this way all the time,* he remembered, *back when I was just a dumb teenage kid.*

He closed his eyes, but he could still feel the heat of the emerald flames turning his body to slush. He ignored the unnerving sensation of his limbs swiftly streaming away, and slid headlong into the blaze. There was a moment of searing heat and pain, then he was through the fiery barrier—and back in one piece. Frosty eyelids snapped open, and he found his "melted" limbs and armaments restored to their original solid state. *Way to go!* he rejoiced.

Now it was the Leader's turn to blink in surprise. His bushy black eyebrows arched halfway up his billboard-size brow. The convolutions of his bulging brain throbbed like the swollen domes of the evil telepaths in that old *Star Trek* episode, the one about the alien zoo. "Impressive," the Leader admitted in a haughty tone. "There must be some degree of intellect in that sculpted ice cube you call a skull, although I must admit that I don't see anything resembling gray matter there."

"You like messing with people's brains?" Iceman said heatedly. "How 'bout I return the favor?" His club and shield at his side, the arctic Iceman didn't lay one frigid finger on the Leader, but the scheming super-villain clutched the enormous hemispheres of his bloated noggin in agony.

"Arrgh!" he gasped. His fungus-green eyes bulged from their sockets. "Wha—what . . . are y-you . . . d-doing . . . to me?" For an alleged megagenius, he seemed to be having trouble stringing words together.

"Freezing the flow of blood to your brain," Iceman explained with relish. He had once used the same trick to bring down another know-it-all telepath, the White Queen. The Leader dropped to his knees, writhing in pain. Done in by the mother of all migraines, the Leader didn't look so arrogant now. "That's for what you did to Rogue and the others," Iceman said harshly. He wondered how much brain damage it would take to get the Leader back down to his original, unmutated I.Q. Bobby was tempted to find out.

That's that, I guess. Iceman savored his easy victory over the infamous mastermind—until a blast of searing heat struck him from behind. His icy physiognomy melted and boiled away, sending a traumatic shock through his entire body. Instinctively, he shifted back to human form to avoid evaporating entirely, but the strain, combined with the blistering heat, was too much for him. One thought raced through his brain an instant before darkness swallowed up his consciousness:

Hadn't the Leader said something about a partner?

Chapter Six

"**W**hat the—?"

For a second there, Captain America had thought the tide of battle was definitely turning in their favor. The Beast and Iron Man were holding their own against Wanda and Rogue, respectively; the Hulk was standing up to Wolverine's frenzied claws, while Iceman definitely appeared to have their true enemy, the Leader himself, on the ropes. Then an unexpected figure materialized behind Iceman, cowardly shooting the frozen X-Man in the back with a bright red burst of flame. Cap watched in alarm as the mutant youth transformed rapidly back into flesh and blood before collapsing onto the floor. The former Iceman lay sprawled in a pool of his own melted substance.

But who had bushwhacked the X-Man? At first, Cap was surprised to see Wolverine appear from nowhere, looking just as he had before the Leader's trans-mat beam snatched him from the quinjet, even though yet another Wolverine, the one in the orange jumpsuit, was still sparring with Hulk as his uniformed double stood over Iceman's vanquished form. Captain America guessed that the hypnotized berserker slashing away at the Hulk was the Real McCoy, so who was this new arrival? An illusion, a Sentinel, or . . . ?

Jigsaw pieces came together in the Avenger's mind as the answer hit him with all the force of an old V-2 rocket. *That blowtorch bit is the giveaway,* Cap thought; all of a sudden, he knew exactly who the Leader's alien partner was.

"Super-Skrull!" he accused the bogus Wolverine. "I should've known you were mixed up in this the minute we saw that saucer."

"Hah!" the imposter barked cruelly, spinning around to face the star-spangled Avenger. "It took you long enough to figure it out, human." Before Cap's eyes, the short, stocky form of the Canadian X-Man morphed into someone else completely. The duplicate gained in height, becoming at least six feet tall, while Wolverine's distinctive yellow uniform darkened to shades of black and purple. The X-Man's mask disappeared and the face below took on a more reptilian aspect, with flaring pointed ears and lime-green scales. Deep furrows segmented his lower jaw, while inhuman red eyes glared at Captain America with undisguised malice. A black skullcap formed a widow's peak above his protruding brows. His right fist, the one that struck down Iceman, smoldered like burning coals. "Are all humans so blind," he taunted, "or only their so-called heroes?"

"It's been you all along," Cap realized, his mind swiftly reviewing the events of the last few days. "Ever since you joined up with us at Avengers Mansion, right after we got back from Niagara Falls."

"Of course," the Super-Skrull gloated. "It was the work of a mere hatchling to infiltrate your allied forces, the better to monitor your pathetic attempts to locate and rescue your captured teammates." Behind the imposing figure of the Skrull warrior, the Leader gradually recovered from Iceman's ingenious attack. Holding a pale green hand to his stricken cranium, he staggered slowly to his feet while casting a venomous gaze at the unconscious Iceman. "I deceived your planet's primitive intelligence operatives as well, when they interrupted my investigation of the X-Men's headquarters."

Cap nodded grimly. He recalled receiving a brief report from Nick Fury about S.H.I.E.L.D.'s violent altercation with "Wolverine" at Professor Xavier's mansion in Westchester. A lot of odd occurrences now made a lot more sense. *No wonder "Wolverine" was able to beat Rock so quickly down in Freehold,* Cap realized; *we had the Super-Skrull fighting beside us and we didn't even know it!*

Now the masks were off, though, and the Leader's silent partner stood revealed. Cap repressed a shudder at the horrendous thought of the Leader and the Super-Skrull working in concert. Ordinary Skrulls were bad enough, given their cunning and innate shape-changing ability, but the Super-Skrull was the most dangerous exemplar of his treacherous breed: a ruthless soldier imbued by Skrull science with all the unique super-powers of the entire Fantastic Four. The combination of the Super-Skrull's raw power with the Leader's corrupt genius made for a genuinely awesome alliance. *Then again,* he thought, *that's what they said about the Axis Powers, too, back during the Big One, but the courage and ability of good men and women prevailed in the end, as it always will.*

"We did all right against your saucer," Cap reminded the Skrull, "just as the brave people of Earth have always overcome the Skrull Empire's devious plots against our liberty."

A frown added to the Skrull's malevolent appearance. "Do not mock the Empire, primate," he warned ominously. "True, your armored comrade cost me a vessel and a squad of loyal soldiers, but it takes more than a lucky shot to destroy me, the supreme embodiment of Skrull military might. My personal force field protected me from the explosion while my gift of invisibility allowed me to retreat unobserved."

It's ironic, Cap thought. In his own twisted way, the Super-Skrull saw himself as the symbol of his Empire's strength and resourcefulness, like the Skrull version of, well, Captain America. *But I represent freedom and decency and equal opportunity for all, not a vicious empire that measures its greatness upon the oppression of other races.* "Your force field? Your invisibility?" Cap challenged the Skrull. "Sound like the powers of Sue Richards, the Invisible Woman, to me."

The Super-Skrull's lips curled back in a snarl, and Cap knew that he had hit a nerve. "My special abilities may have been modeled on the freakish talents of the Fantastic Four, but that makes them no less mine! I have mastered all my gifts, exceeding their aboriginal origins, for the greater glory of the Skrull Empire!"

Having regained his composure and conceited attitude, the Leader joined his extraterrestrial ally, stepping over Iceman and the puddle beneath him. "You must forgive my partner's patriotic declamations, Captain," he said archly. "He gets carried away sometimes—but look whom I'm talking to!" He glanced up at the Super-Skrull, whose scaly hide was a brighter shade of green than his own, closer to the Hulk's chartreuse tint. "If you're quite through exchanging *bon mots* with this flag-wrapped relic, I assume you're capable of eliminating our uninvited visitors before they cause any more damage to this facility."

The Skrull bristled visibly. "Watch your tone, human," he threatened, his voice much deeper than his partner's supercilious tones. "I am no lackey to leap at your command."

Cap was encouraged by this sign of strife between Earth's foes, but the Leader hastened to put his partner at ease. "No offense intended," he assured the glowering alien. "I simply meant that the sooner our mutual enemies are disposed of, the sooner we can proceed to the completion of our grand endeavor."

The Skrull's red eyes widened. "You mean . . . ?" he asked anxiously, his ire at the Leader's preemptory manner apparently forgotten.

"That's right, my martial associate," the Leader said with a self-satisfied grin. "My experiments on our captives have yielded the results we sought. All that remains is to complete the enterprise."

"Excellent!" the Skrull enthused. He lifted a smoking fist in front of his broad chest and hammered the air triumphantly. "Then the future is ours!"

I don't like the sound of this, Captain America thought. Anything that gladdened the hearts of the Leader and/or the Super-Skrull couldn't be good for humanity. "What are you talking about?" he demanded. "What sort of nefarious scheme have you cooked up between the two of you?"

"Wouldn't you like to know?" the Leader teased unhelpfully, then addressed his partner. "A few irritating loose ends remain." He gestured dismissively toward Cap and the other heroes. "If you please . . . ?"

"Very well," the Skrull said readily. "In truth, I have been eager to abandon the masquerade and face our opponents as a warrior should—in combat." He fixed a hostile gaze upon Captain America, and his clenched fists expanded until they were the size of boulders. A thick, lumpish carapace—mimicking the rock-like armor of the Thing—covered his fists and lower arms, but that was just the beginning of the Skrull's preparation for battle. The stony, orangish cudgels ignited spontaneously. Crimson flames, reminiscent of those flaunted by the Human Torch, raged over the Super-Skrull's hands until each rocky fist resembled a meteor burning up as it crashed through the atmosphere. And like meteors, the Skrull's fists flew at Cap, rubbery arms stretching behind them like the elastic limbs of Mr. Fantastic.

Captain America dived out of the way of flaming fists. He'd gotten as much information as he was going to get from the two villains; the time for talking was clearly over. "Heads up, people!" he warned his teammates, still engaged in battle against the brainwashed mutant trio. Not counting the Beast, whom he considered an Avenger, he noted that their X-Men allies had all bitten the dust. Cyclops and Storm were out cold, along with the Vision. *It's up to us now,* Cap realized. "Avengers Assemble!"

He wasn't foolhardy enough to go hand-to-hand against the Super-Skrull. The bionically-enhanced alien was at least as strong as the Thing, which made him only a little less powerful than the Hulk. Instead Cap concentrated on the Leader, who was physically the frailer of the pair. Cap's ever-ready shield soared dependably at the Leader's mushroom-shaped brow; if nothing else, the mad genius's huge head made a remarkably easy target.

Right before the spinning edge of the shield collided with the Leader's skull, however, an unseen force halted the flying weapon and sent it whirling back at Cap, who concealed his disappointment as he plucked the shield from the air with one hand. His shrewd mind took strategic note of the Leader's seemingly miraculous escape; telekinesis, it appeared, could be numbered among the would-be tyrant's mental powers. *That's going to make things a little harder,* he concluded.

He recovered his shield just in time to defend himself from a blazing stream of fire directed at him from the Super-Skrull's rocky fingertips. Although comparable in temperature to that produced by an acetylene torch or flamethrower, the white-hot flames didn't even scratch the polished surface of Cap's venerable shield. "Is that the best you can do?" the Avenger asked defiantly. The streaming fire swept down toward his legs and Cap leaped high in the moon's low gravity, clearing the spurting flames by more than ten feet. Adrenalin mixed with the Super-Soldier Formula in his blood, bringing him to peak fighting condition. "Listen, mister, I knew Jim Hammond, the original Human Torch, and I've fought beside Johnny Storm, too. And I can tell you one thing, you're no Human Torch!"

"As though I would ever aspire to such a demeaning label!" the Super-Skrull retorted. A fist of burning granite pounded against Captain America's shield as the veteran hero landed on his feet. He found his durable buckler, forged from a unique adamantium-vibranium alloy, on the receiving end of what Ben Grimm, the real Thing, colorfully called "clobbering time!" The shield on Cap's arm held up to the piledriver blows, but he could feel the impact all the way through to his bones. "I am more than human, primate," his attacker bragged. "I am Skrull!"

The super-powered alien's torso stretched like taffy as he wrapped himself around Captain America, squeezing the Avenger's ribs like an enormous anaconda. Gasping for breath, Cap managed to keep both arms above the Super-Skrull's constricting coils. He tried to slice through the Skrull's elongated body with the edge of the shield, but the fiendish alien's flesh was just as pliable as the humanoids' had been. As elastic as Reed Richards, to be exact. The dark purple coils bent harmlessly before the striking edge of Cap's shield, readily absorbing the force of his blows. The harder he hit the Skrull, the more the villain's body stretched. *It's like he doesn't have any bones!* Captain America thought, unable to make a dent in the resilient alien.

Cap's own ribs were nowhere near as flexible. Darkness crept up on his vision as the Skrull's winding anatomy crushed the air from his lungs. A tunic of blue chain mail provided Cap with little protection against the Skrull's suffocating squeeze play. "Earth will never surrender to you and your kind!" the living legend grunted, refusing to abandon hope even against the overwhelming power of his alien opponent. "Even if you kill me, others will pick up the fight against you. The spirit of freedom cannot be snuffed out, not even by you and the Leader!"

"The arrogance of your species is truly astounding," the Super-Skrull exclaimed. His dragon-like visage sat atop his attenuated body, bobbing opposite Cap's face like the head of a cobra. "The Skrull Empire has ruled over an entire galaxy since before your species even began to evolve from its crude mammalian forebears. Only a perverse accident of intergalactic history has kept your world from our dominion for so long. Far more important threats to our security, such as Galactus and the hated Kree, have kept the Empire from turning the full force of our mighty battle fleets against your insignificant planet.''

''Plus the fact that we primitive primates have given you a bloody nose everytime you've stuck your shape-shifting snoots into our affairs!'' Cap reminded the Super-Skrull with the last of his breath. Typically overconfident, the Skrull carelessly let his reptilian face come within reach of Captain America's free arms, a tactical lapse the Avenger called to his foe's attention by means of a strong left hook to the Skrull's jaw.

''Ackk!''

The force of Cap's punch propelled the pointy-eared head backwards, stretching the Super-Skrull's scaly neck two feet longer than usual. A pearl-white fang flew from the Skrull's mouth and went skipping across the floor. With the powerful alien momentarily stunned, Cap felt the coils around him slacken. His gloves pressed down hard on the sinuous purple loops as he struggled to slip out of the Skrull's python-like hold. He got halfway free before the Leader spoke up, his aloof and caustic tone conveying more than a full measure of condescension toward the Avenger's David-versus-Goliath struggle against the Super-Skrull:

''A valiant try, Captain America, but I'm afraid there's too much at stake to permit your obsolete heroics to interfere.''

An electrifying mental blast hit the Avenger right behind his eyes, inducing a seizure that caused Captain America to spasm uncontrollably within the serpentine coils of the Super-Skrull. White static and a screeching buzz filled his head from the inside out, then rushed down his spine and out to every inch of his body. His entire nervous system short-circuited at once, and his shield slipped from his fingers. As Cap slumped above the winding rounds of the Super-Skrull's midsection, his best and only weapon hit the floor with a metallic clang that echoed down the corridor.

The Super-Skrull?!

Sitting astride the prone form of the Scarlet Witch, the Beast was appalled by this unwanted revelation. The odds against them had increased geometrically with the addition of another formidable antagonist to the ranks of their enemies. *At least that explains Wolverine's taciturn attitude,* he realized. *I'd thought that "Logan" was acting more laconic than usual.*

Beneath his substantial, simian corpus, the enthralled Witch wrestled to throw off her beastly burden. Hairy palms covered her eyes while equally shaggy feet held down her hands, making the casting of spells an unlikely prospect at best. *An efficacious but not exactly permanent, solution,* the Beast allowed reluctantly, evaluating his improvised means of neutralizing Wanda's highly hazardous hex powers. He could hardly keep the Scarlet Witch constrained thus indefinitely, especially not while his fellow Avengers required his assistance against the rest of their adversaries. Even now, as he looked over his bushy shoulder at the scene behind him, he saw that Captain America was on his own against both the Leader *and* the Super-Skrull, an unenviable position for even America's foremost costumed defender. "My apologies, my dear Ms. Maximoff, for the ungentle methods I am about to resort to," he told his captive; alas, only by rendering Wanda unconscious with a forceful blow to her head could the Beast free himself to come to Cap's aid. He tilted his head back in anticipation of smacking heads with the vulnerable mutant enchantress. One good head-butt should send the Witch off to slumberland, he surmised.

An unshakable grip seized him by the scruff of his neck before he could put his pugnacious plan into action. The Beast possessed the size and mass of a mountain gorilla, but he was yanked backwards, and away from the Scarlet Witch, effortlessly, by someone easily as strong as Wonder Man or the Thing; it required no brilliant feats of ratiocination to deduce that the bionically-blessed Super-Skrull had come after the Beast a few seconds before the hirsute X-Man would have preferred. *That does not bode well for Captain America,* the Beast thought with acute apprehension.

At the cost of a handful of blue fur, pulled out by its roots, the Beast tore himself free from the Super-Skrull's hold, somersaulting forward with an Olympics-worthy dismount onto the tiles. He twirled around to see the Skrull's extendable arm retract back to normal humanoid proportions. The orange, cobblestone fist at the end of the arm bore an uncanny resemblance to the Thing's mutated mitts, and the bare patch at the back of the Beast's neck tellingly testified that the similarity was far more than merely cosmetic. A cool draft blew against the exposed pink skin beneath the indigo fur, adding to the chill the X-Man experienced as he witnessed Captain America's defeat. *Five down, three to go,* he brooded glumly; with only he, Iron Man, and the Hulk left standing, the good guys had well and truly lost the advantage of superior numbers.

"As Sir Andrew Browne Cunningham observed at the

Battle of Taranto,'' the Beast mused aloud, '' 'We are so outnumbered there's only one thing to do. We must attack.' ''

So resolved, the acrobatic X-Man cartwheeled toward the Leader, hoping to lambast the Leader before his prehensile partner could fully unwind from around Captain America. He had no illusions that he could endure long against the Super-Skrull's one-man (or should that be one-alien?) impersonation of the Fantastic Four, but mayhap there was still a chance to quash the hypertrophic brain behind the alien's considerable brawn.

His aspirations to undo the Leader, along with the rest of his shaggy self, collided literally with an invisible wall that brought him slamming to a halt yards ahead of the Leader. *Shades of Sue Richards!* he realized, recognizing a transparent force field when he *didn't* see one. The incongruous solidity of the invisible barrier knocked him back onto his anthropoid *derriere,* which, quite regrettably, landed him at the feet of the Super-Skrull, whose unmistakable shadow fell ominously over the chagrined X-Man. "Gadzooks!" the Beast said with a gulp.

The former Avenger yet entertained notions of eluding the Super-Skrull's bellicose attentions via the expedience of his own unsurpassed agility, but when he strove to bound away lickety-split, he found himself trapped inside a sphere of invisible force that lifted him off the floor as though attached to an ingeniously-camouflaged crane. "You're not going anywhere, mutant," the Super-Skrull declared. The unseen globe rotated on its axis so that, his face and hands pressed against the clear concavity of his invisible prison, the Beast ended up staring into the leering countenance of the Skrull. "And some call your kind *Homo superior!*" he said, disgust dripping from his voice. "You look more like some variety of atavistic throwback to me."

"Says the chap who looks like a *Crocodilus vulgaris* with rhinoplasty," the Beast shot back. "Considering that your own extraterrestrial species is well known to have reached an evolutionary plateau several thousand millennia back, and been genetically stalled ever since, I wouldn't be casting stones at any other planet's more eccentric mutations."

"That is outrageous Kree propaganda!" The Super-Skrull's expression went from disgust to outrage in a nanosecond. "The finest scientists in the known universe have discredited that ridiculous libel."

"Those wouldn't be *Skrull* scientists perchance?" the Beast inquired. If he couldn't actually conquer the Super-Skrull in a physical contest of arms, he decided he'd settle for thwarting his foe at a battle of wits. "Not exactly the most objective of observers."

"As opposed to whom?" the Skrull argued. "The Supreme Intelligence of the Kree, the odious originator of that vile calumny?" For better or for worse, the Beast had definitely gotten beneath the Skrull's metamorphic skin; fossilized hands gripped the transparent globe, shaking Beast and orb alike. "You would believe that Kree-born abomination before the greatest minds of the Empire?"

"Well, they don't call him the Supreme Intelligence for nothing," the Beast pointed out. Personally, he wouldn't trust either Krees or Skrulls farther than he could throw them in heavy gravity, but he saw no reason to share that particular insight with so partisan a commentator. "Now maybe if it was only the Fairly Bright Intelligence, or the Occasionally Correct Intelligence, we might have some reason to doubt his conclusions *vis-a-vis* your long-term evolutionary potential, but the *Supreme* Intelligence . . . ? Sounds like an indisputable authority to me.''

''Silence, you jabbering ape!'' Losing all patience, the Super-Skrull stepped away from the floating form of the Beast. His scaly forehead furrowed in concentration and his invisible cage began to shrink dramatically. The Beast suddenly felt as though he was being crushed inside a transparent trash compactor. The inward pressure forced him to curl into a ball, with his bewhiskered chin pressed tightly against his furry knees, but the pressure only increased until his bones ached from the stress upon them. He felt a stab of profound sympathy for Ororo and her intermittent bouts of claustrophobia; at the moment, he knew just how she felt!

Better that I endure this trial than her, he thought, searching assiduously for a silver lining in an unusually dark and oppressive cloud, but that was small consolation as his abused senses sunk beneath the murky waters of oblivion. *But, my oh my, where is the Mighty Thor when we need him?*

Locked together like two ends of a bolo spiralling out of control, Iron Man and Rogue slammed into the transparent dome surrounding the Leader's violated lunar habitat. For a second, the Golden Avenger feared that the dome wall would crack beneath the combined impact of the two grappling super-heroes, but the Leader had built his lair of stronger stuff than that; once again, Iron Man wished he had time to examine the architecture of the moonbase more thoroughly, perhaps even acquire some samples of the building materials for further analysis later on. *Maybe a synthetic polymer with augmented molecular bonding . . . ?*

He briefly considered smashing through the dome on purpose; certainly, he was better equipped than Rogue to survive in the vacuum outside. But who knew what the resulting explosive decompression could do to the rest of the inhabitants of the moonbase, including the other two brainwashed hostages? No, he concluded, as tempting as the idea of subjecting Rogue to the void was, breaching the dome had to remain a strategy of last resort. *Too bad,* he thought. *I could use the edge. . . .*

Despite her diligent efforts, Rogue had yet to penetrate Iron Man's protective insulation. Thank heavens he kept her away from the Hulk, though; it was all his armor could do to hold together against her astounding base-level strength. He knew he had to discourage her somehow, or it would be only a matter of time before she succeeded in prying off a piece of his iron suit, making him vulnerable to her vampiric touch. *This skirmish has to stay the super-brawl equivalent of safe sex,* he thought wryly, *or I'm done for.*

Taking his cue from nature, specifically the electric eel, Iron Man electrified the outer skin of his armor, sending thousands of volts through the tessellated iron tiles. The powerful galvanic charge made Rogue's hair stand on end and drove the possessed mutant away, at least for the moment. "About time," Iron Man muttered. With Rogue's eager fingers finally retreating from his eyeslits, he could see clearly for the first time since the X-Men's southern-fried succubus latched onto him.

Outside the dome, Tycho's mountainous walls rose in the distance while the Earth shined down from above. Within the dome's see-through walls, broken humanoid fragments littered the paved circular track beneath him. Iron Man wished he could see what was going on deeper within the moonbase, where the X-Men and the other Avengers fought the Leader and his zombified abductees, but keeping Rogue away from that smorgasbord of super-powers had to stay his top priority. The last thing any of them needed at this point was an enslaved mutant possessing all the powers of the X-Men, the Avengers, and the Hulk!

Right now Rogue remained focused on the armored Avenger. She hovered high above the floor, defying the moon's meager gravity, while her green eyes searched for a defect in Iron Man's defenses. His own jets suspending him in the air, Iron Man waited warily for Rogue's next move. *Good thing she doesn't have Cyclops's eyebeams anymore,* he thought. *That cuts down on her offensive options a little.*

Watching Rogue's face for any indication of her intentions, Iron Man was surprised to see her stiffen noticeably, then cock her head to one side, her eyes looking inward, as if listening to some inner message. *A telepathic command from the Leader?* he theorized. What diabolical purpose could that heartless megalomaniac have in mind for his high-flying pawn now?

Without so much as a farewell threat, Rogue zoomed away, abandoning their unresolved duel in favor of a new and more mysterious errand. To Iron Man's alarm, she dived toward the Hulk's rough-hewn entrance to the next corridor. He fired his grapples again, aiming to snag the X-Man a second time, but Rogue was not going to be undone by the same trick twice. Zigzagging through the dome's pressurized atmosphere, she smoothly eluded the grapples and more; as the gauntlets flew past her, she grabbed onto the cables behind them with her bare hands, then gave the tungsten lines a strong yank, jerking Iron Man downward toward the pavement. "Whoa there!" he gasped, pulling out of his unplanned descent only seconds before taking a nosedive into the track below. By the time he stabilized his flight path, however, Rogue had disappeared through the ragged gap in the wall.

Now what? Iron Man worried, retracting his failed gauntlets, which refitted themselves upon his hands. Leery of flying into an ambush, he scanned the concrete walls of the inner cylinder with his sonar to make sure no one was lying in wait on the other side of the make-shift doorway. His sensors detected nothing of the sort, but any plans to pursue Rogue were forestalled when she came rushing back through the entrance with Wolverine in tow. The savage Canadian dangled below Rogue as the two entranced X-Men climbed toward Iron Man; Rogue's bare hands, the Golden Avenger noted, gripped the sleeves of her teammate's orange jumpsuit, avoiding any direct contact with Wolverine's flesh. Even brainwashed, it appeared, Rogue took no chances with her mind-sapping touch.

Without slowing her upward velocity by a single mph, Rogue raised her feral passenger above her head, then flung Wolverine at the Iron Man with all her strength. *Uh-oh,* the targeted Avenger thought, his eyes widening behind his faceplate, *I believe the X-Men call this a "fastball special."*

Reacting by reflex, Iron Man tried to deflect Wolverine with his chest-beam, only to remember too late that Rogue had already shattered the central lens with her fists. Wolverine struck Iron Man like a missile, his adamantium claws slicing through the Avenger's armor like it was made of tin foil. Iron Man grunted in pain as the vicious blades scored his shoulders; warm blood leaked between his skin and the padding beneath the armor. *That's way too close for comfort,* he realized, biting down hard to keep from screaming. The fresh wounds hurt like the devil, and he used his palm repulsors to blow Wolverine away from him before the mutant's claws could inflict any more damage.

Thanks to the minimal gravity, Wolverine fell in slow motion toward the pavement, raising a cloud of pink flakes when he eventually hit the remains of the frozen humanoids. But Iron Man could not spare a second to observe the X-Man's soft landing; primed to exploit the chinks her teammate had carved in the Avenger's armor, Rogue followed up her fastball special with a head-on attack of her own. Iron Man crisscrossed the airspace between them with repulsor rays, but Rogue bulldozed through the coruscating fusillade as if no more concerned about her own comfort or safety than any of the Leader's soulless humanoids. One eye swollen shut, her face bruised and her lips smashed by the cadmium-colored neutron beams, she slammed into Iron Man, her ungloved fingers sliding into the gashes left by Wolverine's invasive claws. Mutant skin touched the raw flesh and blood beneath Iron Man's world-famous armor.

An overwhelming lassitude swept over Tony Stark as all his energy and concentration flowed out of his body through his injured shoulders. But this was more than simply weakness brought on by shock and loss of blood; the very essence of his strength and genius fled his mind and muscles like air escaping from a punctured balloon. Without even the presence of mind to deactivate his boot jets, he veered wildly out of control, smashing through the concrete wall back into the tank containment corridor before crashing headfirst into the tile floor, creating yet another crater inside the moonbase. Wedged upside-down into the bottom of the crater, the Golden Avenger was dead to the world (and the moon) long before fail-safe circuits caused his blazing jets to sputter out.

It had required the vast strength of the Thing, plus repeated verbal commands from the Leader, to pull the rabid Wolverine off the Hulk and convince him to switch partners, but the Hulk didn't care about that. He was just severely ticked off at having his heavyweight slugfest with Wolverine interrupted. "Come back with that mutant!" he roared as Rogue carried his fierce sparring partner away. "I'm not done smashing him yet!"

"Forget that primitive creature," the Super-Skrull instructed. In his black-and-purple uniform, the alien invader stood only a few inches shorter than the Hulk. His hands on his hips, the Skrull posed proudly before the jade giant. Yellow flames licked his stony fists. "Now you face the unrivaled might of the Empire's proudest warrior!"

"Big whooping deal." The Hulk looked unimpressed. "I've whipped your sorry carcass before and I can do it again." He sneered at the bat-eared Skrull soldier standing between him and the Leader. "So you're as strong as the Thing, huh?" He stepped backward, crudely feigning terror by placing a meaty slab of a hand over his mouth. "Ooh, is that supposed to scare me?" He snorted loudly. "Right."

"Do not mock me, barbarian!" The Super-Skrull lifted his hands and unleashed a scorching gout of flame at the earthborn behemoth. He raised his voice to be heard over the angry crackle of the fiery blast. "Fortune may have granted you victory before, but no such capricious twist of fate will save you this time. Now is the hour of your ultimate defeat!"

"Blah, blah, blah," the Hulk responded. The raging firestorm engulfing him did little more than irritate his chartreuse hide, like a really bad sunburn. His skin reddened for an almost subliminal second, then immediately returned to its usual shade of green. The smell of burning hair contaminated the once-pristine atmosphere, but the Hulk acted none the worse for wear. "That's the best part about brawling with Wolverine," he griped. "Unlike the rest of you windbags, he doesn't mouth off when he gets down to business." He snuffed out the ineffectual flames by clapping his hands together with stupendous force. "You wanna rumble? Shut up and fight!"

"Hell-Hounds of the Black Nebula!" the Super-Skrull swore vehemently. "You will pay for your insolence, Terran!" His boots remaining firmly planted where they were, the Skrull stretched toward the Hulk, seeking to ensnare the green giant in those very same coils that had so effectively immobilized Captain America. The alien's elastic torso wrapped tightly around the Hulk's gigantic form, but the gamma-spawned monster was infinitely stronger than the star-spangled Avenger, and he pulled the thick, purple strands of Skrull away from him as if they were made of well-chewed bubble gum. No matter how relentlessly the coils squeezed their prize, they could neither restrain the Hulk nor even restrict his movement.

Reluctantly acknowledging the failure of his ploy, the versatile Skrull abruptly switched tactics. Quickly unspooling from the Hulk, he resumed his usual proportions several feet away, then focused his will on the advancing ogre. "Prepare to surrender, Hulk," he warned. "As you shall see, I need not even touch you to vanquish you utterly!"

Like the Beast before him, the Hulk found himself enclosed in an invisible force field, yet holding the ever-incredible Hulk was an altogether different proposition than trapping one loquacious Avenger. Seven feet, one thousand pounds of unfettered fury hammered at the transparent cage, each cataclysmic blow sending an excruciating pulse of psychic feedback streaming back to the mind of the Super-Skrull. Slimy perspiration broke out over the Skrull's lime-green brow and his lizard-like eyes bulged from the grueling mental exertion required to maintain his force field against such awesome opposition. "Wraiths of the Void!" he cursed under his breath, his chest heaving in exhaustion. "This is impossible! My powers are drawn from the raw cosmic energy of the universe itself. They cannot be overcome by mere brute force!"

"Ain't nothing mere about it, Skrully," the Hulk grunted. Bulging veins stood out like cables atop his grotesquely exaggerated musculature. Locking his immense fists together, he delivered a double-handed blow to his unseen prison. The Super-Skrull gasped out loud from the transferred impact of the titanic wallop; it was like the alien's own brain was being pounded upon and not just an invisible energy construct. Ramming his shoulder into one side of the besieged bubble, the Hulk threw his entire weight (or the closest lunar equivalent) against the crumbling force field, which shredded into insubstantial wisps of bio-electricity as the huge monster stampeded through the barrier and grabbed the shaken Super-Skrull by the throat. Trembling from fatigue, and wheezing through his snout, the Skrull emitted a hoarse, choking sound.

"You know, I never noticed before—" the Hulk began, lifting the Skrull off his feet like Darth Vader interrogating a recalcitrant rebel soldier. Unlike the stunned Skrull, the jade giant wasn't even breathing hard. "—but you're almost as ugly as my old pal, the Abomination. All you need is a few more warty bumps on your head and you'd look just like him." A malicious grin bared the Hulk's great white teeth. "That's going to make knocking your block off a lot more fun."

Prior to carrying out his threat, however, a scarlet radiance fell over both the Hulk and his intended victim. The roseate glow made the two combatants' green skin look like differing shades of muddy brown instead. "What the—?" the puzzled Hulk asked, blinking against the bright red light. "Where's that coming from?"

Looking away from the gasping Skrull, the Hulk spotted an auburn-haired woman standing next to the unconscious body of the Beast, her slender fingers extended toward the pair of inhuman monsters. Even though she was wearing an unflattering orange jumpsuit in place of her usual gypsy duds, the Hulk recognized the Scarlet Witch—and wondered what exactly the brainwashed mutant babe was up to. "You'd better not be pulling one of your stinkin' hexes on me, witch!" he hollered. " 'Cause no hocus-pocus hoodoo can stop the Hulk, and I'm not above proving it by stomping you flat!"

Despite his churning anger, a peculiar sensation came over the irate Hulk. His heart began to pound less violently, his pulse slowing to something close to resembling ordinary human circulation. The swollen veins along his arms and shoulders retreated beneath his chartreuse epidermis, which no longer seemed to be stretched quite so tightly over his densely-packed muscles. *If I didn't know better,* he thought, *I'd swear it was the Change starting!*

But that wasn't possible. Was it?

His right hand still gripped around the Super-Skrull's throat, the Hulk lifted his other hand up before his face. Was there something screwy about its color? At first, the Hulk hoped that it was just the scarlet glow of the Witch's hex sphere that gave his upraised palm a disturbingly pinkish tint, but the more he stared at his open hand, the more obvious its transformation became. "No!" he bellowed, but his voice lacked its customary depth and volume. "Not now. *Not now!*"

Emerald eyes, rapidly fading to brown, widened in dismay. Groping his face with shrinking fingers, he felt his jawline narrow, and the beginnings of a scruffy beard begin to sprout from his chin. The sloping forehead straightened out. A squat, pug nose grew thinner and more refined, until the Hulk couldn't even recognize his own profile. There was no denying it now; he was turning back into that spineless weakling, Banner! Puny, helpless Banner!

His outstretched arm could no longer support the Super-Skrull's imposing physique. The Skrull gasped for air as he dropped from his stricken captor's weakening grasp; he was now considerably taller and heavier than his shrunken opponent. With the last vestiges of the Hulk's legendary rage, a thin, greenish figure howled and shook his scrawny fists at the heavens. "This can't be happening!'' he cried out, his fearsome roar dwindling to an indignant yelp. ''Not at a moment like this!''

''It does seem rather improbable,'' a languid voice said with obvious amusement. The Leader strolled across the floor to smirk at his longtime nemesis, whom he could now look directly in the eye. ''But then, making the improbable inevitable happens to be the specialty of our own dear Specimen #2.'' He nodded approvingly at the mesmerized Scarlet Witch. ''Her singular talents prove more useful all the time. I really must seriously consider cloning her one of these days.''

Clutching his scaly throat, which still bore the imprint of the Hulk's huge fingers, the Super-Skrull looked Banner over with a visible mixture of relief and regret. The slender physicist grabbed onto his oversized trousers to keep them from sliding to the floor. ''This pathetic human is the Hulk?'' the Skrull asked, shaking his head in disbelief. He towered over Banner, who squinted up at the warlike alien through weak, myopic eyes.

''Amazing, isn't it?'' the Leader confirmed. ''Now do me a favor and beat him senseless.''

Chapter Seven

The Super-Skrull hated being on the moon.

Ex-Commander K'lrt, once the greatest hero of the glorious Skrull Empire, repressed a shiver of superstitious dread. Ten million Earth-years ago, on this same barren satellite, his revered ancestors had been savagely massacred by the treacherous Kree, commencing ten thousand millennia of bitter enmity between Kree and Skrull. Even though the Kree themselves had recently fallen beneath the sway of the avian Shi'ar, that primordial bloodbath yet loomed large in the cultural memory of the Skrull Empire, thus accounting for K'lrt's unease. The sooner he and the Leader left this accursed place behind, the happier he would be.

"I could have defeated the Hulk on my own," he insisted once more. "You had no right to let your mutant thrall intervene in our contest."

He paced impatiently about the Transformation Chamber, soon to be the site of his long-awaited apotheosis, and the first way station on his road back to the Empire—and to redemption. The Chamber, located two levels below the bottom of the great crater, occupied the entire sub-basement and was the size of a municipal arena on one of the Empire's lesser colony worlds, such as Morani Prime, say, or Kral IV. The matte-black floor of the Chamber rose like an inverted bowl toward the illuminated platform at the center of the room, around which the Leader's three mutant slaves stood at attention. It was upon that platform, K'lrt knew, that he would finally achieve the power that would allow him, after many long cycles of exile and disgrace, to reclaim a place of honor within the Empire. He could scarcely wait for the historic experiment to begin.

"My apologies," the Leader said, sounding less than repentant, "but there were larger matters at stake than your personal honor as a warrior. I could not afford to endanger our grand endeavor just so you could test your mettle against a mindless menace like the Hulk. Trust me, I know too well how the best-laid plans can be reduced to chaos by that meddlesome brute."

Loudspeakers transmitted the Leader's voice from above, where the mutated human resided in a lighted control bulb overlooking the entire rotunda. Glancing upward, K'lrt could discern the swollen cranium of the Leader through the transparent walls of the blister, which was affixed to the ceiling directly above the central platform. The Leader's hands danced over an intricate control panel as he made the final adjustments to his apparatus in anticipation of the crucial experiment to come.

"You think like a scheming palace courtier, not a warrior born," K'lrt reproved. Even after many weeks of plotting and preparation, including the excavation and construction of this lunar base, it still felt odd to be allied with a human, of all creatures, even if the greenish cast of the Leader's skin made him slightly more presentable in appearance than the rest of his barbaric species. "But I am willing to forgo my satisfaction as a soldier in this instance, provided you can truly deliver on your promises—and give me the power I desire.''

"*We* desire," the Leader corrected. "And have no fears; careful study of our original specimens, along with the data we appropriated from the Mutant Research Centre in Scotland, has brought certain success well within our grasp." Lighted indicators flickered on and off around the base of the transformation platform as the Leader keyed in the last few settings. The steady hum of computers underscored the quiet of the chamber. "I certainly hope your esteemed Empress appreciates all we have accomplished under her royal patronage."

"The Empress is wise," K'lrt said simply. In fact, the all-powerful Empress of the Skrull Empire had no knowledge of their operations these past few weeks, for it had been far longer than that since the Super-Skrull had last held his rightful place among the elite of the Empire. Cruel reversals of fortune, invariably brought about by the stubborn resistance of Earth's superpowered defenders, had reduced the once-proud Commander to a homeless exile, a Skrull without an Empire. The memory of past failures sullied his reputation, making him hunger to restore his good name, but the Leader knew none of that.

Although skilled in the mysteries of science, especially for a primitive Terran primate, the Leader had no way of tracking the fickle caprices of imperial politics. K'lrt had led the human to believe that he had the full backing of the Skrull Empire behind him, whereas, in truth, he commanded no more than a small handful of faithful supporters, such as the loyal soldiers who'd perished when the human called Iron Man had the temerity to fire upon their scout ship. *Your sacrifice will not be forgotten, my fallen comrades,* he resolved. *When I am restored to power and glory, I will see to it that your names are duly entered into the annals of the Empire's heroes.*

All the more reason not to let the Leader know that he had been misled until the experiment was complete—and K'lrt had the power to return to the imperial court in triumph. Would the Empress then honor the promise the Super-Skrull had made on her behalf, granting the Leader a world of his own within the Empire's vast borders? K'lrt resisted the temptation to smile at a private joke; frankly, he doubted the Leader would ever have the opportunity to raise the issue with the Empress. Once their work together was concluded, he fully intended to dispose of his gullible human "partner." Why give the dishonorable Terran renegade a chance to share his scientific secrets with any other Skrull? To ensure his preeminence within the Empire, the power they unlocked must remain K'lrt's alone.

Intent on changing the subject, the Skrull wandered away from the platform to inspect their latest prisoners of war. A series of vertical plastic tubes were embedded in the circular wall of the rotunda. There were twelve tubes in all, eight of which contained a defeated member of the ill-fated rescue mission. Tranquilizing gas filled the interior of each tube, ensuring that the captives stayed unconscious and that, perhaps most importantly, Bruce Banner remained pink-skinned and powerless for the time being. Secure metal cables ran from the base of each suspension niche, connecting the tubes to the central platform like the spokes of an enormous wheel. All had transpired just as the Leader had anticipated, and so their prisoners had a vital part to play in the upcoming experiment.

He paused before the translucent cylinder containing the Terran android known as the Vision. "It is unfortunate," K'lrt commented, "that this irritating mechanism had already been defeated by the time I saw fit to reveal my true identity. Not too long ago, he interfered with an important mission I undertook in the service of the Empire; I would have enjoyed personally revenging myself for that past indignity."

A weary sigh escaped the Leader's loudspeakers. "Has anyone ever told you that you dwell too much on yesterday's defeats?" The human's hectoring tone offended K'lrt. "You need to keep your extraterrestrial eyes on the future, my morose friend. A new day is dawning . . . figuratively speaking, of course. Here on the moon, the sun won't actually rise for another 27 and two-thirds earth-days, but I trust you get my point. Leave your checkered past buried in the ashes of history. Tomorrow belongs to us."

Your memory is long enough where the Hulk is concerned, K'lrt thought silently. From the beginning, the Leader had insisted on factoring the Hulk into all their calculations and strategizing; indeed, he seemed constitutionally incapable of conceiving of a master plan that did not include the destruction of the Hulk as a major component. *So be it,* the Skrull reflected, inclined as ever to indulge the mutated Terran scientist on this particular matter. After all, K'lrt himself bore no great love for that monstrous savage. *Let the Leader have his revenge against the Hulk, so long as he completes the work at hand.*

"How much longer must I wait?" he demanded. "I thought all was in readiness."

"Patience," the Leader replied from above. "This is delicate work, requiring the precise calibration of my instruments. Rest assured, we shall proceed imminently."

That had best be the case, K'lrt thought balefully. Such forced inactivity chafed upon his nerves. He was a soldier, a Skrull of action, not a self-professed intellectual like the Leader, content to tinker with his scientific toys until the heat death of the universe, or so it seemed. Spying on their enemies in the guise of Wolverine had kept K'lrt fruitfully occupied while the Leader conducted his preliminary experiments on the kidnapped mutants, but the time for reconnaissance and research had long since passed; he was eager to reap the bounty he had awaited for so long.

He marched away from the niche holding the Vision, and his gaze fell upon the mute and motionless form of the real Wolverine, waiting with his fellow thralls for the Leader's next command. Although his eyes remained open, he appeared to possess no more animation or volition than the anesthetized prisoners in their suspension tubes. *If only all humans could be so docile and easily managed,* K'lrt thought; it occurred to him that he would have to deal with Leader's mutant pawns once he eliminated the Leader. *A simple enough task, once I attain the supremacy I seek.*

Of the dozen tubes nestled in the wall, four remained empty; proof that not even the Leader's amplified intellect had been able to estimate the exact number of Terran champions who would arrive at the moonbase in search of their absent comrades. Contemplating the unoccupied tubes, K'lrt regretted that Nightcrawler had been injured too badly to accompany his teammates on the rescue mission; the mutant's ability to teleport short distances without the aid of trans-mat devices could have added to the harvest ahead. . . . Still, at least the extra tubes could be employed to store the remains of the Leader's mind-controlled puppets. K'lrt looked forward to presenting the bodies of Earth's impertinent protectors as trophies for the Empress. What a proud and triumphant day that would be!

"There!" the Leader declared from his perch. "I can now state with total confidence that we are ready to begin. Kindly take your place upon the pedestal, if you please."

At last! Keen anticipation filled K'lrt as he stepped onto the transformation platform. Humming cables, radiating outward from the pedestal, linked him to the prisoners in their clear plastic cylinders. "Are you certain it will work?" he asked anxiously. Now that the moment had finally arrived, he dreaded the possibility of yet another failure. What if the experiment was unsuccessful? What they were trying had never been attempted before . . . !

"Well, there's no time like the present to find out," the Leader answered, rather too blithely for the Skrull's liking. "Brace yourself."

An instant later, a lambent green glow washed over the Super-Skrull, causing every cell in his body to resonate with the arcane energies transfiguring him. K'lrt had not deigned to learn all the technical intricacies of the process—that's what technicians and other underlings were for—but he understood the basics well enough. The Leader was using a modified form of his gamma-powered trans-mat technology to modify the Skrull's DNA on a molecular level, using genetic templates based on those of their mutant test subjects, adapted to achieve compatibility with the uniquely metamorphic properties of Skrullian DNA. According to the Leader, the process would only work on a Skrull, a happy accident of fate that guaranteed that the Leader could not simply perform the experiment upon himself, even if the mutated human hadn't also needed K'lrt and his followers to construct the moon base and capture the three mutants required to make this glorious moment possible. *Fate intended me for this epic accomplishment,* the Super-Skrull felt certain. *My destiny is at hand.*

The transforming radiance lasted only a heartbeat, but when it was over, the Super-Skrull felt stronger than he had in years, even more powerful than he had been many years ago, when an entire network of Skrull satellites had beamed cosmic energy directly into the bionic implants in his body, as opposed to the situation in recent years, when his powers had merely been fueled by whatever ambient cosmic energy was available. But all that had changed now. His limbs throbbed with unfathomable might. His eyes glowed with awesome power, held barely in check. He could sense minute fluctuations in air currents and temperature, feel the atmospheric moisture and barometric pressure responding to his whims. His sense of balance, of coordination and poise, felt infinitely heightened. He could see, hear, smell better than ever before.

"Well?" the Leader asked, looking down on him from his observation bulb. K'lrt could catch the scent of the Terran's sickly cologne from many feet below the

Leader's perch. "Don't just stand there. Let's see a test run."

Very well, the Skrull thought. He focused his gaze on one of the empty tubes along the wall. Crimson energy, identical to the beams projected by the X-Men's Cyclops, burst from his eyes, shattering the plexiglass tube into a hundred pieces. Even the Leader's blank-eyed mutant slaves flinched at the explosive sound of the vacant tube breaking apart beneath the force of the K'lrt's eyebeams. *Impressive,* K'lrt thought, pleased by the destructive effect of the crimson rays. He longed to test them against a living target, perhaps even the Leader.

But K'lrt was just getting warmed up. He bounded from the pedestal, executing a flawless handspring that turned into a series of backwards somersaults, eventually landing him on his feet several yards away. The strenuous gymnastics induced neither dizziness nor shortness of breath; K'lrt found himself in peak physical condition, as though he had just completed a rigorous course in basic training at the Skrull Military Academy. Glancing down at his boots, he noted that his feet had grown significantly larger, and that he had gained an opposable big toe on each foot. He could always change them back the way they were, as any Skrull could, but for now he chose to let the huge simian paws remain, as physical evidence of his transfiguration.

Thunder echoed in the sublunarian chamber. Lightning flashed overhead as an impossible rainstorm manifested inside the sealed enclosure. K'lrt laughed out loud, letting the cool raindrops stream down his face, throwing out his arms to welcome the torrential downpour. "Careful with those thunderbolts!" the Leader chided him, no doubt uncomfortable with the lightning's close proximity to his elevated control bulb, but K'lrt didn't care; he basked in the fury of the tempest, revelling in his effortless command of the elements.

The sheer power of it all was intoxicating. Testing himself further, he made the temperature drop dramatically, transforming the soaking rain into a blizzard of snow and ice. As a cold-blooded reptile, bred by evolution to thrive in a much warmer climate, the Skrull should have been miserable in the freezing snowstorm; instead, the ice flowed over his body like a second skin, one that felt just as natural as his own. The frosty glaze moved as he moved, as snug and comfortable as his soldier's uniform. He held out a frozen hand and watched in delight as an icy copy of Captain America's shield formed out of the falling sleet. K'lrt waited until the frigid disk was complete, then hurled the shield at the hanging bulb containing the Leader. The mutated human mastermind yelped in alarm, but the arctic weapon bounced harmlessly off the bottom of the plastic blister, ricocheting back into K'lrt's grip with perfect accuracy.

"Yes!" the Skrull rejoiced. He crushed the imitation shield to powder, then raised icy fists above his head in victory. Thunder roared in synch with his exalted spirit. "Success! The power is mine!"

"So it appears," the Leader agreed. Like all over-educated pedants and scholars, he could not resist the compulsion to cap his scientific achievement with a lecture. "By combining the essential ingredients of Rogue and the Scarlet Witch's genetic gifts, along with the shape-shifting capacity of your singular species, you can now assume the form *and* the abilities of any being you encounter."

K'lrt could not contain his joy. This was almost too good to be true; unlike his deceased soldiers, who had required technological aids to simulate the powers of the X-Men when they raided the Terrans' airborne command center, he truly possessed the intrinsic abilities of the captured X-Men and Avengers. There were limitations, of course; his altered DNA could not provide him with copies of his enemies' mechanical armaments, such as Iron Man's armor, Wolverine's adamantium claws, or any of the Vision's purely artificial functions, but that deficiency was of little consequence. With all the organic capabilities of two mighty teams of super-beings at his disposal, plus the raw strength of the incredible Hulk, what need did he have of mere weaponry?

"Wolverine's mutant healing factor was also necessary to the procedure," the Leader added, continuing his lecture, "to protect your body from the enormous stresses involved, which might otherwise prove fatal even to a Skrull." K'lrt resented the implication of weakness and fragility on his part, but chose to say nothing, too pleased by the exercising of his new abilities to bother quarreling with the Leader; there would be time enough to punish the human later, before terminating him once and for all. "As an added bonus," the Leader observed, "that same healing factor has repaired in you whatever defect prevented Cyclops from turning his optic blasts on and off at will." The green-skinned human inspected a display on his control panel. "Hmm, a cursory survey of that X-Man's neural pathways suggests that it was a childhood brain injury that ultimately cost Cyclops control over his eyebeams. You, of course, suffer no such impairment."

K'lrt was not surprised by the Leader's favorable diagnosis; he fully expected to wield the humans' powers with greater skill and daring than they ever had, just as he had always utilized the special abilities of the Fantastic Four with far more ruthlessness than that hated quartet could ever employ. Unlike Reed Richards and his insufferable clan, he was not restrained by human concepts of mercy or misplaced compassion. As a warrior, he knew there was no place for high-minded scruples on the battlefield.

Thinking of the many deadly uses to which he had put the strength of the Thing or the flames of the Human Torch raised an unsettling doubt in his mind. Had the Leader's procedure produced any negative effect on his original abilities? He prayed to Sl'gur't, eternal God of Battle, that the changes made to his genetic structure had not stripped him of the valuable powers provided by his bionic implants.

Raising a rime-coated hand before his eyes, he watched with relief as his frozen fist burst into flame. A rocky shell formed beneath the fiery blaze, then his wrist extended halfway across the rotunda before snapping back to its original length. To complete his test, K'lrt concentrated until his entire forearm disappeared from sight, concealed by a veil of invisibility. He nodded in approval; he was all he had been—and more.

No longer am I merely the Super-Skrull, he concluded with mounting pride. *I have become—the Ultimate Skrull!*

Which meant that the Leader had served his purpose. The bottom half of K'lrt's body ignited, blasting the Skrull off the floor of the rotunda. He rose until he was level with the Leader's hanging bulb and could look the arrogant mammal in the eyes. Behind the clear plastic of his observation blister, the Leader raised a quizzical eyebrow, clearly unaware of his increasingly precarious situation. *By the Sacred Halls of Val'ka'mor,* the Ultimate Skrull thought, *how could a sentient lifeform be so brilliant and at the same time so unwitting?* K'lrt had waited for this moment ever since his first encounter with the Leader, many weeks ago; if anything, the mutated human was even more presumptuous and disrespectful than the rest of his irksome breed. "The Leader" indeed! Even the human's chosen pseudonym betrayed his overweening ego. *As if the accident of his enlarged brain truly made him the equal of a Skrull!* K'lrt laughed out loud, a harsh and unforgiving sound.

"May I ask what you find so amusing?" The Leader regarded his jubilant partner with galling nonchalance. More than that, his tone sounded patronizing in the extreme, as if he too saw no point in continuing the pretense of an equal partnership. "Besides your new and improved talent for mimicry, that is."

Mimicry! K'lrt seethed at the dismissive term. Time to teach the ill-mannered primate a lesson he would remember for the rest of his inevitably brief existence. "I have borne your impudence long enough!" he declared. "Let you be the first to feel the wrath of the Ultimate Skrull!"

Dispensing with the fire of the Human Torch, he let Storm's tethered winds hold him aloft. Membranous wings grew beneath his arms, the better to glide upon the breeze, but K'lrt was not done exploiting the female X-Man's gifts. The Leader was frightened by the lightning of a few minutes ago? *Let us see how he reacts to being the target of such potent electrical fury.* Blue sparks leaped between K'lrt's gloved fingers, and the scent of ozone entered the atmosphere, as the Skrull kindled the raw galvanic potential of the air and sent a jagged thunderbolt crashing against the Leader's perch.

"*Et tu*, Skrull?" the Leader responded with transparently insincere regret. To K'lrt's disappointment, his lightning had no visible effect on the bulb enclosing the Leader; the clear plastic blister was more durable than he had anticipated, a testament to the human's undeniable scientific ingenuity. *No matter,* the Skrull resolved; hiding inside his plastic bubble would only prolong the Leader's demise, giving the conceited monkey more time to tremble at his approaching end.

"Go ahead, cringe behind your flimsy cage," he told the Leader, letting Cyclops's eyebeams join the lightning beating against the hanging bulb. "I don't want you to perish *too* quickly."

K'lrt's one concern was that the endangered Leader would call upon his mutant slaves to defend him, forcing the Skrull to waste time contending with Wolverine and the two females before he could satisfy his desire to see the Leader dead. Curiously, however, the human made no effort to sic his super-powered servitors upon the Skrull; the entranced mutant trio remained as they were, standing inertly upon the floor below. A scowl crossed K'lrt's face as doubt and suspicion cast a shadow over his earlier exultation. Why was the Leader, a physical weakling, not more terrified by the invincible Skrull warrior he had so foolishly created? A wary K'lrt began to sense that something was amiss, even as he redoubled his efforts to demolish the Leader's elevated sanctuary.

"K'lrt, K'lrt, K'lrt," the Leader said reprovingly. The Skrull could barely glimpse his former partner through the dazzling blaze of crimson force beams and white-hot bolts of lightning, but he could too readily imagine the Leader shaking his head like a disappointed schoolmaster. "If I were you, I wouldn't do this," the human advised. "I *really* wouldn't do this."

The Skrull's ire boiled over. How dare this overreaching aborigine address him so familiarly? A fierce thunderclap shook the underground chamber and K'lrt clenched his fists in rage. To his surprise, he felt something shift beneath the skin of his hands; a moment later, six bony protrusions, three on each hand, tore through flesh and glove alike, jutting out from the backs of his hands like claws.

Exactly like claws.

K'lrt admired his lethal new appendages. Although made of rigid bone and not adamantium, they clearly bore a kinship to Wolverine's infamous claws. *An unexpected blessing,* the Skrull decided. He retracted the claws experimentally, then extended them again, nodding with approval as the osseous blades slid in and out of their subdermal sheaths. There was a touch of pain as the claws sliced through his skin on their way out into the open, but nothing a warrior could not endure. The punctured flesh healed swiftly, too, before a single drop of Skrullian blood could leak from the insignificant wounds. The hurt fled, but the curved talons stayed.

His vicious-looking claws reinspired K'lrt's zeal to penetrate the Leader's seemingly impervious command bulb. How he longed to use his new claws to lobotomize the human's abnormally large brain, then dissect it one hemisphere at a time! Ruby-red eyebeams blinked out of existence, and the lightning ceased to lighten, as the Skrull took a more hands-on approach to breaching the Leader's defenses. A forceful gust of wind carried him closer to the bulb so that his arms scarcely needed to stretch to reach the transparent plastic. Upon closer inspection, he was gratified to see that his lightning had partially melted portions of the bulb, creating blurry ripples in the clear material. *A promising start,* the Skrull thought, leering at the Leader.

"Take a good look at your handiwork, human!" K'lrt taunted the cowardly scientist. With one hand, he froze the surface of the bulb while his other hand, positioned a few feet away, heated a different section to searing extremes. The clash of contrasting temperatures was more than the sturdy plastic could endure unscathed; spidery cracks spread across the region betwixt the hot and cold zones, leading the Skrull to grin in anticipation. He slashed out with his claws, which sliced through the weakened material with ease, allowing him to carve a circular window in the protective bubble. The excised plastic fell with a crash onto the platform below. "I must thank you for these wonderful new powers," K'lrt insisted, "before I deprive you of your unworthy human existence!"

Although backed away from the simultaneously chilled and heated plastic, the Leader still looked disturbingly unconcerned. He made no move to summon reinforcements, even from so close at hand, but simply eyed a digital counter upon one of his black wristbands. "Five, four, three, two," he counted down calmly, like a humanoid metronome. "One."

The wind suddenly fled from beneath K'lrt's wings and the Skrull dropped like a stone, or at least a stone falling in low gravity. He grabbed onto the bottom edge of the hole in the bulb, but the razored plastic was sharp and cut his fingers before he thought to form a rocky shell over them. Letting go instinctively, he plunged slowly toward the black steel floor. His gradual descent gave him plenty of time to flame on, and he rose again, enveloped in a sheath of red-orange fire, to confront the full implications of his abrupt tumble from the heights.

He knew at once that something distressing had occurred. Although his original powers remained in place, his magnificent new abilities had vanished. His eyes no longer tingled with extradimensional force. His ultra-keen senses had scaled back down to their former levels. He held no sway over the wind or temperature, nor had his muscles retained any memory of their recent acrobatic prowess. Even his skeletal claws sank back into his hands, where they promptly ceased to exist.

The Ultimate Skrull was gone, leaving only a mere Super-Skrull behind.

"What treachery is this?!" he demanded of the Leader. A barrage of fireballs, directed all around the command bulb, expressed his volcanic displeasure, but K'lrt knew he could not incinerate the Leader just yet, not until he understood the calamity that had befallen him. That this was almost certainly what the Leader had planned did not make it any easier for the Skrull to curb his more-than-justifiable lust for vengeance. "What have you done?!"

The flaming Skrull hovered near enough the Leader's perch that the mutated human did not need to rely on his loudspeakers to be heard. "Just because, unlike some people, I was not born and raised in the distant Androm-eda Galaxy, that does not make me a gullible, provincial dupe," the Leader said. "Did you truly believe that I would bestow so much power upon you without taking a few sensible precautions to protect my own interests?'' The Leader rolled his eyes in scornful disbelief. ''Please! If anyone has cause to be incensed here, it should be me, given how insultingly you underestimated my intelligence.''

K'lrt gave little weight to the Leader's complaints. Of course he regarded all humans with contempt; that was the natural order of things! ''Enough,'' he insisted, uninterested in the Terran's self-serving rationalizations. ''Tell me what you have done to my powers.''

''The genetic templates I superimposed on your alien DNA contain, by deliberate design, a chromosomal command to switch off after an elapsed period of time,'' the Leader explained, brazenly gloating over his perfidy. ''As a result, the treatment is only temporary; without periodic renewals, you will invariably lose your new-found capacities.''

So there it was, the unexpected snag in his plans. Although part of him craved the Leader's annihilation more than ever, K'lrt forced himself to re-evaluate the situation more objectively. A good commander knew when to revise his strategy in response to an unforeseen change in conditions, and it seemed that his vexing alliance with the upstart human genius would have to extend longer than the Skrull had originally planned. ''I see,'' he said gruffly. ''I suppose I should have expected nothing better from a creature such as yourself.'' Another concern troubled him far more than the Leader's betrayal. ''Of what value are these new powers if they last no longer than this? I cannot constantly flee from battle to renew my strength, and not even I can promise that every conflict will be resolved within a matter of minutes.''

The more he contemplated the problem, the more discouraged he became. Had he labored so hard, and sacrificed the lives of his soldiers, merely to secure a momentary advantage? Perhaps he should simply kill the Leader after all; such transient powers were hardly worth tolerating the human's odious presence.

''The duration of the time-limit can be adjusted,'' the Leader assured him. ''For the purposes of the present demonstration, I judged that you would require a 'wake-up call' almost immediately, since I'd calculated, quite accurately as it turns out, that you would attempt to, er, redefine our relationship not long after the completion of our experiment.'' The Leader inspected the hole in his bubble, cautiously running a pale green finger along its edges. ''In the future, your heightened powers can be programmed to last for hours, even days, depending on your needs and expectations. But they *will* expire eventually, you can be sure of that.'' An infuriating smile stretched beneath the furry black growth upon the Leader's upper lip. ''Back on Earth, we call that 'planned obsolescence,' and it's an essential hallmark of our economic system.''

More proof of your barbarity, the Skrull thought bitterly; it came as no surprise that the Terran's primitive civilization was built upon premeditated sabotage. He kept his opinion to himself, however; despite his righteous anger, K'lrt had to admit that the Leader had done an effective job of making himself indispensable to the Skrull's objectives—at least for the present. *The day will come,* he vowed privately, *when I shall find a way around this ''planned obsolescence,'' and then you will rue the day you dared to deceive the most fearsome Skrull of all!*

But for now the Leader had to remain a necessary, if

grossly unpalatable, part of K'lrt's plans. "What do you want?" the Skrull asked the grinning, mutated monkey.

"Merely the continuation of our earlier agreement and agenda," the Leader answered blandly, shrugging his scrawny shoulders as though the matter was hardly worth mentioning. "I look forward to a grateful welcome to the Skrull Empire, and the planet you promised me." He stroked his fuzzy lip with his fingertip. "I've always found contact with extraterrestrial intelligences to be highly stimulating, you know, ever since I made the acquaintance of the Watcher many years ago, near the beginning of my illustrious career. That particular close encounter ended badly, yet that has never discouraged me from seeking out new opportunities beyond the stars."

K'lrt let the Leader reminisce while he refocused his attention on his larger ambitions. The human's trickery was a setback, true, but the Skrull's overall objectives stayed the same. His splendid new powers would serve as his passport back into the good graces of the Empire, where he could swiftly overwhelm all opposition to rise to a position of power second only to the Empress herself. Then, once he was securely installed at the head of the awesome Skrull military machine, he would lead the Empire to victory over the Shi'ar and, by extension, the despicable Kree, before quashing all of the Empire's intergalactic rivals once and for all. The Brood, the Badoon, the Z'nox, the Dire Wraiths . . . all would fall before the supreme power of the Ultimate Skrull and his mighty fleets. Who could predict how far he might rise? If the current Empress proved uncooperative or shortsighted, perhaps it might even be time to sire a whole new dynasty, beginning with Emperor K'lrt the First . . . !

"And what of Earth?" he asked the Leader. At the back of the Skrull's mind was the hope that the human might ultimately settle for dominion over the planet of his birth, once that minor world was rid of its irksome super-heroes. "Have you no interest in ruling your own kind?"

"You can have that misbegotten sinkhole for all I care," the Leader replied, crushing K'lrt's hopes of an easy solution to the problem of his burdensome ally. "As I've told you repeatedly, I would prefer to start afresh elsewhere in the universe."

He tapped his control panel and a holographic image of the Earth appeared in the air between K'lrt and the command bulb. "Nevertheless," the Leader added, a malicious gleam in his eyes, "I do think we should leave my native world something of a good-bye gift."

"What did you have in mind?" the Skrull asked, curious despite his unhappiness at the Leader's continued existence. If anything, he hated Earth, site of innumerable past defeats and humiliations, even more than he loathed the haunted satellite beneath whose barren crust he and the Leader now resided. As eager as he was to return to the splendors of the Empire, he also relished the prospect of doing lasting harm to the miserable warren the humans called home.

"I thought you'd be interested," the Leader said, chuckling to himself. His fingers tapped over the controls and the holographic globe was replaced by a series of three-dimensional blueprints and schematics. K'lrt recognized the images as diagrams of the internal workings of the gamma-powered robots his soldiers had hijacked from the humans' helicarrier. "Although the prototypes for the Gamma Sentinels have all been disabled by our adversaries, we can easily reconstruct them using the resources of this moonbase." The Leader looked as smug and pleased with himself as a Xandarian thistle-cat. "One of the advantages of my homegrown humanoids is that they are a virtually inexhaustible source of free labor."

"And then?" K'lrt prompted.

"The plan is elegant in its simplicity," the Leader stated. "The second generation of Gamma Sentinels will lure Earth's remaining heroes into action by attacking key population centers, then detonating once the heroes are within the destruct radius of their built-in gamma bombs. The Fantastic Four, the Thunderbolts, the New Warriors, the Inhumans . . . every misguided conglomeration of metahuman vigilantes will be destroyed, ending forever the possibility of them interfering with my— I mean, *our*—future activities."

A most intriguing proposition, K'lrt thought, approving of the Leader's genocidal plot. The idea of purging Earth of its indefatigable champions went a long way toward soothing a martial spirit nettled by the Leader's pernicious subterfuge. The unworthy denizens of that backwards world had far too often played a pivotal role in interstellar affairs; they would be doing the whole cosmos a favor by putting the humans in their place at long last. The Super-Skrull particularly enjoyed the notion of Reed Richards and his meddlesome family being reduced to radioactive ashes.

"Make it so," he said.

Chapter Eight

Viridescent light briefly hid the Super-Skrull from the Leader's view, so he glanced down at the lighted panel before him. According to the gauges monitoring various aspects of the genetic superimposition, the second implementation of the Skrull/mutant synthesis program was proceeding as smoothly as the first. All pertinent variables were well within designated parameters while entropic flux had been kept to a minimum. *Matter transportation makes genetic recoding* so *much easier,* the Leader reflected, *not to mention less invasive.* Just beam in a different amino acid here, rearrange some chromosomes there and, *voila,* a considerably more super Super-Skrull. *Quite an impressive accomplishment, if I do say so myself.*

It bothered the former Samuel Sterns not at all that his own human tissues lacked the natural elasticity needed to survive the transformation; what need had he for Hulk-like muscles or ocular death-rays? He was a thinker, not a fighter, and more than content to become the power behind the Skrullian throne. He already possessed the only asset he would ever need: his own incomparable brain.

The emerald radiance above the transformation platform faded, and the re-refashioned Skrull stepped down from the pedestal. The Leader waited, more or less patiently, while his literal-minded alien partner predictably tested each and every one of his restored super-powers. Bone claws? Check. Eyebeams? Check. Ice? Check. Lightning? Check. Acrobatics . . .

Sighing, the Leader filed his nails and amused himself by playing several imaginary games of chess simultaneously, until finally the Skrull was finished. "Feeling better now?" the Leader asked flippantly. He was eager to proceed to the next item of business.

"It will do," the Skrull answered brusquely. Ice-coated hands thawed out, revealing black gloves underneath. Knife-edged claws withdrew into their sheaths. "For how long this time?"

Now that his point had been made, the Leader could afford to be magnanimous. "A full twenty-four hours," he promised. "More than enough time to break in your new abilities like a pair of new shoes." He glanced down at the chronometer on his control panel; according to his rough calculations, it would take approximately 48.932 hours to manufacture and dispatch a new set of Gamma Sentinels. Allowing for 5.375 more hours to entice their super-heroic prey onto ground zero, the Leader estimated that he and Commander K'lrt would be ready to depart for the Skrull throneworld by the end of the week, well before the next lunar sunrise.

But first there was a more vital item on his agenda. "Time to execute Dr. Banner," the Leader announced cheerfully. He had been saving Banner's demise as a special treat with which to reward himself after the success of the experiment; it would be both expedient and enjoyable to eliminate Banner, and thereby the Hulk, before saying farewell to the Milky Way forever. "The end of one chapter of my illustrious career," he commented, appreciating the symbolism, "and the beginning of the next."

The Skrull shrugged, incapable of truly comprehending the pivotal significance of this moment. "Cannot you simply place the human under your control, like you have these three?" he asked, gesturing at Wolverine and his distaff confederates. "The Hulk could be a valuable weapon in our arsenal."

"Sadly," the Leader explained, "the Hulk has always been immune to my mental manipulations, thus our perpetual antagonism." Memories of past defeats at the Hulk's hands made the present moment all the more sweet. "Speaking from painful experience, let me assure you that our fortunes can only be enhanced by the Hulk's swift removal from this vale of tears."

The Leader contemplated the other tubes, containing his new collection of X-Men and Avengers. To be scrupulously honest, he had not quite made up his mind what to do with the rest of their new prisoners. Now that he had the various mutants' genetic templates in his database, along with schematics of Iron Man's armor and the Vision's construction, not to mention the formula for Captain America's fabled Super-Soldier Serum, there was really no need to keep the hostages alive, but it really seemed a shame simply to extinguish their lives when their legendary powers and talents could still be brought under his irresistible Leadership.

The Hulk, on the other hand, had to die. Now.

"So be it," the Skrull agreed. "I doubt any will mourn the brute." He approached the tube holding Banner's unconscious form. A spear of ice formed in the Skrull's hands, its point aimed at Banner's heart. "It seems a shame, however, to sully my new gifts on such a menial task, against so defenseless and unworthy a foe. I am a soldier, not a butcher.''

''You feel this killing is beneath your standards for wholesale slaughter?'' the Leader asked, amused by the Skrull's archaic scruples and code of honor. ''Very well. There's no reason you should have to stoop to so easy an execution, not while other options present themselves.'' He pressed the touchpad on his wristband and the plastic tube surrounding Banner descended into the floor, leaving the slender scientist exposed. An electro-magnetic stasis field kept Banner standing upright in his niche. ''Specimen #3, kindly terminate Dr. Banner if you please.''

Alert to the Leader's command, Wolverine marched toward the open niche. *Snikt.* Silver blades slid from his hands.

Kill Banner. Kill. Kill.

The order cut through the murk in Logan's head like a lighthouse beacon shining clear and strong through a heavy fog. Soggy and thick, the fog lay over his mind, making it hard to think, let alone figure anything out, but he knew he had to kill the sleeping man in front of him, that much was certain. The Leader's voice and Logan's thoughts were one and the same.

Or were they?

Kill Banner. Kill . . . Banner?

The only other light in the fog came from the smoldering red rage at the back of his mind, the primal blood-lust that burned right on the borderline between his murky awareness and his unconscious mind. That bestial blaze fought back against the fog, granting him shadowy glimpses of dim shapes lurking within the murk, away from the piercing light of the Leader's commands. In the faint red glow, he could almost make out the barest outlines of other priorities, maybe even another point of view.

Kill Banner?

He felt confused, but he couldn't guess why. The voice in his head, the only thoughts he could truly hear, could not be misunderstood. His orders were simple and clean, just the way he liked them.

Kill Banner. Kill.

Logan peered at his prey, propped up lifelessly in a recess in the wall. The man looked dead, but Logan could hear Banner's heartbeat, slow and regular. He could smell the scent of life on the man's pink skin, as well as the noxious reek of the chemicals drugging his blood. Banner's scrawny chest rose and fell evenly. His exposed throat provided an easy target for Logan's claws. Maybe too easy.

Kill . . . who?

To the Leader's surprise, Wolverine paused before striking. The orange-suited mutant, whom the Leader had believed to be under his complete control, stood before Banner's niche, staring at his intended victim as if uncertain what to do. The X-Man's murderous claws hung at his sides, when, according to all reasonable expectations, they should have already been buried in Banner's flesh. *I don't understand,* the Leader thought. *It's not even like I'm asking him to go against his own nature. The man's a natural-born killer after all.*

Wolverine's inaction did not go unnoted by the Skrull. ''Is something wrong, human?'' he asked the Leader, sounding pleased that the Leader might have encountered a problem. An unseemly smirk appeared upon his reptilian countenance. "Are you still certain you can handle this 'easy execution' on your own?"

The Leader's cheeks turned a darker shade of green. *This will not do,* he thought, embarrassed and annoyed at losing face in front of the arrogant Skrull. "Specimen #3," he repeated, clicking the volume on his loudspeakers up a notch. "You have your orders. Terminate Banner."

Down on the floor, Wolverine raised his claws until their points nudged Banner's throat. The Leader nodded approvingly, feeling his aggravation pass from him. *This is more like it,* he thought, looking forward to Banner's last choking gurgles. After so many years, and too many frustrating escapes from the Leader's brilliantly-devised deathtraps, the long, ugly, violent rampage of the Hulk was coming to an end. "And none too soon," the Leader whispered. In a very real sense, Wolverine's claws would do what that original gamma bomb explosion should have accomplished years ago: eliminate Robert Bruce Banner for good.

Snikt. Wolverine's claws retracted into his hands, leaving Banner's throat unscratched. "What are you doing?" the Leader gasped, taken aback by the mutant's unprecedented disobedience. Adding insult to Banner's lamentable lack of injury, the Super-Skrull laughed out loud at the Leader's failure.

"On second thought," the Skrull mocked, "perhaps you are not ready to rule an entire world just yet. Perhaps we can find you an island in a pond somewhere. A small island."

Very funny, the Leader thought, deciding that the only

thing more annoying than the Super-Skrull's warrior's code was his feeble sense of humor. *I must nip this minor insurrection in the bud promptly,* he decided, *before the vainglorious Commander forgets who is really the Leader here.*

Tapping out a rudimentary command on his wristband, the Leader immediately teleported himself down to the floor of the Transformation Chamber. Obviously, he had underestimated Wolverine's volatile nature, but that was nothing a second dose of direct telepathic contact couldn't remedy. Studiously ignoring the Skrull's skeptical gaze, the Leader came up behind the recalcitrant mutant, who remained transfixed before Banner's dormant form, his feral eyes riveted on the defenseless physicist's jugular. The muscles in Wolverine's face twitched randomly, evidence of an ongoing inner conflict. His entire body vibrated with tension, his dense black mane bristling like a cat's. A low growl rumbled up from deep inside him.

Clearly, the Leader concluded, Wolverine had not thrown off his mental shackles entirely, but was merely caught in a psychological limbo somewhere between free will and perfect obedience. *Time for a booster shot,* he thought, laying his hands against Wolverine's temples. The X-Man's lack of height made his head easier to reach than, say, the Skrull's. Mental energy flowed from the Leader's fingertips into the mutant's skull, bringing clarity to his disordered thoughts. "Kill him," the Leader instructed. "Now."

KILL HIM NOW!

The command flared inside Logan's head like a mushroom cloud, stronger and brighter than before. Paradoxically, the clearer the command, the deeper the fog became, wrapping around his thoughts, making it difficult to think anything else except. . . .

KILL HIM NOW!

Banner's jugular throbbed a few inches away. Logan could already taste the blood, imagine the man's life bleeding out through the gashes Logan's claws would make. It was simple. Easy. All he had to do was cut and slice and claw and tear, just like the voice inside his head insisted.

KILL HIM NOW!

The claws leaped from the backs of his hands, sliding out in their grooves the same way his thoughts seemed to be guided in just one direction, channeled inexorably toward a single, inescapable goal. And yet, despite the relentless mental tide tugging him toward the kill, something felt wrong. Kill Banner? Why? Banner was no match for him. Tackling the Hulk was one thing; the bonfire at the back of his brain blazed hotter at the thought of pitting his claws against the green-skinned giant's grizzly-sized bulk. But Banner? This skinny, pink sitting duck? Banner couldn't even run away from Logan's claws, let alone fight back with any hope of survival. What sort of prey was that?

KILL BANNER! KILL!

Logan wanted to kill someone alright, but not Banner. Whether it was his mutant healing factor at work, or just plain cussedness, he resisted the compulsion to strike out at the helpless man. Killing Banner in cold blood went against his instincts, no matter how inescapable his orders to the contrary. The Leader's command still shone as intensely as before, but he found he could distance himself from its strident neon imperative, keeping it apart from the other shapes emerging from the fog. The blood-red glare of his raw animal will illuminated the fogbound landscape of his mind.

His gaze flicked from side to side, spotting Rogue and the Scarlet Witch out of the corners of his eyes. He became aware of another presence directly behind him, pressing upon his temples. *My Leader,* he understood, then corrected himself. *No,* the *Leader.* His eyes glanced over at Rogue again, as a plan came together in his mind. *This is the Leader's fault. He's done something to me, something to all of us.*

Angry veins pulsed in his temples. Logan's teeth ground together violently. His claws jerked in and out of his clenched fists, while his fingernails dug into the palms of his hands, drawing blood. The pain made it a little easier to ignore the flashing billboard in his head. Fighting his own rage as well, Logan mustered enough sanity to figure out what needed to be done.

KILL BANNER NOW!

"No!" Logan snarled. He spun around and grabbed the Leader by the shoulders, lifting the startled super-villain off his feet. Before the Leader could reassert his control, Logan flung the mutated mastermind at another of his brainwashed victims. "Rogue, darlin', catch!"

As the Leader barrelled headfirst toward the entranced X-Man, Rogue instinctively threw out her hands to halt the collision. Her bare fingers could hardly miss the Leader's elephantine cranium and she caught the bulbous projectile with both hands.

Atta girl! Logan thought, grinning wickedly despite the lingering fog in his mind. Before his eyes, Rogue's entire body stiffened as though an electric current was passing through her. Her eyes bulged in surprise as the Leader's staggering I.Q. poured into her brain, which expanded to accommodate her enormous new intellect. Her smooth brow mushroomed in size, both cerebral hemispheres swelling up like balloons beneath her chestnut hair. Her rosy skin took on a greenish complexion that clashed with her ugly orange jumpsuit.

As for the Leader, he emitted a sickly groan before sagging against Rogue, who hurriedly dropped him like a hot potato. The sound of the villain's limp body hitting the floor was like music to Logan's ears, even if the Leader's final command still reverberated within the X-Man's skull, freezing him in place.

KILL BANNER NOW!

With her newly-acquired super-smarts, it took Rogue less than a second to assess the situation. Zooming past the dumbfounded Super-Skrull, she lightly brushed her fingertips across Logan's throbbing forehead. He experienced a moment of weakness, typical of hands-on treatment from Rogue, but the brief infirmity passed quickly, taking with it any vestiges of the Leader's control. The fog lifted in his brain, and the Leader's intrusive voice fell silent at last. *About flamin' time,* he thought; for the first time in who knew how long he could literally hear himself think. Just as he'd hoped, Rogue had used her borrowed mental powers to undo the hold the Leader had placed over both their minds. "Good work, darlin'," he told her. "Don't forget the Witch, too."

"Right on it!" Rogue drawled, streaking away toward the enslaved Avenger. Wide-eyed and alarmed, the Super-Skrull's gaze jumped back and forth between Logan, Rogue, and the collapsed Leader. Then he grasped what Rogue was up to, and his extendable arms stretched after her, desperate to stop her from freeing Wanda as well. Flaming stone fists, looking like catapulted mounds of red-hot coals, headed on an intercept course for Rogue's colossally enlarged skull.

"Forget it, bub!" Logan growled, leaping at the Skrull. The gravity was so low he might as well have been flying. *That's right,* Logan remembered. *We're on the moon.* He felt like he had just woken up from a long, uneasy sleep, his brain full of discordant images that he only half-recalled. *When in blazes did the Skrulls get mixed up in this mess anyhow?*

He slammed into the Skrull, the weight of his adamantium skeleton driving the alien backwards and away from Rogue. The Skrull grunted in surprise, the top half of his body stretching to absorb the force of Logan's assault while the Skrull's boots remained firmly planted on the floor. Logan slashed at the Skrull's face with his claws, only to be blocked at the last minute by some sort of invisible force field. *Yeah, yeah,* Logan thought, unimpressed. He recognized the Super-Skrull from a barroom brawl in Manhattan a few years back. *A one-man Fantastic Four, I remember.*

The force field expanded outward, shoving Logan away from the alien warrior. His back crashed into the wall, but Wolverine endured the impact stoically. He'd done what he'd set out to do; give Rogue time to snap the Scarlet Witch out of her trance. Looking across the rotunda, he saw Magneto's only daughter blink and shake her head after a glancing touch from Rogue, who hurriedly brought the other woman up to speed. "Watch out for this character!" he warned Rogue and the Witch, nodding at the Skrull. "He's got plenty of tricks!"

"More than you can imagine, mutant!" the Skrull bragged, apparently unworried by the former hostages's three-to-one advantage over him. A thick, blue layer of ice formed over his left fist while his right remained aflame. His eyes glowed an ominous shade of red, and a crimson beam lashed out at Logan, who dodged the beam by diving to one side an instant before the incandescent ray shattered the floor where he had been standing. "Surrender or face the unlimited power of the Ultimate Skrull!"

What the—? Logan thought. *That was just like one of Cyke's beams.* Alert eyes scanned the arena-sized chamber, registering for the first time that others besides Banner were suspended in the transparent plastic tubes. *Scott, 'Roro, Cap, Hank, Bobby, Shellhead, and the Vision,* Logan spotted, scowling; *looks like the bad guys have half of the X-crew here, plus the Avengers to boot.* He wished he could borrow the Leader's memories from Rogue, just so he had a better idea of what was going down. All he could dredge up now were vague recollections of fighting Iron Man and/or the Hulk. *Feels like I missed a good chunk of this flamin' yarn.*

"Never!" the Scarlet Witch declared, responding to the Skull's demand that they surrender. Her accent betrayed her Balkan roots. "When have you ever known an Avenger to yield to the likes of you, Skrull? We've beaten you before and we will again."

"Ha!" the Skrull laughed harshly. "You three could not even escape my underlings. What hope do you have of defeating the champion of the Skrull Empire?"

"Your underlings?" Wanda echoed, sounding puzzled. Confusion creased her brow momentarily, then the truth sunk in. "Of course . . . the puppets!" She eyed the Skrull with renewed anger and determination. "A clever trick, but you no longer have surprise and deception on your side." Her fingers assuming arcane and esoteric configurations, she cast a hex sphere over the hostile Skrull. A shimmering globe of scarlet light surrounded her foe, but the Skrull looked unafraid. With a gesture from his frost-covered hand, he dispelled the hex, which popped like a soap bubble, leaving the Scarlet Witch visibly shocked. "How did you do that?" she demanded. "It's impossible!"

"No, it ain't," Rogue corrected her. Her voice even sounded a little like the Leader's now. "This scaly carpetbagger's got all our powers, plus our friends' powers besides." She tapped her inflated noggin. "Ah know just how the Leader did it—and it works! The Skrull's a lot more dangerous than before."

Nuts! Logan thought. Like the Super-Skrull wasn't enough of a challenge before the Leader souped-up his powers. Claws extended, Wolverine warily circled the alien, keeping both eyes on the Skrull as he spoke to Rogue. "Guess that eliminates you putting the touch on him, right?"

"'Fraid so, sugah," Rogue said, rising into the air above Wanda. "We'd just cancel each other out, like he and the Witch just did." She cracked her knuckles loudly, then faced the Skrull with her bare fists.

"The female speaks truly," the Skrull gloated. "I am the sum of all your talents and more." Bony claws jutted from his fists like calcified parodies of Logan's own adamantium blades.

"Watch it, chum," Logan warned. "You're gettin' dangerously close to copyright infringement there." He risked a glance at the Leader, who had not yet recovered from Rogue's one-of-a-kind whammy. *There's the brains of this outfit,* he reminded himself. *Better put him under wraps before we get caught up in a rumble with*

E.T. here. He sprang at the Leader's comatose body, ready to trade the swell-headed mutate for a ride home, if that's what it took to get the X-Men and the Avengers back on their native soil. The Skrull wasn't the only one who could take hostages.

Logan's pounce brought him smack against another invisible force field, shielding the Leader from harm. "Believe me, mutant," the Skrull asserted, "I wish I could permit you to wield those admirable claws against my duplicitous accomplice, but I still have need of that vexing human." He drove Logan away from the Leader with a concentrated burst of optic rays. "You and the two females, on the other hand, have become expendable."

So what else is new? Logan thought.

Rogue's brain felt stuffed to busting by the Leader's accumulated knowledge and intellect. She doubted if even Professor X had this much raw data and processing power crammed into his skull, even if the Leader's memories came tainted with an undertone of heartless evil and cruelty that was impossible to mistake. Although it left a bad taste in her mouth, the villain's sinister inclinations didn't mess up Rogue's head too much; she'd zapped too many bad guys with her hungry fingers to be seduced by the slimy underside of the Leader's soul. *The Skrull's our big problem now,* she thought, her allegiances and priorities back in order at last.

You didn't have to be a super-genius to realize that the Super-Skrull, endowed with the powers of a whole passel of super-types, was going to be one tough customer. A stolen memory showed her the alien warrior taking out both Captain America and Iceman—and that was *before* the Leader multiplied the Skrull's abilities!

"Mine is the ferocious power of the elements!" Commander K'lrt exulted, raising his arms above his head. The Leader's psyche provided Rogue with the Super-Skrull's real name. "Feel the coldness of my contempt for you Terran rabble!"

A savage winter storm awoke within the underground chamber. Biting winds howled in fury, driving Wolverine and the Scarlet Witch back from their alien enemy. Freezing sleet and snow pelted the heroes, coating their limbs with a frigid glaze that weighed them down even as it chilled them to the bone. *Must be mixing Bobby and Ororo's powers,* Rogue realized. Only she could make any headway at all against the unnatural blizzard; the southern-born X-Man flew into the wind, fighting to reach the all-powerful Skrull at the center of the tempest.

The wind chill factor had to be a hundred below. As invulnerable as she was, Rogue still felt the awful cold. The arctic wind blew against her face, turning her lips blue and chapped. She shivered uncontrollably as she flew, her teeth chattering loud enough to be heard over the wailing of the storm. Ice covered her outstretched arms and legs; if not for the moon's lesser gravity, she wasn't sure she could have stayed aloft. Her fingers lost all feeling, making her pine for her gloves—and not for the usual reason. *Brrr!* she thought. *This is no kind of weather for a Mississippi gal like me.*

Slowly, stubbornly, she jetted into the blizzard. Powerful headwinds fought her every inch of the way, but she dived toward the Skrull, who started flinging fireballs and lightning bolts at her. Crimson eyebeams joined the Skrull's anti-aircraft fire, turning the turbulent atmosphere into an aerial obstacle course worthy of the

Danger Room. *Thank goodness for all those training sessions!* Rogue acknowledged, banking sharply to avoid K'lrt's eyebeams as they came sweeping toward her. The familiar red beams reminded her of Cyclops and the other imprisoned X-Men; knowing that her teammates had come all the way to the moon just to rescue her, Logan, and Wanda only fueled her determination to teach both the Leader and the Super-Skrull a lesson they'd never forget. "R-r-ready or not," she whispered through frozen lips, "h-h-here I c-come!"

She let a couple fireballs hit her, just to warm up a little. The roiling globes of flame melted most of the frost away, while doing no more harm to her impervious skin than a hot tub; thankfully, the homely orange duds she was wearing turned out to be fireproof, too. She luxuriated in the toasty feeling of warm flames racing over frost-bitten cheeks, which was surely not what the homicidal Skrull had in mind. *He's still not used to his new crop of super-powers,* she deduced. *His attacks are getting in each other's way.*

Then a thunderbolt struck Rogue between her shoulderblades at the same time that a scarlet hex bolt disrupted her nervous system, triggering an epileptic fit.

The snowstorm blinded Wanda Maximoff, making it all but impossible to see what was happening, let alone aid in the battle against the Super-Skrull. The fierce wind, excruciatingly cold, whipped her auburn tresses about wildly, so that she was constantly tugging her hair away from her face. Wet, clumpy flakes of snow, mixed with stinging pellets of hail, bombarded her without surcease. New fallen snow, as clean and white as the snowy peaks of Wundagore Mountain where she was born, piled up past her ankles, burying her bare feet beneath a carpet of frozen moisture. *This is ridiculous,* she thought angrily, hugging herself tightly and shivering. *How are we supposed to defeat the Super-Skrull in the face of this imitation Ice Age?*

To her surprise and frustration, she glimpsed the unmistakable scarlet glow of a hex bolt through the swirling snowfall, proving that the Skrull was successfully copying her powers even as she searched futilely for shelter from the storm. Who was the target of the imitation hex bolt, she wondered. Rogue? Wolverine? It tormented her to imagine her own mutant magic employed against her X-Men allies, but what could she do to halt the Skrull's protean onslaught? The remorseless blizzard hid the alien villain from her hexes as effectively as any smoke screen or natural camouflage.

''Witchie!'' a gruff voice called out from nearby. Wanda recognized Wolverine's raspy tone and attitude even if she couldn't make out the X-Man amidst the tempest-tossed snow. ''Forget the Skrull!'' he shouted over the keening wind. ''Wake up Cap and the others!'' His claws scraped against something hard and crystalline, drawing Wanda's attention to a transparent tube embedded in the wall behind her. Turning her back on the Skrull and his storm, she peered past the deluge of falling snow until she spied Cap's red-white-and-blue figure suspended motionlessly within the tube. Similar tubes flanked the patriotic Avenger on both sides, but Wanda could only faintly glimpse the costumed individuals trapped therein. *Had the Leader and the Super-Skrull captured all of the Avengers?* she fretted. *What about the Vision?* She thought she spotted her ex-husband's diamond-shaped emblem on one of the entombed figures, but it was hard to tell in the storm. "Vision?" she whispered, her breath misting in the chill air.

"Hurry it up!" Wolverine hollered. His claws clacked loudly against the clear plastic cylinder and Wanda discerned his stocky, snow-flecked outline against a stretch of black wall between two tubes. His head dipped beneath his shoulders as he crouched before the vicious wind. "Rogue's on her own versus the Skrull, so make it fast!"

Yes, of course, Wanda thought. As deputy leader of the Avengers, it felt odd to be receiving orders from an X-Man, but now was no time to argue about protocol. Although her fingers shook from the cold, that didn't stop her from gesturing at the nearest containment tube, conjuring a hex bolt that leaped from her numb fingertips to the apparatus controlling the tubes. Eldritch energy lit the vicinity, casting scarlet shadows upon the snow and revealing Wolverine in his orange prisoner's garb. He nodded with satisfaction as, one after another, the tubes malfunctioned "spontaneously," releasing their captives. Looking more than a little dazed, Captain America staggered into the snow, instinctively snatching up his shield from where it lay at the bottom of his tube. "What the devil?" he exclaimed as the first blast of wind now struck his chiseled features. "Where are we?"

All along the wall, other heroes slowly came back to their senses. Wanda spotted the Vision, just as she'd thought, as well as the Beast, Cyclops, Storm, and more. From the looks of them, they all needed a few minutes to recover from whatever sort of suspended animation the Leader had consigned them to. If nothing else, Wanda guessed, the bracing cold had to be a brutally effective wake-up call.

"Way to go, Witchie," Wolverine said. He helped a frail-looking man in torn brown trousers stumble through a particularly deep snowdrift. Wanda recognized the shivering human as Dr. Bruce Banner only seconds before the man's skin began to turn an auspicious shade of green. "Things are lookin' up!"

I hope so, she prayed.

Rogue's eyes rolled backward, so that only their whites could be seen. Her jaws locked together and she nearly swallowed her tongue. Limbs flailing out of her control, she crashed into the snow at the Ultimate Skrull's feet.

The hex-induced seizure passed quickly, yet left the X-Man shaken and unhappily impressed by K'lrt's rapid mastery of his purloined powers. "Guess he's a quick learner," she muttered, lifting her head from the snow. Her bottom lip bled where she'd bitten it during her fit, and she spit a dollop of fresh blood onto the frozen whiteness beneath her. "Serves me right for gettin' cocky."

"You deserve the same thing every upstart primate deserves," K'lrt stated. His disdainful words came from only a few feet above her. "Extinction."

"Oh yeah?" Rogue asked, scrambling onto all fours and staring straight ahead at the Skrull's knees. "Don't go countin' your critters 'fore they're cooked, you two-legged gator!" Without even bothering to get back on her feet, she launched herself into K'lrt, butting him in the abdomen with her head.

It was like diving headfirst into a trampoline. K'lrt's elastic torso absorbed her charge, then bounced her back onto the snow. *Dang!* the aggravated mutant thought. The no-good Skrull had too many weirdo powers to keep track of. "Okay then," she decided. "Let's get down to basics."

She threw a roundhouse punch at K'lrt's scalloped jaw, her fist connecting with solid bone this time, instead of living rubber. As she'd figured, their mirror-image absorption powers canceled each other out, allowing them to exchange blows without trading memories. *Good,* she thought. *That makes things simpler.*

K'lrt took her blow without giving an inch, something not many opponents this side of the Juggernaut could do. From the looks of him, the alien soldier relished the opportunity for a little hand-to-hand combat. A grin stretched across his lizard-like face. Red eyes filled with baleful satisfaction as he swung a rocky fist at Rogue's head. "You are formidable for your kind, female," he warned her, "but you're no match for the Ultimate Skrull!"

"Says who?" Rogue countered, blocking the blow with her right arm. "The only thing ultimate here is your outerspace-sized ego!"

Despite her bravado, however, K'lrt had her worried. The sheer strength of his punch startled her; she was lucky she hadn't fractured her arm by throwing it in the way of his fist. Just how strong was this character anyway? Not even Colossus had ever hit her that hard.

Feinting with her left, she slugged the Skrull with her right, catching him right above his bulging brows. Hoping for a knock-out, she was disappointed when K'lrt responded instead with a glancing blow that left Rogue's head ringing. She barely ducked beneath his follow-up swing in time to avoid another piledriver punch. Groggy and on the ropes, she kicked a pile of snow into the Skrull's face, just to slow him down for a sec. *I need a breather,* she realized, still feeling woozy from that shot to her head.

The Super-Skrull's head and shoulders ignited into flame, melting away the offending snow. "Foolish mammal!" he taunted Rogue. "Such childish tactics cannot save you. Do you not realize that I now possess the cumulative strength of the Hulk, the Thing, the Beast, Captain America, and even yourself? Nothing in this solar system can equal my might. Certainly not an ignorant harpy out of her element and her depth."

He ain't joking, Rogue admitted to herself. The Leader's memories confirmed K'lrt's boasts. *If one of those Hulk-plus haymakers connects with my head, I'm history.* An old-fashioned slugfest was out; she didn't stand a chance of beating the Ultimate Skrull in an ordinary scuffle. Instead she rapidly searched the Leader's borrowed memories for a way to defeat the amplified power of the hostile alien.

Fortunately, the Leader's powers of concentration kept pace with his encyclopedic store of knowledge. Inspiration struck within nano-seconds, and Rogue looked to the command bulb overhead, abandoned ever since the Leader beamed down to the floor at the beginning of Wolverine's rebellion. *The answer's up there,* she grasped at once. *That's the only way.*

She had to hurry, though. She needed the Leader's technical know-how to carry out her plan, but she could already feel the villain's mutated brainpower beginning to slip away from her. The length of her physical contact with her victims determined how long she held onto their captured attributes; unfortunately, she'd only touched the Leader for a few seconds. *Darn it,* she thought, *I should have hung onto his swelled head a little bit longer, back when I had the chance.* With the downed mastermind protected by K'lrt's force field, there was no way to renew her claim on the Leader's smarts. It was now or never.

"See you later, bat-ears!" She fled her lopsided boxing match with the Skrull, taking off into the air. K'lrt's elongated arms chased after her, unwilling to surrender their prey. Rogue felt her prefrontal lobes start to shrink down to their standard dimensions; would she still have enough scientific expertise to pull off her scheme? That might depend on how quickly she got away from K'lrt. A petrified fist, unbelievably strong, closed around her ankle and she struggled to yank her foot free. "Hey, y'all!" she yelled at the various X-Men and Avengers below. "Somebody get this grabby alien offa me!"

The snow had died down while Rogue and the Super-Skrull traded knuckle sandwiches. Banner was in the throes of his eye-popping transformation into the Hulk, greenish muscles piling onto the cursed scientist's shivering physique, when Wolverine heard Rogue's heartfelt cry for assistance. Peering upward into a fading flurry of snowflakes, Logan saw that the airborne X-Man was tethered to the floor by one of the Skrull's unnaturally extendable arms. The lasso-like limb began to retract before Logan's eyes, dragging Rogue back down toward the triumphant Skrull.

Sorry, bub, Logan thought, rushing toward the Skrull with his silver claws out front, *not while I'm still breathing.* He didn't wait for the rest of the heroes to recover from their anesthetized incarceration within the Leader's tubes. Loping briskly across the snow, he slashed out at the Skrull's outstretched arm. "The lady said let go!'' he growled, thrusting another set of claws at the Skrull's reptilian face.

Over three meters long, the targeted arm was too pliable to slice clean through, yet Logan managed to saw through the Skrull's uniform to the scaly flesh beneath, scratching the surface of the alien's skin. ''Aggh!'' the Super-Skrull croaked in surprise and pain. He whipped his injured arm away from Wolverine's claws at the same time that he used his eyebeams to repel the savage X-Man before Logan's claws could spear his face. A blast of concussive force sent Wolverine rocketing away from his enemy, but, despite the bruising impact, Logan knew he'd done his part. A sense of predatory satisfaction suffused his being as his sensitive nostrils caught the unearthly scent of the Skrull's spilled blood. *Nobody messes with the X-Men and ends up unscarred,* he thought ferociously. *Nobody!*

His minor flesh wound healed instantly, but the Super-Skrull could neither forget nor forgive the X-Man for drawing first blood. Intent on avenging his honor, the Super-Skrull released Rogue and charged Wolverine, an icy javelin materializing in his hands. He threw the spear with superhuman force, driving it through the X-Man's midsection and into the wall behind him. ''Hah!'' the Skrull laughed cruelly, enjoying Logan's plight. ''I always thought you would make a fine trophy!''

Impaled on the frozen lance, pinned to the chamber wall like a bug in an entomologist's display case, Wolverine let out a bestial howl. He tried to grab onto the icy shaft and pull it out of his guts, but its slick surface was made even slipperier and harder to hold by the warm blood gushing from his perforated stomach. *Healing fac-*

tor or no healing factor, he thought, grimacing, *this hurts like blazes.*

He couldn't even shake the spear free from the wall; the Super-Skrull had propelled the javelin too hard and too deeply for that. Now the Skrull was coming in for the kill, and Logan knew he couldn't get off the blasted spike before the Skrull turned him into a casualty of war. *Never expected to cash in my chips on the moon, of all the crazy places,* Logan mused, as his internal organs stubbornly tried to repair themselves despite umpteen inches of unyielding icicle, *but I guess I had a good long run.*

"Prepare to die, Terran!" the Skrull asserted, brandishing his claws of bone; he clearly appreciated the irony of slaying Wolverine with replicas of Logan's own infamous claws. "May your afterlife be as backwards and odious as your planet!"

The skeletal blades shot toward Logan's throat—only to shatter against a huge green palm that dropped between the Skrull and his intended victim. The Skrull shrieked in agony as his organically-grown claws splintered into pieces. His mouth opened so wide Logan could see past the alien's fangs and down his throat. Not a pretty sight, but Logan wasn't complaining.

"Forget that," the incredible Hulk rumbled, shoving the Skrull backwards with a sweep of his gargantuan arm. "Nobody clobbers that Canadian runt but me."

"What he said," Iron Man added, his amplified voice ringing out over the spacious rotunda. The armored Avenger was just one of several heroes coming to Logan's aid. "Sort of."

Casually, with just one hand, the Hulk tugged the bloody ice-spear out of both the wall and the impaled

X-Man. The gamma-spawned behemoth broke the frozen
lance over his knee while Wolverine slid down onto the
snow, leaving a gruesome trail on the black steel wall.
Logan clutched his stomach and bit down on his lip as
his punctured entrails painfully reknit. *That's one I owe
you, big guy,* he thought, grateful that, for once, the Hulk
had remembered whose side he was supposed to be on.

Who'd have guessed it?

K'lrt scanned the wintry battlefield, reminiscent of the
arctic ice caverns of B'hamma Prime. It seemed that all
of the Terran champions had been roused from stasis;
both Avengers and X-Men fanned out around him, stak-
ing out positions from which to launch a unified attack.
He identified Captain America and Storm to his left,
while Cyclops and the Scarlet Witch readied themselves
to the right. The Beast, the Hulk, and Iceman spread out
before and behind him. Iron Man and the Vision circled
overhead, casting their humanoid shadows over the outnumbered Skrull. "All right, Skrull," Captain America
said sternly, and K'lrt was appalled by the human's sanc-
timonious posture and tone. The Avenger's shield,
branded with primitive tribal emblems, stood guard upon
the human's bended arm. "We can do this the easy way
or the hard way. That's entirely up to you."

"And you'll hand over the Leader, too, if you know
what's good for you," the Hulk added sullenly. Unlike
Captain America, the mighty brute did not bother to hide
his essential barbarousness behind a facade of unde-
served dignity. "Me, I'm just looking for a chance to
knock your alien butt into orbit."

K'lrt did not grant the Terrans' hollow threats and
ultimatums the honor of a reply. *Let them come,* he

thought confidently. With his awe-inspiring new powers, he could vanquish them all, thanks to the Leader's scientific acumen. Looking beyond the ring of Terran insurgents, K'lrt noted that the victimized Leader was starting to stir for the first time since being struck down by his former slave. Although still unconscious upon the floor, the Leader groaned weakly. His fingers scratched fitfully at the carpet of snow while his puny body contracted into a fetal position to conserve his body heat. *A pathetic sight,* K'lrt appraised in disgust. Perhaps the overbearing genius would be less presumptuous after this near-debacle, brought on solely by the Leader's overweening vanity and ultimate incompetence. In the final analysis, he reflected, it is the warrior who wields the power that matters, not the lowly technician who labors to forge the weapons, but has no place upon the battlefield.

He cast a contemptuous glance at the Leader's elevated command bulb, only to see Rogue fly into the empty transparent blister through the opening K'lrt himself had carved in the Leader's protective bubble. For the first time, he felt a tremor of apprehension: what in the name of sacred Skrullos was that troublesome female doing up there? A sobering realization struck him with the force of a runaway comet; until the Leader recovered from Rogue's parasitic touch, the rebellious human possessed all of the Leader's vast knowledge—including the secret of the Skrull's new powers!

"No! This cannot be!" His cold blood went cooler as a chill rushed down his malleable spine. Surrounded as he was by a motley assortment of X-Men and Avengers, K'lrt knew that he could not possibly thrash all his foes before the mutant wench worked her mischief in the command bulb. Invisibility, it was plain to see, was the better part of valor.

Abruptly, the Ultimate Skrull vanished before the startled eyes of Earth's intransigent defenders, rising unseen into the air with all the speed at his command. *Rogue must die,* he resolved, *before another minute passes!*

"Easy does it," Rogue murmured as she sat down upon the revolving seat at the center of the hanging bulb. An illuminated control panel, consisting of an intimidating array of colored touchpads and gauges, circled her like a ring. The anxious X-Man gulped as she tried to make sense of the bewildering controls, with the help of the Leader's swiftly fleeing super-genius. *Well I'll be!* she thought. *This blamed set-up looks more complicated than all that Shi'ar hardware back in the Danger Room.* Her greenish-white forehead wrinkled as she examined the controls, racking the Leader's pillaged brilliance for whatever hints might be hiding there before her extra gray matter evaporated completely.

The console *looked* familiar, kind of, but the more she tried to tap into the requisite expertise, the faster her stolen memories seemed to recede. *K'lrt's a sitting duck right now,* she reminded herself, biting her wounded lip in frustration. *All I've gotta do is push the right dang buttons!*

But which ones?

"Mutant sow!" Without warning, K'lrt appeared right outside the bulb, glaring at her with murderous fury. Copying Rogue's own powers allowed him to fly without wind or flames. "Leave those instruments alone!" he ordered Rogue angrily. Close up, his alien features looked more ugly and inhuman than ever. Overlapping layers of sea-green scales glinted beneath the harsh artificial lighting. Pointed ears flared like miniature devil-wings along the sides of his skull. Deep grooves segmented his lower jaw into puffy green pouches. Yellow fangs gleamed like daggers. "You'll pay for trespassing where you do not belong, you human maggot!" Snake-like eyes glowed Cyclops-red.

"'Fraid you're behind the times," Rogue rejoindered. She hit the Skrull with the only weapon against which he had no defense: one of the Leader's telepathic mind-blasts. K'lrt reeled backwards, clutching his head in shock and agony as every synapse in his brain blazed with psychic fire. "Maggot ain't been part of the X-Men for some time."

A trace of the Leader's own deep disdain for his alien accomplice filtered into Rogue's knowing smirk as the Super-Skrull tumbled backwards through the air. *Figures,* she thought, *that the Leader wouldn't provide his partner with any protection from mental attacks.* Every no-account scoundrel wants to keep an ace up his sleeve.

Meanwhile, she was running out of time and pilfered memories. Her overstuffed skull was literally shrinking by the moment, wringing the Leader's boundless intellect and erudition from her head like water from a sponge. Tense fingers rested lightly upon the control panel, anxious to put the Skrull out of his misery but hesitant to make a mistake. *Don't think about it,* she decided. *Just trust that the knowledge's still back there— somewhere—and let your fingers do the walkin'.*

Relying more on habit than conscious design, she activated the trans-mat projectors, experiencing a surge of relief as her hands tapped out the appropriate commands.

A dazzling burst of emerald light enveloped the stunned Skrull, transporting him at once down onto what Rogue now recognized as the transformation platform. His mind still dazed by her telepathic jolt, K'lrt looked about uncertainly, momentarily puzzled by his instantaneous relocation. "Don't let him budge from that platform!" Rogue shouted via the Leader's loudspeakers.

Avengers and X-Men both responded without hesitation. A shimmering violet tractor ray, courtesy of Iron Man, locked the baffled Skrull in place, while Iceman anchored K'lrt to the pedestal with great slabs of glistening ice. As if that wasn't enough, the Hulk's massive hands dropped heavily onto K'lrt's shoulders. *Careful,* Rogue thought, *don't touch his skin; that lizard's still got my absorbing powers.*

Thankfully, the Hulk kept his big hands on K'lrt's dark purple uniform, even as the Scarlet Witch cast an eerie occult glow over the proceedings, shielding the other heroes' efforts from any Skrull-generated hexes. Looking down from her perch beneath the ceiling, Rogue was impressed, and mildly surprised, at how well the two teams worked together. *Nothing like a pair of A-number-one crums like the Leader and the Skrull to get us heroes to put aside our differences.*

At the last minute, the Ultimate Skrull caught on to his predicament. "No!" he raged. "You can't!" Shards of ice went flying as he thrashed wildly in a desperate attempt to escape the platform, but the Hulk's strength, coupled with Iron Man's magnetic beam, could not be shaken off as easily as Iceman's hastily constructed frozen shackles. Flames erupted from the trapped Skrull, yet the Hulk did not withdraw his hands from the inhuman torch. Despite his augmented power, K'lrt was unable to flee the pedestal fast enough.

"Too late, sugah," Rogue said, pressing the final button. Her brain had nearly shrunk to normal, and her formerly green-tinted complexion was a rosy pink once more, but that didn't matter now. The Leader had taught her everything she needed to know. "You're toast," she announced.

A green aura surrounded K'lrt, outshining even the blazing flames racing over his body.

The Leader awoke in time to see the Super-Skrull transfixed in the glow of the transformation process. *That musclebound fool!* he cursed the alien, realizing instantly that all their schemes were being undone. How in creation had K'lrt managed to let their adversaries maneuver him into such a vulnerable position?

It was all those blasted mutants' fault, he recalled, climbing slowly to his feet. He tottered unsteadily as a dizzy moment made the chamber seem to spin around him. First Wolverine, then Rogue; both X-Men had turned on him, setting in motion a catastrophic chain reaction that had apparently led to the overthrow of the so-called Ultimate Skrull. Bitter resentment drove the last vestiges of grogginess from his mind. *After all my painstaking preparations and planning . . . what a waste!*

His infallible brain assessed the situation faster than the most advanced super-computer, informing him to a statistical certainty that the day was lost. Nearly a dozen pig-headed super-heroes were running rampant through his dangerously fragile moonbase, whose existence had no doubt been exposed to S.H.I.E.L.D., the Fantastic Four, and lord knows whom else. Worst of all, his blundering partner was almost surely being stripped of the near-omnipotence that the Leader had labored so hard to bestow upon him. *It's enough to drive a lesser mind insane,* he brooded darkly. Once again his visionary undertakings had been trampled beneath the thoughtless heels of inferior beings, an historical atrocity on the same order as the burning of the Great Library of Alexandria or Galileo's infamous inquisition. He shook his capacious head sadly. Would the light of his genius ever prevail over the unthinking violence of the Hulk and his costumed kin?

Still, he had learned two valuable lessons from this maddening exercise in futility: 1) Never marry your ambitions to another's agenda, even if your potential ally comes from a more advanced civilization beyond the stars, and 2) never underestimate the notorious X-Men. He'd already known how destructive to his plans the Hulk and the Avengers could be; now Charles Xavier's infamous band of mutant renegades had earned a place of distinction upon the long list of the Leader's archfoes. Next time he would be sure to include the X-Men's annihilation in his plans, along with the demise of the Hulk and those other super-powered vandals. "And there will be a next time," he whispered venomously. "Of that, there can be no question."

"LEADER!"

The booming epithet came from the Hulk, who had finally noted his old enemy's recovery. Letting go of the glowing Super-Skrull, and turning his meter-wide back on the transformation platform, the Hulk stomped toward the Leader, undiluted malice in his emerald eyes. "You're not getting away this time, Sterns!" he bellowed. Years of nonstop antagonism stoked the fury in his reverberating voice. "It's payback time!"

"I fear we'll have to settle our accounts later, my misbegotten nemesis, but I'll leave you something to remember me by." The Leader calmly pressed a button on his wristband, and a series of explosions, coming from the very foundations of the secluded moonbase, rocked the chamber. *Excellent,* he thought; once initiated, the base's self-destruct sequence could not be aborted by any save himself. A sardonic smile upon his face, he tapped new instructions into his wrist controls. "*Adieu,* Hulk, though I suspect we'll meet again."

"NO! NOT AGAIN!" The Hulk lunged at his perennial foe, but the calculating genius, ever prepared for any eventuality, departed in a flash of viridescent light a heartbeat before the Hulk's huge arms closed around him.

Only the Leader knew where he had disappeared to.

On the platform, another luminous green halo faded, taking with it the Ultimate Skrull's precious new powers. Aghast and infuriated by this noxious turn of events, K'lrt attempted desperately to summon a storm, fire force beams from his eyes, transform his flames to ice, cast a hex . . . anything! But his utter failure at any of these feats only confirmed what he already knew and lamented. His augmented abilities were gone.

He was merely a Super-Skrull once again.

"Meddling animals!" he accused his persecutors. An invisible force shield freed him from Iron Man's tractor beam. He spitefully kicked the last remaining chunks of ice away from his legs. "How dare you rob me of what was rightfully mine? By the Lost Treasures of Tarnax IV, I vow eternal vengeance upon you all!"

"Big talk," Iron Man said, his smug human visage blessedly concealed behind his primitive battlesuit. "From where I'm standing, Skrull, you're in no position to talk."

"You tell him, Iron Man!" Iceman blurted. The callow X-Man sprouted icy spikes along his shoulders and upper arms. He flaunted a frozen club clenched in his crystalline fist. *How appropriately aboriginal,* K'lrt thought in scorn.

"Our armored associate speaks for us all," the Beast asserted, looking only slightly more bestial than his irksome fellow primates. Hairy blue knuckles brushed the floor as he moved with a revoltingly simian gait to join Iceman and the others. "Those who trade in forcible abductions and shameless super-power poaching can hardly claim to be the wronged party in this particular contretemps."

All this barking, mammalian chatter offended K'lrt's highly-sensitive ears. To perdition with his lost invincibility, he was ready to fight on. Even with nothing more than the powers of the Fantastic Four and his proud Skrull heart, these impudent humans would learn that the Super-Skrull was no cowardly Kree to be cowed by their laughable prowess and authority. "Do your worst, humans," he challenged. "The Super-Skrull fears you not!"

His flaming fists thickened dramatically, the unstable molecules of his black gloves allowing his hands to mimic those of Benjamin Grimm. A roiling fireball sparked within his grip, but before he could hurl it at the insolent Beast, the buried chamber quaked violently. The powerful tremors nearly toppled K'lrt from the pedestal, and he swung his arms wildly to retain his balance. At first he thought an unexpected moonquake had struck, then he recalled that Earth's lifeless satellite was geologically dead as well. More explosions sounded overhead, from the upper levels of the lunar base, and the Skrull realized what was transpiring. "Computer!" he shouted loudly to the voice-activated machinery in the habitat's walls. "Terminate self-destruct sequence!"

"Negative," a robotic voice reported from the loudspeakers in the ceiling, even as fiery blue sparks gushed from the elevated command bulb to fall like suicidal fireflies on the heads of the Skrull and his adversaries. The Leader's sophisticated apparatus immolated itself in a spectacular eruption of electric pyrotechnics, leading K'lrt to hope that Rogue had been consumed in the conflagration as well. "Abort command denied due to supreme executive override."

Supreme? K'lrt knew of only one sentient being who possessed the sheer effrontery to place himself above the Skrull in the computer's hierarchy of command. "Leader!" he roared, searching the shaking rotunda for his faithless partner. "You craven worm, what treachery is this?"

His irate gaze fell upon the Leader only an instant before that base and perfidious villain teleported himself to safety, leaving the lumbering Hulk empty-handed. The depths of K'lrt's contempt for his departed ally plummeted to absolute zero; he knew desertion when he saw it. *Someday, Leader,* he swore a solemn oath, *you will rue your dishonorable retreat!*

To complete his unhappiness, he saw Rogue soar free of the imploding command bulb, unscathed by the fiery holocaust devouring the Leader's equipment. "Shoot!"

she exclaimed, zipping over the Super-Skrull's head. "Who started the fireworks?"

The shuddering moonbase began to tear itself apart. Jutting blocks of steel and concrete thrust up through the convex floor, creating irregular crevices and jagged monoliths across the base of the rotunda. K'lrt abandoned the unsteady pedestal, using his torchfire to lift him above the convulsing floor. Those Terrans who could fly—Iron Man, Storm, and the Vision—joined Rogue in the air, while the other humans scrambled as best they could to cope with the chaos beneath their feet. Iceman tried to rise above the explosion-wracked floor on a rising pillar of ice, but another turbulent perturbation shattered the foundations of his frozen column, sending him falling toward a gaping chasm from which volcanic gouts of flame emerged. "Yikes!" he yelped as he plunged toward what K'lrt hoped would be a scalding death.

Iron Man dived to rescue Iceman, but the arctic X-Man demonstrated that he required no assistance; taking advantage of the weakened gravity to slow his fall, he extruded an ice-slide ahead of him that carried the endangered mutant safely over the perilous fissure. "Watch out below!" he whooped as he slid to a soft landing in a surviving snowdrift. A second later, his translucent head rose from the piled snow and looked around at the crumbling chamber, taking in the incendiary paroxysms laying waste to the moonbase. "Correct me if I'm wrong, gang," he called out to his teammates, "but I think it may be time to get out of here!"

Cracks opened up in the ceiling and a solid steel beam crashed downward, dropping between K'lrt and Storm as they flew toward each other. The beam nearly hit Cyclops, but Captain America threw himself at the X-Men's dour co-leader, carrying them both out of the path of the falling girder. "Thanks for the save, Captain!" Cyclops said after catching his breath. The heavy beam slammed into the floor only a few feet away, raising a cloud of pulverized cement and tile. "That could have flattened me!"

"My pleasure, X-Man," the Avenger answered. He brushed clinging snow and powdered concrete from his garish costume. "Good soldiers watch out for each other—even on the moon!"

K'lrt found the humans' self-congratulatory banter nauseating. He sought to break up their mutual admiration session with a stream of searing fire, but a surprising gust of wind blew the flaming spray away from his targets, so that the bright orange flames merely scorched the fallen girder instead. "Dorrek's Ghost!" the foiled Skrull swore. Having only recently wielded the very same control over the currents of the air, K'lrt had no difficulty naming the source of the untimely wind. "Storm!"

"Well, Skrull?" she said, swooping between K'lrt and her gravity-bound cohorts. Elemental energy suffused her eyes, making them shine with an electric luminosity. "Your secret hiding place is destroying itself before your eyes. Will you save yourself from the mounting cataclysm—or waste your life in fruitless conflict?"

As much as he loathed admitting it, there was wisdom in what the mutant female said. K'lrt could not deny that their battlefield was rapidly becoming a tomb; despite his intense craving for vengeance, he knew that only a dolt or a martyr waged war atop a sinking ship—and the Super-Skrull was neither.

"The choice is yours, Skrull," Storm stated with galling strength and composure. Her snow-white tresses billowed from the wind raising her up through the air. "Shall we battle to our shared destruction—or live to fight another day?"

"Curse you, witch!" he snarled at her, unable to refute the relentless logic of her argument. The clangor of crashing walls somewhere above them only added to the maddening inevitability of his decision. Gnashing his sharpened canines, K'lrt shook a blazing fist at Storm and her abhorrent fellows. "Beware the future, Terran filth!" he proclaimed defiantly. "Humanity will yet learn to dread the wrath of the Super-Skrull!"

"Ah, go ahead and scram already!" Wolverine shouted back at him, impertinent to the last.

Another day, mutant, K'lrt vowed, then rose like a solar flare through the roof of the devastated chamber, leaving a trail of hellfire in his wake.

Looking uncannily like Johnny Storm at his most torrid, the Super-Skrull fled at great speed, the extreme heat of his bombastic exit melting through the decaying ceiling and creating a vertical escape route from the doomed rotunda. *And none too soon,* Ororo thought, grateful that the malevolent alien warrior had not insisted on a battle unto death. With both their foes having chosen retreat over further confrontation, the X-Men and their noble allies could concentrate on the more vital task of escaping the disastrous demise of the Leader's lunar habitat. "Iron Man!" she called to the armored hero she had come to trust completely over the course of their joint crusade. "This chamber will not long endure. I suggest we take advantage of the exit provided by the Super-Skrull."

"Sounds good to me," the Avenger agreed, jetting closer to Storm, who saw her own countenance reflected in his polished faceplate. Iron Man pointed upward at the hole in the ceiling. "I've got a fix on the quinjet's homing beacon. It's two levels up and about forty-three degrees to the northwest."

"Then lead the way, my friend," Storm told him. "I shall ensure that none of our comrades are left behind." Gliding down over the agitated floor of the rotunda, where Cyclops and the others scrambled to avoid thrusting mounds of concrete rubble, she got everyone's attention by means of an emphatic thunderclap. "Listen to me!" she cried out, certain that all eyes were upon her. "Iron Man has discerned the shortest route back to our spacecraft. All who are able, follow after him as swiftly as possible. I will summon a wind mighty enough to carry the rest of you to safety."

Bright Lady, she prayed, *let us all depart this place in haste.* It was all too evident from the fitful trembling of the chamber's walls that the Leader's once-sturdy sanctuary was no longer a safe haven from the deadly vacuum outside. *I fear that every moment lost may cost us dearly.*

The newly-melted exit was at least thirty meters above the floor, but that posed no difficulty for the Vision, who wafted weightlessly upward, and Rogue, whose tremendous strength enabled her to carry the Beast and Cyclops as well. Likewise, the brawny legs of the resolutely self-reliant Hulk propelled him up and out of sight within seconds. That left only Iceman, Captain America, and the Scarlet Witch stranded upon the unstable floor of the rotunda. "Can your winds support the four of us?" Captain America asked, clearly concerned for Storm's own safety.

"With so little gravity to contend with, easily," she assured him. Unwilling to expend another valuable moment in discussion, Storm proved her point by harnessing the imperiled atmosphere to lift both she and her passengers higher and higher above the floor until they passed through the circular opening the Super-Skrull had left behind. "Careful," she warned, "the edges of the aperture may still be hot."

"No problem, 'Roro," Iceman said, his ebullient voice tinkling like crystal chimes. A layer of frost formed over the molten edges of the hole. "I've got that covered!"

"Good teamwork," Captain America commented approvingly. "The X-Men work well together." Storm knew that was high praise coming from the chairman of the Avengers.

"Yes," the Scarlet Witch added. Her accent bore a disturbing similarity to Magneto's, but Storm resolved not to hold that against her. "Over the last day or so, I've been impressed by Rogue and Wolverine's resources and performance under pressure."

"Thank you," Storm replied, accepting the praise on behalf of her teammates. Following Iron Man's directions, she carried her complement of heroes two levels beyond the collapsing rotunda. To her dismay, she saw evidence of similar demolition elsewhere in the moonbase; all through the multi-level complex, flames and explosions undermined the structural integrity of the entire outpost. But Storm refused to give in to despair, choosing to hope for the best. "If nothing else, this terrible ordeal may ultimately strengthen the bonds between our two teams."

"It already has," Wanda Maximoff insisted, and Storm wondered at the conviction in the woman's voice.

Reaching the appropriate level, they found both the Beast and Cyclops waiting for them. "See?" the shaggy X-Man informed his fellow alumni of Professor Xavier's academy. "I told you they'd be along shortly. In the immortal words of FDR, we have nothing to fear but fear itself."

"That and explosive decompression," Cyclops said grimly, giving voice to Storm's own direst apprehension. "Wolverine and the others are clearing the way to the quinjet. Let's not keep them waiting."

Once her fellow travelers' boots were securely lowered onto the floor of the upper level, Storm set free the obedient wind and hurried after Scott and Hank. Captain America, Iceman and the Scarlet Witch kept pace with her as they ran for their lives. *How much longer,* she worried, *would the base's life-support mechanisms survive the cascade of destruction the Leader set in motion?*

As they had discovered earlier, upon their initial exploration of the moonbase, this level was laid out in a series of concentric circles, with no obvious portals between each ring. *I suppose you don't require doors,* she surmised, *when teleportation requires only the press of a button.* The ring they now traversed clearly held the Leader's personal quarters; unlike the sterile, futuristic decor that predominated in the other sections they had visited, this donut-shaped region was comfortably, even cozily, appointed with lush orange carpeting, walnut bookshelves, and elegant sofas and chairs. Subdued

lighting provided a meditative ambience completely be-
lied by the seismic jolts shaking the very walls of the
sumptuously-furnished domicile. Leatherbound volumes,
whose titles and contents Storm had no time to observe,
toppled from their shelves, landing on the carpet with a
muffled clatter. *The Leader lived well,* she thought. *A
pity he could not leave the rest of us to also enjoy the
comforts of home.*

"Let's go, people!" Cyclops urged them on. Storm
saw that Iron Man had marked the trail by leaving behind a string of luminescent white pellets, no doubt
released from a hidden cache in his laudably well-
equipped armor. To further ensure that they did not lose
their way in the tumult and confusion, Iron Man had also
laser-burned an arrow on the ceiling. "This way!" Cyclops shouted redundantly. "Hurry!"

The Beast bounded over to Storm's side. "Is it just
me," he asked glibly, trotting down the corridor as he
spoke, "or is this headlong dash also providing you with
a truly remarkable sense of *déjà vu?*"

Storm knew just what he meant. Only days ago, at
the very outset of the present crisis, the three of them—
Cyclops, Beast, and herself—had run through a holographic Danger Room simulation that bore an uncomfortable resemblance to their current circumstances. In
that exercise, the trio of X-Men had rushed madly
through an imploding Shi'ar space station, striving desperately to reach a waiting space shuttle before the artificial environment gave way to the killing void of outer
space. The striking, if coincidental, parallels with the
real-life race against time now in progress only added to
her anxiety, especially when she recalled that all three
X-Men had ultimately "died" in that earlier exercise,

when the collapse of the station's wall had sucked their entire party into the chill of space. Her memories of those final frightening seconds, right before the holographic routine ended, were all too vivid. *Blackness all around me, and a freezing cold . . . !*

"Let us hope for a better outcome this time," she said, as more detonations rocked the lunar headquarters. As in the simulation, the diminished gravity seemed to add wings to her feet. She was eager to leave the moon behind and return to the warm embrace of Mother Earth. Claustrophobia, never far away, chafed at her nerves, reminding her just how cramped and precarious the moonbase truly was. *Gods of earth and air,* she entreated, *your daughter is far from your green hills and fragrant skies. Pray do not forsake me in this dreadful place.*

The lack of visible doorways could not slow the likes of the Hulk, Iron Man, and Rogue. Rounding the curve of the corridor, Storm and her fellow stragglers came upon an enormous rent in the outer wall of the Leader's disintegrating bastion of domesticity. "Through here!" Cyclops beckoned and Storm required no further urging. They left the residence ring, running quickly across the width of a wide hallway lined with exploding metal tanks. Storm recognized the site of their lost battle against the mind-controlled hostages, even as she and the others now ducked pieces of flying shrapnel.

Jagged chunks of metal bounced off Captain America's shield until Storm conjured up a gale to blow much of the airborne detritus away from the fleeing group, while Iceman simultaneously raised an icewall to defend them from lethal fragments coming at them from the opposite direction. "Holy smokes!" he marveled. "This whole place is one big deathtrap!"

"Succinctly and unimpeachably put, o' refrigerated buddy o'mine," the Beast concurred. His unequalled dexterity had allowed him to evade the deadly shrapnel with aplomb, and he soon led the way ahead of his more acrobatically-challenged comrades. "An expeditious egress is manifestly in order!"

Despite his flippant manner, the Beast was not mistaken. They were undeniably running out of time. The tiled walkway buckled beneath Storm's feet, venting gusts of hot gas and ionized plasma which she and the others were forced to dodge as they ran, trusting on skill and determination to avoid the hazards which sprang up in their path. Temporarily shielded by wind and ice, they sprinted across an ever-shifting obstacle course toward a convenient new cleft in the next outermost wall. "Come one, come all!" the Beast beseeched them, his agile gymnastics bringing him first to the rough-hewn doorway. "After you, ladies and gentlemen!"

Storm darted through the yawning gap. *Was this wide portal torn open by the Hulk's strength or by Iron Man's repulsor rays?* she wondered, then decided it didn't matter. It occurred to her that, unlike during the ill-fated practice session, this time they had the Avengers and the Hulk on their side, not to mention Rogue, Iceman, and Wolverine. Such valiant allies *had* to make a difference, or so she hoped.

Intent on fending off harmful missiles with her winds, Storm was the last to take the escape route extolled by the Beast. The hole in the wall led to a familiar stretch of blacktop, still dusted with the brittle remains of the Leader's unliving humanoids. Her spirits soared as she saw the opening of the ice tunnel leading to the Avenger's quinjet. With admirable speed, Iceman had expanded the frozen tube back out to their vessel. Glancing rapidly through the transparent dome surrounding the Leader's base, she saw that Iron Man and the Vision were already seated in the cockpit of the spacecraft, preparing for take-off. "The Goddess be praised," she murmured. Even now she could perceive a delicate spiderweb of cracks spreading across the surface of the dome. The quaking pavement threatened her balance and she stumbled awkwardly toward the entrance of the tunnel. *Almost there,* she thought.

A deafening bang sounded behind her and a burst of red-hot flame gushed from the improvised doorway from which she had emerged only seconds before. Another few moments, she realized, and she would have been incinerated.

Time to leave, she concluded. Hank McCoy obviously felt the same. "Now boarding," he said, waiting by the tunnel entrance for the last of his teammates. "Avenger Airlines, Flight 101, departing Luna for New York City, Planet Earth. Sorry, no drinks or meals will be served until we reach our destination." He stretched a hairy palm toward Storm. "May I see your boarding pass, please?"

Ororo smiled at her friend's whimsical ways and stepped fleetly toward the frigid tube, but the sudden clutch of wet, gooey fingers held her back. Looking down in alarm, her blue eyes widened at the shocking sight of a smooth pink hand rising from a wide puddle of glistening ooze. "Goddess!" she gasped, comprehending in an instant what had happened. The heat from the explosions was thawing out the frozen bits and pieces of the humanoids, allowing the unnatural creatures to recreate themselves from the residue of their earlier defeat!

"Zounds!" the Beast exclaimed, nearly in unison with her own horrified outburst. The disembodied hand squeezed its sticky fingers around her right calf, holding onto her with surprising strength, while all over the remnant-strewn track, other scraps of pink plastic began to wriggle and stir back to life. A nearby puddle of thick, viscous, rosy syrup flowed across the pavement to merge with the pool of liquescent plastic from which the clutching hand arose. The beginnings of a humanoid head and shoulders took shape as the growing puddle swiftly achieved cohesion. Storm saw another set of damp fingers rising toward her, reaching out greedily. . . .

She tugged hard to free her leg from the avid humanoid hand, but she could not break free from its grip. Tenacious pink strands of goo stretched between the puddle and the sole of her black vinyl boot. The Beast grabbed onto her arms with both hands and added his own gorilla-like strength to hers. At first his assistance did no good; Storm felt like she was glued to the floor like a mouse trapped on an adhesive snare. Worse yet, she heard the telltale hiss of the atmosphere escaping through minute cracks in the quivering dome. If the quinjet did not leave immediately, the Avengers, the Hulk, and the other X-Men might all be obliterated by the moonbase's final catastrophic death throes.

"Go!" she ordered the Beast. "Leave me, and tell the others to take off at once! You mustn't risk all for my sake!"

The furry X-Man merely tightened his grip on Storm's wrists and pulled all the harder. "Funny, I thought braving overwhelming odds was part of the job description,'' he said, interrupting his commentary with a grunt of exertion. ''Besides, who's going to water all your flowers back at the Institute? The Hulk's the only one here with a green thumb, but somehow he doesn't strike me as botanically-inclined.''

Storm realized there was no arguing with her courageous teammate, and she feared that her arms would be yanked from their sockets before her leg escaped the grasp of the partial humanoid. Then her foot squeaked out of her boot, leaving only the empty footgear stuck between plastic fingers. Storm thought she was free—until the creature's second hand closed around her left ankle. She could have wept from the injustice of it all, of coming so close to saying farewell to the dying moonbase, only to be stalled by the relentless humanoids at the very brink of freedom, but instead she redoubled her strenuous efforts to get away, balancing uncertainly on one foot to avoid placing her other foot back in the mucilaginous pink muck congealing beneath her. Would the humanoids even notice the loss of atmosphere when the dome shattered, or were they unbreathing as well as unliving? Through the clear wall of the dome, now veined with dozens of hairline fractures, Storm took one last look at the planet of her birth, shining like a precious blue gem in the heavens. She thought the Earth had never looked so beautiful.

A sudden flash of light threw a scarlet tint over all she viewed, making the blue-green orb briefly resemble the red planet Mars. The incarnadine radiance had an even more drastic effect upon the semi-formed humanoids, causing their solid components to liquefy once more, so that ruddy heads and hands and fingers dissolved rapidly, the glutinous pink jelly streaming back down onto the pavement. "Good thing I decided to see what was keeping you two," the Scarlet Witch observed from beneath the crystalline arch of the ice tunnel.

Storm tugged again and her foot easily pulled away from the last thinning tendrils of goo. Snatching up her discarded boot from a spreading puddle of rose-colored fluid, she hurried into the tunnel after the Beast and Wanda, not even sparing a second to thank the Witch for her highly opportune hex. There would be time enough later for expressions of gratitude, after they left the Leader's booby-trapped lair. Broken flakes of the decaying dome rained down upon the top of the ice tube as Storm sprinted toward the open door of the quinjet.

Waiting inside the aircraft, the Beast grabbed Storm by the shoulders and physically hauled her into the quinjet. Captain America called to Iron Man as Ororo hastily strapped herself into her seat. "That's everybody! Get us out of here—on the double!"

"You don't need to tell me twice," Iron Man said. Powerful engines roared to life, and surging gee-forces shoved Storm into the cushions of her seat as the quinjet executed an instant vertical take-off that carried them hundreds of feet above the lunar surface in a matter of seconds. Craning her neck to peer out of a porthole to her left, Storm watched in silence as the domed moonbase disappeared in a split-second bonfire of burning oxygen. Within moments, all that was left was a faint cloud of smoke and dust rising from somewhere within the Tycho Crater.

Storm looked away from the moon, preferring to watch the Earth grow in size ahead of her, as the quinjet carried them home.

Epilogue

The shady, secluded garden behind Avengers Mansion could not have been more different from the barren, gray wastes of the moon. A high iron fence separated the mansion's backyard from nearby Central Park, but the sounds of a warm summer night in the city penetrated the privacy of the Avengers' refuge. Rogue leaned against the bark of a leafy maple tree and watched her teammates confer with the Avengers under more congenial and social circumstances than their hectic lives usually permitted. Mutant outlaws mingled with celebrated heroes, but Rogue kept her distance from the milling crowd of costumed adventurers. Although the tranquil garden was infinitely preferable to the Leader's pain-wracked laboratories, a lingering sense of melancholy clung to Rogue's mood.

"Somethin' botherin' you, darlin'?" Wolverine asked, approaching her. Like her, he had discarded his orange prison togs for his usual uniform, a spare suit of which was kept stored in the Blackbird, currently hangared in the docking bay on the top floor of the mansion. Out of respect for the Avenger's strict no-smoking policy, he gnawed on a wad of chewing tobacco instead. "You're lookin' down."

"It's nothin'," she lied. "Just an old-fashioned case of the blues, I reckon."

"Don't go blowin' smoke at me, Rogue." Logan spat

254

a squirt of brown juice onto the manicured lawn, then eyed her carefully. "I know you too well. What's the matter?"

She realized there was no fooling Logan. His instincts were too sharp. "Well, you remember when ah borrowed the Leader's memories back on the moon?" He nodded, unlikely to have forgotten such a decisive turning point in their battle against the Leader and his alien accomplice. "Turns out that the Leader had discovered a cure for my absorbin' power, some kind of drug that could temporarily turn off the whole nasty business, makin' it safe for me to touch or be touched." Her throat tightened at the thought, remembering too many frustrating moments of affection thwarted and passion denied. "The Leader knew the secret, which meant that ah knew it, too, for a little while." She tapped her head with her forefinger, all too aware of the protective glove now covering her hand. "It was all up here, but now it's gone. Ah've racked my memory, but ah can't remember a single dang ingredient of the formula, just that it worked and ah used to know why."

"That's a tough break," Wolverine agreed. He laid a comforting hand on her shoulder. "But maybe it's just as well. You don't want to owe your happiness to a crum like the Leader." Rogue heard the anger in his voice when he mentioned the sadistic genius who had experimented so cruelly upon both of them. "You'll find a way to get around your powers someday, and you won't have to go wading through some slimeball's sleazy memories to do it."

"Ah hope so," she said, crossing her fingers. "Ah'm not getting any younger, y'know."

Logan cracked a wry smile. "Trust me, kid, you don't have a clue about gettin' older."

Rogue remembered that no one, not even the Professor, knew how old Logan really was, only that he'd been the best there was for as long as anybody could recollect. *Guess I am just a spring chicken compared to him.*

"Excuse me." An accented voice broke into their conversation. Rogue was surprised to see Wanda Maximoff coming over to join them beneath the spreading boughs of the old maple. "I hope I'm not interrupting."

In her colorful gypsy garb, the European Avenger looked a whole lot more like a Scarlet Witch. A long red cloak hung from her shoulders while a pointed headdress, not unlike the one Storm sometimes wore, rested atop her billowing auburn curls. Her bright red, two-piece outfit was skimpier than Rogue recalled from the last time the X-Men bumped into the Avengers, but Wanda pulled the look off without seeming at all trampy. Silver bracelets jangled softly as she walked toward the two X-Men.

"Nah," Logan answered her, making room for the Witch to stand beside them. "Rogue and I was just jawin', that's all." He looked up at the Avenger, who was several inches taller than he was. "What's up, Witchie?"

"Call me Wanda," she insisted warmly. "How are your injuries, Wolverine?"

Fresh white bandages girdled Logan's waist where the Ultimate Skrull had skewered him with his frozen spear. "Can't complain," he said gruffly. "I heal fast, in case you haven't heard. Thanks for asking, though."

"I'm glad you're recovering," Wanda said, before turning her sights on Rogue, who felt distinctly uncomfortable beneath the other woman's scrutiny. She and the Witch hadn't exactly hit it off up on the moon, especially when they first found themselves trapped together in that awful lab. *Can't much blame her for hating me,* Rogue thought, *considering what I did to Ms. Marvel.* She braced herself for whatever parting shot the Witch had in mind.

"I wish to apologize, Rogue," Wanda began, catching the startled X-Man completely offguard. "I fear I treated you too harshly before. What happened to Carol was a tragedy, but it's obvious that you've turned your life around since then. Given that my own checkered career also began with an ill-advised stint among the Brotherhood of Evil Mutants, I should have been more forgiving." She offered the younger woman her hand. "Perhaps we can both move on and place our dubious pasts behind us?"

"Gladly!" Rogue agreed, taking Wanda's hand and shaking it firmly, all the while being careful not to crush the Witch's hand with her super-strength. That both women wore gloves provided a double layer of protection to the heartfelt handclasp. Rogue felt a heavy burden of guilt slip from her shoulders; maybe all that violence and suffering at the hands of the Leader and his Skrull stooges had been worthwhile after all, if it meant that she could finally bury the hatchet with one of Carol Danvers' closest friends. *Still,* she thought cautiously, *now is probably not the time to mention that fling I had with Wanda's daddy down in the Savage Land . . . !*

Captain America was busy comparing notes with Cyclops and Storm when the Beast came bouncing out of the back door of the mansion, rejoining the informal gathering in the garden. "Felicitous news, my distinguished colleagues!" he announced cheerily, attracting the attention of all present, even Bruce Banner as he lurked silently on the fringes of Cap's discussion with the X-Men's co-leaders. Cap paused to listen to what the Beast had to say. *Good news is always welcome,* he thought, *particularly after a long and arduous mission.*

The Beast sprang onto the top of a marble birdbath before launching fully into his spiel. "A few long-distance calls at Tony Stark's expense have yielded reassuring status reports on some of our absent associates. From Scotland, the good doctor MacTaggert reports that our friend, the esteemed Kurt Wagner, is recovering nicely from the fractured ankle he sustained in battle against the late, unlamented Gamma Sentinels, although Moira complains that Nightcrawler's frequent *bamf*ing has left her labs and medical facilities fairly reeking of brimstone.

"Furthermore, I'm delighted to bear glad tidings of our fellow X-Men, who have at last returned to Westchester after the successful completion of their business in Antarctica. Professor X and the others look forward to hearing more about our own lunar excursion upon our return to the ivy-covered walls of the Xavier Institute."

Cap noted that even the steadfastly serious Cyclops lightened noticeably at the Beast's news report. *No doubt he's eager to be reunited with his wife,* Cap deduced, remembering that Cyclops and Jean Grey, the former Marvel Girl, had wed not long ago. "Sounds like happy endings all around," he commented to his mutant guests.

"Indeed," Storm agreed, taking a sip from a cup of hot tea provided by Edwin Jarvis's impeccable hospitality. "Would that all our struggles could end on so harmonious a note."

"There's no reason they shouldn't," Cap stated. A lamp over the back porch cast a warm glow upon the nocturnal scene. An electrostatic force field devised by Tony Stark kept the outdoors reception free of mosquitos and other pests. "In my experience, the positive efforts of good men and women will always ensure peace and victory in the end."

"I wish I could share your optimism, Captain," Cyclops said. An uncanny glow burned steadily behind the ruby lens of his visor, making it impossible to read the X-Man's eyes. "But in a world where our own government can finance and develop projects like the Gamma Sentinels, we mutants have learned that sometimes the best we can hope for is an occasional lull in a never-ending battle against hate and prejudice."

"Wish I could say you was wrong about that, junior," a deep, raspy voice intruded from the shadows under a rear corner of the mansion. A tall figure wearing a worn brown trenchcoat stepped into the light, revealing the voice to belong to none other than Nick Fury, Executive Director of S.H.I.E.L.D. A stark black eyepatch concealed his scarred left eye, but the surviving eye looked over Cap and the other heroes without a hint of trepidation at arriving uninvited and unannounced amidst such a formidable assembly. "Best I can promise," he said to Cyclops, "is that you ain't the only one bothered by Sentinels and garbage like that."

"Fury," Captain America greeted the veteran, whom Cap had known since they first fought together against the Axis powers during World War II. "I don't recall Jarvis letting you in."

Fury snorted, biting down hard on the unlit cigar clenched between his rugged jaws. "A quarter-century in the cloak-and-dagger business teaches you a few things," he remarked, "like how to make a quiet entrance when you want to." He glanced to his left, where Bruce Banner, clad in hand-me-downs from Steve Rogers's closet, had begun to creep quietly toward the door. "No need to make tracks on my account, Doc," Fury stated. "Likewise for your mutant buddies." He looked squarely at Cyclops and Storm and raised his voice loud enough to be heard all through the garden. "Get this straight, heroes. I ain't here—not officially, that is. Who you Avengers want to hang out with in your free time is none of my beeswax. I just wanted to let you know that I've pulled the plug on the entire Gamma Sentinels project."

"Good to hear it," Cap said. As far as he was concerned, the very idea of robot policemen manufactured specifically to hunt down mutants, whose only crime was being born different, was a blatant violation of everything America stood for. He liked to think that the federal government's occasional forays into Sentinels and Mutant Registration Acts were misguided aberrations that hardly reflected the mainstream of American thought and history, but such shameless incidents only made it harder for concerned citizens, like Cyclops and his mutant teammates, to trust the nation Cap had proudly spent his life defending. "I hope this really is the last we've seen of the Gamma Sentinels and their ilk."

"Well," Fury hedged, "I wouldn't be surprised if there's still a few more anti-mutant initiatives hidden in the black ops budgets of other agencies, but I can tell you this: S.H.I.E.L.D. is out of the Sentinels business for good.'' Fishing around in the pockets of his trenchcoat for a lighter, he eventually gave up and stuck his cigar into one of his coat's interior pockets. ''After all the ruckus those prototypes caused, no one's goin' to have the nerve to even breathe the word 'Sentinel' around me for another decade or so.''

''I wish I could believe you, Fury,'' Cyclops said grimly. Beside him, Storm solemnly nodded in accord. ''With all due respect, though, you'll forgive me if the X-Men take your promises with a grain of salt. We've heard such assurances before.''

Captain America was saddened but not surprised by the X-Man's suspicious attitude. *Perhaps that's truly the lasting difference between the Avengers and the X-Men,* he thought soberly. *As officially-sanctioned heroes, the Avengers fight on behalf of the very same system that the outlawed X-Men regard with mistrust and apprehension.*

Only time would tell which team saw the future most clearly. . . .

Greg Cox is the author of the Iron Man novels *The Armor Trap* and *Operation A.I.M.* In addition, he was the author of *Star Trek: The Q Continuum* trilogy as well as several more *Star Trek* novels, and a nonfiction book on *Xena: Warrior Princess*. Greg served as coeditor of two science fiction/horror anthologies (*Tomorrow Sucks* and *Tomorrow Bites* with T.K.F. Weisskopf), and he has also published many short stories in anthologies ranging from *Alien Pregnant by Elvis* to *100 Vicious Little Vampire Stories* to *The Ultimate Super-Villains* to *Other-Were*. Greg lives in New York City.

George Pérez, one of the most renowned artists in comics, is best known for his stints on *The Avengers, Fantastic Four, Justice League of America,* and *The New Teen Titans* (which he also cowrote and coedited). Other noteworthy efforts include his work on *UltraForce, The Silver Surfer* (as writer), *Isaac Asimov's I-Bots, Sachs & Violens,* and *The Incredible Hulk: Future Imperfect.* He coplotted and drew *Crisis on Infinite Earths*, and wrote and drew the revamp of *Wonder Woman* (both for DC). Recently, George returned to the series that made his career, Marvel's *The Avengers*, where he collaborates with writer Kurt Busiek. George lives in Florida.

CHRONOLOGY TO
THE MARVEL NOVELS AND
ANTHOLOGIES

What follows is a guide to the order in which the Marvel novels and short stories published by BP Books, Inc., and Berkley Boulevard Books take place in relation to each other. Please note that this is not a hard and fast chronology, but a guideline that is subject to change at authorial or editorial whim. This list covers all the novels and anthologies published from October 1994–September 2000.

The short stories are each given an abbreviation to indicate which anthology the story appeared in. USM=*The Ultimate Spider-Man*, USS=*The Ultimate Silver Surfer*, USV=*The Ultimate Super-Villains*, UXM=*The Ultimate X-Men*, UTS=*Untold Tales of Spider-Man*, UH=*The Ultimate Hulk*, and XML= *X-Men Legends*.

X-Men & Spider-Man: Time's Arrow Book 1: **The Past** [portions]
by Tom DeFalco & Jason Henderson
   Parts of this novel take place in prehistoric times, the sixth century, 1867, and 1944.

CHRONOLOGY

"The Silver Surfer" [flashback]
by Tom DeFalco & Stan Lee [USS]

The Silver Surfer's origin. The early parts of this flashback start several decades, possibly several centuries, ago, and continue to a point just prior to "To See Heaven in a Wild Flower."

"In the Line of Banner"
by Danny Fingeroth [UH]

This takes place over several years, ending approximately nine months before the birth of Robert Bruce Banner.

X-Men: Codename Wolverine ["then" portions]
by Christopher Golden

"Every Time a Bell Rings"
by Brian K. Vaughan [XML]

These take place while Team X was still in operation, while the Black Widow was still a Russian spy, while Banshee was still with Interpol, and a couple of years before the X-Men were formed.

"Spider-Man"
by Stan Lee & Peter David [USM]

A retelling of Spider-Man's origin.

"Transformations"
by Will Murray [UH]
"Side by Side with the Astonishing Ant-Man!"
by Will Murray [UTS]

CHRONOLOGY

"Assault on Avengers Mansion"
by Richard C. White & Steven A. Roman [UH]
"Suits"
by Tom De Haven & Dean Wesley Smith [USM]
"After the First Death . . ."
by Tom DeFalco [UTS]
"Celebrity"
by Christopher Golden & José R. Nieto [UTS]
"Pitfall"
by Pierce Askegren [UH]
"Better Looting Through Modern Chemistry"
by John Garcia & Pierce Askegren [UTS]
   These stories take place very early in the careers of Spider-Man and the Hulk.

"To the Victor"
by Richard Lee Byers [USV]
   Most of this story takes place in an alternate timeline, but the jumping-off point is here.

"To See Heaven in a Wild Flower"
by Ann Tonsor Zeddies [USS]
"Point of View"
by Len Wein [USS]
   These stories take place shortly after the end of the flash-back portion of "The Silver Surfer."

"Identity Crisis"
by Michael Jan Friedman [UTS]
"The Doctor's Dilemma"
by Danny Fingeroth [UTS]
"Moving Day"
by John S. Drew [UTS]
"Out of the Darkness"
by Glenn Greenberg [UH]

"The Liar"
by Ann Nocenti [UTS]
"Diary of a False Man"
by Keith R. A. DeCandido [XML]
"Deadly Force"
by Richard Lee Byers [UTS]
"Truck Stop"
by Jo Duffy [UH]
"Hiding"
by Nancy Holder & Christopher Golden [UH]
"Improper Procedure"
by Keith R.A. DeCandido [USS]
"The Ballad of Fancy Dan"
by Ken Grobe & Steven A. Roman [UTS]
"Welcome to the X-Men, Madrox . . . "
by Steve Lyons [XML]

 These stories take place early in the careers of Spider-Man, the Silver Surfer, the Hulk, and the X-Men, after their origins and before the formation of the "new" X-Men.

"Here There Be Dragons"
by Sholly Fisch [UH]
"Peace Offering"
by Michael Stewart [XML]
"The Worst Prison of All"
by C. J. Henderson [XML]
"Poison in the Soul"
by Glenn Greenberg [UTS]
"Do You Dream in Silver?"
by James Dawson [USS]
"A Quiet, Normal Life"
by Thomas Deja [UH]
"Chasing Hairy"
by Glenn Hauman [XML]
"Livewires"
by Steve Lyons [UTS]

"Arms and the Man"
by Keith R.A. DeCandido [UTS]
"Incident on a Skyscraper"
by Dave Smeds [USS]
"One Night Only"
by Sholly Fisch [XML]
"A Green Snake in Paradise"
by Steve Lyons [UH]
   These all take place after the formation of the "new" X-Men and before Spider-Man got married, the Silver Surfer ended his exile on Earth, and the reemergence of the gray Hulk.

"Cool"
by Lawrence Watt-Evans [USM]
"Blindspot"
by Ann Nocenti [USM]
"Tinker, Tailor, Soldier, Courier"
by Robert L. Washington III [USM]
"Thunder on the Mountain"
by Richard Lee Byers [USM]
"The Stalking of John Doe"
by Adam-Troy Castro [UTS]
"On the Beach"
by John J. Ordover [USS]
   These all take place just prior to Peter Parker's marriage to Mary Jane Watson and the Silver Surfer's release from imprisonment on Earth.

Daredevil: Predator's Smile
by Christopher Golden
"Disturb Not Her Dream"
by Steve Rasnic Tem [USS]
"My Enemy, My Savior"
by Eric Fein [UTS]

These all take place after Peter Parker's marriage to Mary Jane Watson, after the Silver Surfer attained freedom from imprisonment on Earth, before the Hulk's personalities were merged, and before the formation of the X-Men "blue" and "gold" teams.

"The Deviant Ones"
by Glenn Greenberg [USV]
"An Evening in the Bronx with Venom"
by John Gregory Betancourt & Keith R.A. DeCandido [USM]
  These two stories take place one after the other, and a few months prior to The Venom Factor.

The Incredible Hulk: What Savage Beast
by Peter David
  This novel takes place over a one-year period, starting here and ending just prior to Rampage.

"Once a Thief"
by Ashley McConnell [XML]
"On the Air"
by Glenn Hauman [UXM]
"Connect the Dots"
by Adam-Troy Castro [USV]
"Ice Prince"
by K. A. Kindya [XML]
"Summer Breeze"
by Jenn Saint-John & Tammy Lynne Dunn [UXM]
"Out of Place"
by Dave Smeds [UXM]
  These stories all take place prior to the Mutant Empire *trilogy.*

X-Men: Mutant Empire Book 1: Siege
by Christopher Golden
X-Men: Mutant Empire Book 2: Sanctuary
by Christopher Golden

CHRONOLOGY

X-Men: Mutant Empire Book 3: **Salvation**
by Christopher Golden
These three novels take place within a three-day period.

Fantastic Four: To Free Atlantis
by Nancy A. Collins
"The Love of Death or the Death of Love"
by Craig Shaw Gardner [USS]
"Firetrap"
by Michael Jan Friedman [USV]
"What's Yer Poison?"
by Christopher Golden & José R. Nieto [USS]
"Sins of the Flesh"
by Steve Lyons [USV]
"Doom²"
by Joey Cavalieri [USV]
"Child's Play"
by Robert L. Washington III [USV]
"A Game of the Apocalypse"
by Dan Persons [USS]
"All Creatures Great and Skrull"
by Greg Cox [USV]
"Ripples"
by José R. Nieto [USV]
"Who Do You Want Me to Be?"
by Ann Nocenti [USV]
"One for the Road"
by James Dawson [USV]
These are more or less simultaneous, with "Doom²" taking place after To Free Atlantis, *"Child's Play" taking place shortly after "What's Yer Poison?" and "A Game of the Apocalypse" taking place shortly after "The Love of Death or the Death of Love."*

"Five Minutes"
by Peter David [USM]

CHRONOLOGY

This takes place on Peter Parker and Mary Jane Watson-Parker's first anniversary.

Spider-Man: The Venom Factor
by Diane Duane
Spider-Man: The Lizard Sanction
by Diane Duane
Spider-Man: The Octopus Agenda
by Diane Duane
These three novels take place within a six-week period.

"The Night I Almost Saved Silver Sable"
by Tom DeFalco [USV]
"Traps"
by Ken Grobe [USV]
These stories take place one right after the other.

Iron Man: The Armor Trap
by Greg Cox
Iron Man: Operation A.I.M.
by Greg Cox
"Private Exhibition"
by Pierce Askegren [USV]
Fantastic Four: Redemption of the Silver Surfer
by Michael Jan Friedman
Spider-Man & The Incredible Hulk: Rampage (Doom's Day Book 1)
by Danny Fingeroth & Eric Fein
Spider-Man & Iron Man: Sabotage (Doom's Day Book 2)
by Pierce Askegren & Danny Fingeroth
Spider-Man & Fantastic Four: Wreckage (Doom's Day Book 3)
by Eric Fein & Pierce Askegren
   Operation A.I.M. *takes place about two weeks after* The

Armor Trap. *The "Doom's Day" trilogy takes place within a three-month period. The events of* Operation A.I.M., *"Private Exhibition,"* Redemption of the Silver Surfer, *and* Rampage *happen more or less simultaneously.* Wreckage *is only a few months after* The Octopus Agenda.

"Such Stuff As Dreams Are Made Of"
by Robin Wayne Bailey [XML]
"It's a Wonderful Life"
by eluki bes shahar [UXM]
"Gift of the Silver Fox"
by Ashley McConnell [UXM]
"Stillborn in the Mist"
by Dean Wesley Smith [UXM]
"Order from Chaos"
by Evan Skolnick [UXM]
   These stories take place more or less simultaneously, with "Such Stuff As Dreams Are Made Of" taking place just prior to the others.

"X-Presso"
by Ken Grobe [UXM]
"Life Is But a Dream"
by Stan Timmons [UXM]
"Four Angry Mutants"
by Andy Lane & Rebecca Levene [UXM]
"Hostages"
by J. Steven York [UXM]
   These stories take place one right after the other.

Spider-Man: Carnage in New York
by David Michelinie & Dean Wesley Smith
Spider-Man: Goblin's Revenge
by Dean Wesley Smith
   These novels take place one right after the other.

X-Men: Smoke and Mirrors
by eluki bes shahar
   This novel takes place three-and-a-half months after "It's a Wonderful Life."

Generation X
by Scott Lobdell & Elliot S! Maggin
X-Men: The Jewels of Cyttorak
by Dean Wesley Smith
X-Men: Empire's End
by Diane Duane
X-Men: Law of the Jungle
by Dave Smeds
X-Men: Prisoner X
by Ann Nocenti
   These novels take place one right after the other.

The Incredible Hulk: Abominations
by Jason Henderson
Fantastic Four: Countdown to Chaos
by Pierce Askegren
"Playing It SAFE"
by Keith R.A. DeCandido [UH]
   These take place one right after the other, with Abominations *taking place a couple of weeks after* Wreckage.

"Mayhem Party"
by Robert Sheckley [USV]
   This story takes place after Goblin's Revenge.

X-Men & Spider-Man: Time's Arrow Book 1: **The Past**
by Tom DeFalco & Jason Henderson
X-Men & Spider-Man: Time's Arrow Book 2: **The Present**
by Tom DeFalco & Adam-Troy Castro

X-Men & Spider-Man: Time's Arrow Book 3: **The Future**
by Tom DeFalco & eluki bes shahar
These novels take place within a twenty-four-hour period in the present, though it also involves traveling to four points in the past, to an alternate present, and to five different alternate futures.

X-Men: Soul Killer
by Richard Lee Byers
Spider-Man: Valley of the Lizard
by John Vornholt
Spider-Man: Venom's Wrath
by Keith R.A. DeCandido & José R. Nieto
Captain America: Liberty's Torch
by Tony Isabella & Bob Ingersoll
Daredevil: The Cutting Edge
by Madeleine E. Robins
Spider-Man: Wanted: Dead or Alive
by Craig Shaw Gardner
Spider-Man: Emerald Mystery
by Dean Wesley Smith
"Sidekick"
by Dennis Brabham [UH]
These take place one right after the other, with Soul Killer *taking place right after the* Time's Arrow *trilogy,* Venom's Wrath *taking place a month after* Valley of the Lizard, *and* Wanted Dead or Alive *a couple of months after* Venom's Wrath.

Spider-Man: The Gathering of the Sinister Six
by Adam-Troy Castro
Generation X: Crossroads
by J. Steven York
X-Men: Codename Wolverine ["now" portions]
by Christopher Golden

CHRONOLOGY

These novels take place one right after the other, with the "now" portions of Codename Wolverine *taking place less than a week after* Crossroads.

The Avengers & the Thunderbolts
by Pierce Askegren
Spider-Man: Goblin Moon
by Kurt Busiek & Nathan Archer
Nick Fury, Agent of S.H.I.E.L.D.: Empyre
by Will Murray
Generation X: Genogoths
by J. Steven York
These novels take place at approximately the same time and several months after "Playing It SAFE."

Spider-Man & the Silver Surfer: Skrull War
by Steven A. Ronan & Ken Grobe
X-Men & the Avengers: Gamma Quest Book 1: **Lost and Found**
by Greg Cox
X-Men & the Avengers: Gamma Quest Book 2: **Search and Rescue**
by Greg Cox
X-Men & the Avengers: Gamma Quest Book 3: **Friend or Foe?**
by Greg Cox
These books take place one right after the other.

X-Men & Spider-Man: Time's Arrow Book 3: **The Future** [portions]
by Tom DeFalco & eluki bes shahar
Parts of this novel take place in five different alternate fu-

tures in 2020, 2035, 2099, 3000, and the fortieth century.

"The Last Titan"
by Peter David [UH]
  This takes place in a possible future.

MARVEL® Comics

X-MEN®

star in their own original series!

BP Books, Inc.

MARVEL®

Ⓑ BOULEVARD

☐ **X-MEN: MUTANT EMPIRE: BOOK 1: SIEGE**
   by Christopher Golden   0-425-17275-9/$6.99
When Magneto takes over a top-secret government installation containing mutant-hunting robots, the X-Men must battle against their oldest foe. But the X-Men are held responsible for the takeover by a more ruthless enemy...the U.S. government.

☐ **X-MEN: MUTANT EMPIRE: BOOK 2: SANCTUARY**
   by Christopher Golden   1-57297-180-0/$5.99
Magneto has occupied The Big Apple, and the X-Men must penetrate the enslaved city and stop him before he advances his mad plan to conquer the entire world!

☐ **X-MEN: MUTANT EMPIRE: BOOK 3: SALVATION**
   by Christopher Golden   0-425-16640-6/$6.99
Magneto's Mutant Empire has already taken Manhattan, and now he's setting his sights on the rest of the world. The only thing that stands between Magneto and his conquest is the X-Men.

®, ™ and © 2000 Marvel Characters, Inc. All Rights Reserved.

Prices slightly higher in Canada

Payable by Visa, MC or AMEX only ($10.00 min.), No cash, checks or COD. Shipping & handling: US/Can. $2.75 for one book, $1.00 for each add'l book; Int'l $5.00 for one book, $1.00 for each add'l. Call (800) 788-6262 or (201) 933-9292, fax (201) 896-8569 or mail your orders to:

Penguin Putnam Inc.
P.O. Box 12289, Dept. B
Newark, NJ 07101-5289
Please allow 4-6 weeks for delivery.
Foreign and Canadian delivery 6-8 weeks.

Bill my: ☐ Visa ☐ MasterCard ☐ Amex _____ (expires)
Card# _____
Signature _____

Bill to:
Name _____
Address _____ City _____
State/ZIP _____ Daytime Phone # _____

Ship to:
Name _____ Book Total $ _____
Address _____ Applicable Sales Tax $ _____
City _____ Postage & Handling $ _____
State/ZIP _____ Total Amount Due $ _____

This offer subject to change without notice.   Ad # 722 (3/00)